UPSIDE DOWN

N.R. WALKER

COPYRIGHT

Cover Art: N.R. Walker & SJ York
Editor: Boho Edits
Publisher: BlueHeart Press
Upside Down © 2019 N.R. Walker

BLURB

Jordan O'Neill isn't a fan of labels, considering he has a few. Gay, geek, librarian, socially awkward, a nervous rambler, an introvert, an outsider. The last thing he needs is one more. But when he realises adding the label *asexual* might explain a lot, it turns his world upside down.

Hennessy Lang moved to Surry Hills after splitting with his boyfriend. His being asexual had seen the end of a lot of his romances, but he's determined to stay true to himself. Leaving his North Shore support group behind, he starts his own in Surry Hills, where he meets first-time-attendee Jordan.

A little bewildered and scared, but completely adorable, Hennessy is struck by this guy who's trying to find where he belongs. Maybe Hennessy can convince Jordan that his world hasn't been turned upside down at all, but maybe it's now—for the first time in his life—the right way up.

UPSIDE DOWN

N.R. WALKER

CHAPTER ONE

JORDAN O'NEILL

> Asexuality is defined by the absence of something.

I READ THE LINE AGAIN, and another time for good measure, then I mumbled it to myself out loud. "Asexuality is defined by the absence of something."

I squinted at the screen. "Oh, you can fuck right off," I muttered and looked up, directly into the horrified face of a customer. She had those lines above her top lip, like she'd spent a good portion of her sixty-something years scowling. It made her mouth look like a cat's butthole. Her coral-coloured lipstick bled into the lines around her mouth, and I had to make myself not stare. And now not think of cats and their puckered, coral-coloured buttholes. *So gross.* "Oh, not you, obviously. I wasn't saying that to you. I happen to like cats. Not their buttholes, necessarily, I was just..."

"He was just taking these for me. Hello, Mrs Peterson, how are you today?" Merry said as she slid a pile of books from the counter into my arms. She shoved me out from behind the counter and smiled at the now-glaring woman. I was going to suggest Mrs Peterson stop scowling, or at least buy a half-decent lip filler, but thought better of it. I reshuffled the pile of books in my arms, which Merry hadn't even alphabetised yet, and disappeared into the stacks. It gave me time to bang my head on the top row of books and die of frustrated embarrassment.

Working at the Surry Hills library certainly had its perks. Hiding in the stacks from irate customers with feline buttholitis of the mouth being my all-time favourite perk. Books, a close second. Working with Merry a well-placed third. Okay, so well, maybe working with Merry could be better than books... especially when she understood my awkwardness and social ineptitude and bailed me out of situations like she did just now with Mrs Peterson. It also didn't hurt that she reminded me of the Hobbit she was nicknamed after: short, funny, loyal, though thankfully she was absent the huge, hairy feet. Her real name was Meredith, but Merry suited her perfectly.

But in all seriousness, I loved my job. *Loved* it. There was routine, order, everything was catalogued, numbered, and shelved accordingly. It was organised, neat, and usually quiet most of the time. Except on Tuesdays when they held Library Time for preschoolers and there were book readings and sometimes a finger puppet show. Or on Wednesdays when they held their community computer courses for aged folks. Not that they were loud the way thirty preschoolers running through the stacks was loud, but when there were fifteen elderly people all speaking up so they could hear themselves talk, it was kind of noisy. Thursdays, on the other hand, were usually quiet. The only community group that met that day was the local mime actors club, so they didn't make any noise, really. Except for that first time, not long after I'd started, when I was walking past as they were finishing up and the room erupted in applause, causing me to almost drop my armful of books. It startled me so much I'd done an Oscar-worthy rendition of Samuel L Jackson being TASERed and let out a "Motherfucker" to end all motherfuckers. The biggest sacrilege of the whole performance was that a 1952 dust jacket edition of Hemingway's *Men Without Women* hit the floor. It was completely unscathed. My ego, however, not so much.

Fridays were typically busy. English Language Workshops during the day, then Book Club on Friday nights. Because this was Surry Hills, hipster central, it was where all the nerds and geeks could come to be awkward introverts together. I quite often spent my Friday nights in a room full of like-minded people, avoiding eye contact and dying inside every time someone tried to make small talk.

That's the thing about me.

I'm an awkward, introvert book nerd, sci-fi geeky twenty-six-year-old librarian, with brownish-ginger hair. Oh, and I'm a gay man. I'm also an expert in Percy Shelley, Lord Byron, and Wordsworth... or just all French Revolutionary poets in general, really. I also have to wear some item of clothing that is perfectly colour-coordinated with my shoes, and I have an inclination to say motherfucker an awful lot. Oh, and there is also a very good chance I'm asexual.

The jury was still out on that. Actually, that wasn't true; the jury had been in for some time, I'd just been resisting their verdict. I didn't need another label. I had enough of them. I had enough hang-ups, quirks, traits, and societal boxes to tick and squeeze myself into.

I didn't need one more.

But I couldn't decide if having one more label was causing my anxiety to spike or if not having the label confirmed was what gave me anxiety. Maybe I needed the label. Maybe everyone could fuck the fuck off and let me live in my anxiety bubble of non-asexualness. Maybe whoever wrote that article online and said "asexuality is defined by the absence of something" can fuck off too.

And that's where I was up to when Merry found me, with my forehead pressed up against *The Subtle Art of Not Giving a F*ck* in the How Ironic section, mumbling to myself. "You doing okay, Jordan?" she asked.

"To define asexuality by the absence of anything infers that something is missing and therefore incomplete or insufficient." I looked at her. "I am not any of those things, and I resent the implication—"

She put her hand up and spoke over me. Gently, but firmly, like she knew how to deal with me, or something. "The article goes on to explain that by definition, the absence of sexual attraction makes it difficult to label and the resulting struggle to identify with something that is, by definition, the lack of something."

I sighed petulantly. "I didn't read that far."

"I gathered."

"Did Mrs Peterson seem okay?"

Merry smiled. "Of course, she was fine."

"I'm sorry about that, and I'm really thankful you swooped in to save me. Again. So, thank you."

"That's okay. I left a massive pile of returns for you to shelve as payment."

I glanced at my watch. It was almost five...

"Plenty of time," she said with a knowing smile. "I would never let you miss your bus. God forbid you miss seeing him."

"I regret the day I ever told you," I grumbled. She smiled, so I poked my tongue out at her but made quick work of the returns so I could be at the bus stop outside the library at 5:06. I couldn't be late.

I was done by five on the dot, grabbed my satchel, and wrapped my scarf around my neck. It wasn't too cold yet, but the blue of the scarf matched my shoes. I wore charcoal trousers and a long-sleeve white button-down shirt as a standard dress uniform, so every day I added a little colour where I could. And it had to match. Because I didn't spend the first eighteen years of my life in the closet and not come out with some sense of style.

I met Merry at the doors of the library and we headed out together. I only had to walk a whole ten or so metres to the bus stop and she headed up Crown Street toward her flat. "We still going tomorrow night?" she asked as I stood in line.

"Ugh," I said, making a face.

"Jordan, you're going tomorrow night," she said, holding my gaze. "*We* are going tomorrow night. Don't bother calling in sick tomorrow. I know where you live."

"That sounds a lot like a threat."

"Because it is," she said with a smile.

"I'll need to go home first and get changed," I said in a last-ditch effort to bail.

"That's fine. And if I catch the bus with you back to your place," she leaned in and whispered, "I'll finally get to see your guy."

My stomach knotted with dread. "I never should have told you."

She looked over my shoulder and nodded. "Speaking of which."

My bus. The 353 from the city to Newtown. Right on time at 5:06.

"Say hello to him for me," she said with a smile and waved me off as she turned and walked up the street to her place.

She knew damn well I'd never speak to him, let alone be conversational enough to make any kind of greeting on her behalf. I mean, Jesus fuck, I'd only ever made eye contact with him once and I'd almost died. Literally. He'd looked up once and caught me staring at his beautiful face, I'd stumbled up the narrow aisle, almost fell, took out some poor kid with my messenger bag, and landed in the lap of a nun who, for the record, probably could have done without my "fucking motherfucker" expletive as I fell. On the bright side, *Headphones Guy* wore noise-cancelling headphones and was oblivious, and I'd slid into a seat up the back with nothing more than a bruised ego and death-stares from the nun. The whole experience had been horrifying.

So no, Merry, I wouldn't be saying hello to Headphones Guy any time soon, thank you very fucking much. I glared at the back of her head as she walked away until the bus came to a stop and the doors opened. I got on, tapped my Opal card on the swipe screen, and went toward the back. And, just like every day, I scanned the faces until I saw his, careful not to make eye contact.

I got lucky because I scored a seat across the aisle, two seats back, which meant I could stare at his side profile until he got off at the Cleveland Street turn. He had kind of pale skin, brownish-black hair and the scruff to match. Not a full beard, just enough though. He always wore jeans or pants, a shirt and a jacket, and usually boots. I wondered where he might work to dress like that. His clothes were all brands I couldn't afford, so he had to work somewhere that paid half-decent money. He came from the city every day, yet he never wore a suit like every other guy who worked in the city. He had long fingers that would clutch the rail on the bus as he got off, and blue eyes and pink lips, and I wondered what his voice sounded like. I wondered a lot about him...

I wondered what music he listened to with those headphones. What his playlists looked like. Was it the latest charts, or was it jazz or blues? I could see him listening to some jazz-fusion, or an obscure band that no one had ever heard of, and maybe the sales clerk at the indie music store kept one-off vinyls behind the counter for him.

I wondered why he caught the bus. If he made such good money like his outfits suggested he did, why didn't he drive? Did he even own a car? Not many people in Surry Hills did, I allowed, so maybe that wasn't too strange. I certainly didn't drive or own a car. I couldn't afford one, but maybe he could? He'd only been catching the bus for six months now, and I wondered where he came from. What brought him here?

I wondered where he lived. Was it a one-bedroom studio? Did he share a flat? Did he live with someone? I wondered if he was single, spoken for, married. I wondered if he had tattoos, and I wondered what he smelt like. I bet he smelt so good...

And I wondered why I bothered with such daydreams when I knew, even on the slightest chance he might look my way again, that once I told him I didn't like sex, he'd probably laugh and wish me good luck. He would've dodged a bullet and I would have taken one, right to the heart. Again.

It was pointless.

I sighed and sank back in my seat, but I still couldn't look away from his profile. He was so intriguing, gorgeous in an unconventional kind of way, even from this angle. The line of his neck, his jaw, his temple, his cheek.

And that was when I noticed. It wasn't the light from outside the bus playing with the light of his face, it was a tear. A motherfucking tear.

He was crying.

My Headphones Guy was crying. Actual tears. Silent, heartbreaking tears.

He didn't wipe them away. He just sat there and let them fall, and so help me God, that made it worse.

And the noise fell away as though it was me wearing the noise-cancelling headphones. The chatter, the traffic, all became silent, and I wondered what on earth had happened to hurt him in such a way?

I wanted to ask him if he was okay. I wanted to reach out and tell him everything would be fine.

Of course, I couldn't. I couldn't exactly call out to a stranger on the other side of a crowded bus and ask if he was okay, could I? Well, I could, but not without drawing the attention of every passenger, and my Headphones Guy couldn't hear me anyway because he had his headphones on. Then, before I could do or say anything, the bus turned onto Cleveland Street and he shook his head, wiped his cheeks, and glanced around to see if anyone had noticed.

Of course I had.

He stood and hurried off the bus. He didn't look up, he never did. He kept his head down, kept his headphones on, and the bus pulled away.

―――――――

"YOU LOOK TERRIBLE." Merry frowned as she studied me. "You're not stressing about tonight, are you? You'll be fine, Jordan," she said, squeezing my hand. "You might even be surprised how much you enjoy it."

"No, it's not that," I replied, uncurling my scarf from around my neck and opening my locker. Truth be told, I hadn't thought anymore about our plans for tonight.

"What is it?" She was more concerned now.

"My guy," I started, but then immediately felt foolish for calling him *my* anything. "You know, Headphones Guy. He was crying on the bus yesterday."

"Crying?"

I nodded. "Not sobbing. Just staring out the window while silent tears rolled down his cheeks."

"With his headphones on?"

"Always."

"Wow."

"I know, right? And so of course, I spent the entire night wondering what happened. I could barely sleep."

"If it's any consolation, your red shoes and scarf match your bloodshot eyes really well."

I sighed. "I'm not thanking you for that. That was not a compliment and I refuse to reward inflammatory behaviour."

"I meant it as a compliment."

I looked around dramatically. "Alexa? Alexa, what is a compliment? Merry needs a refresher."

"Alexa isn't connected here," Merry replied. Then she smiled and held up her phone and pretended to examine my face. "Siri, what are some beauty tips for exceedingly large bags under bloodshot eyes?"

I pursed my lips at her. "Siri, what is a bitch?"

Merry laughed and put her phone into her pocket. "I was joking, Jordan."

"Then your delivery needs work."

Merry smiled. "Coffee first?"

"Yes, please." I groaned and threw my messenger bag into my locker and locked it. I held my foot up. "But seriously, would you look at these fucking shoes? Are they just not everything?" They were red suede desert boots.

"They're gorgeous."

I bumped her hip with mine as we walked toward the kitchenette. "Of course they are."

"Maybe his grandpa died."

"What?"

"Headphones Guy. Maybe that was why he was crying."

I sighed and took my cup from the cupboard. I looked inside it to double check it was clean and that no one had used it, then proceeded to make my third cup of coffee for the morning. "Maybe. Or maybe he lost a priceless art piece and the insurer did a number on him but there was a double-cross and—"

"You watched *The Thomas Crown Affair* last night too?"

I nodded and added a dash of skim milk to my coffee. "Pierce Brosnan is kinda dreamy."

"I'm still catching the bus with you to your place this arvo, right?"

"Yeah, why?"

"Then I'm going to say something to him when we get on the bus this afternoon."

"Who? Pierce Brosnan?"

"No, you idiot. Headphones Guy."

I was positively stricken. "You absolutely will not!"

"I absolutely will too," she replied, smiling evilly as she stirred her coffee. "I'll get a name so at least we can stop calling him Headphones Guy. And find out what he actually does so you don't have to keep making up the weirdest jobs ever."

"If you do, I'll be so embarrassed I'll be forced to quit and move and join the witness protection program."

Merry stared at me. "Siri, what is an overreaction?"

"Siri, don't answer that, so help me fucking God."

"Jordan," Mrs Mullhearn chided me from across the staffroom, not even glancing up from her iPad. She was two hundred years old and was the scary librarian from every school kid's nightmares. "What have we said about using the f-word?"

I deflated. "That it's only necessary in emergency situations."

"Was it an emergency situation?"

I frowned. "No. Sorry."

Merry barely hid her laughter the whole way out, and I nudged her with my elbow. "You will not speak to Headphones Guy on the bus this afternoon, or Lord Jesus fucking help me I will die."

Mrs Mullhearn looked up this time with a frown, and I gave her my best 'sorry' face, but we all knew I wasn't. Sorry, that is.

Merry laughed and teased me the whole day. By the time work was done and we were waiting for the bus, I was about to hyperventilate with anxiety. But then the only thing possibly worse than Merry actually speaking to my Headphones Guy on the bus was Headphones Guy not being on the bus at all.

"He's not here," I whispered as we walked up the aisle. We managed to get a seat for both of us and she could clearly see there was no guy on the bus with red headphones.

"It's your fault," I told her. "You jinxed me. And now

I'll be left wondering all weekend what happened to him and if he's okay because he was upset yesterday, or what if his grandad *did* die, or what if something horrible happened and he's in hospital? It could be like *While You Were Sleeping,* only him with someone else because you jinxed me."

Merry looked me in the eyes and held my gaze. "Jordan, breathe. I'm sure he's fine. You're fine."

"And you're making me go to this meeting tonight where I may as well just wear a sign with FREAK written in neon fucking letters."

"That's not true. Everyone there will be the same as you. You'll see."

"How do you know? You can't know. That's an improbable equation, and you're just guessing and that makes you a lying liar that lies, and that's worse."

Merry took a deep breath. "Alexa, please add Valium to my shopping list."

An hour later, after I'd changed outfits three times and had to put my head between my knees and do some deep breathing exercises so I didn't freak the complete fuck out, Merry actually got me to the meeting. It was being held in a small function room out the back of a hotel on Elizabeth Street. It was busy with drinkers and partygoers, and I might have even drowned my anxiety in vodka if I wasn't almost freaking out already. There were about seven or eight people there, though I was too nervous to make eye contact or even look at anyone, really. Until Merry made me stop and take a breath.

She faced me, took my hands, and gave them a squeeze. "Look around the room. You'll see everyone is just like you. It's fine, you're fine, okay?"

I took a breath. My lungs felt too small for air but too

big for my chest, but I looked around the room and found the person at the front who was obviously running the meeting, smiling with a clipboard in his hands, and I wanted to positively die.

"Oh fucking fuckity motherfucking fuck," I whispered.

"What is it?"

"There was probably another reason why Headphones Guy wasn't on the bus this afternoon which might not have had anything to do with you or your ability to jinx me," I managed to say before running out of breath. My next line came out high-pitched and squeaky. "Because he's standing at the front of the room."

CHAPTER TWO

I WAS NERVOUS BUT EXCITED, like I was before every meeting. I'd attended similar group sessions for years but this was my fifth time as host and organiser. I'd only been in Surry Hills for six and a half months and on leaving behind my North Shore support group, and discovering Surry Hills didn't have one, it was suggested I start my own. It was only early days, but the turnout had been good and consistent and positive, and that was all I could hope for. I wasn't a huge fan of the venue, but with short notice and basically zero budget, I couldn't very well complain.

Some familiar faces arrived. The women: Bonny, Leah, Sabina, and Nataya. And the two guys: Glenn and Anwar. The very first meeting I'd had, only two people turned up. Leah and Sabina. Then the next meeting Anwar made three, then by meeting four we had six. And this meeting saw two new people walk in. They came in together and could have been a couple, I wasn't sure. I certainly didn't like to assume. But by the way she smiled with ease and how he looked to be almost hyperventilating, I got the impression he was here for himself and she was his support person.

She was shortish, maybe five feet one, and had a piercing in her cheek punctuating her dimple. She had a short black fringe and her hair was in Princess Leia buns on the sides of her head; she wore a mustard coloured knee-length skirt and a purple cardigan. She looked friendly and fun and I liked her before I'd even spoken to her.

He, on the other hand, looked like a ball of nerves. He was tall and trim, and he had a bit of a beard happening. His brown hair was short, he wore dark blue jeans and a yellow sweater and bright yellow shoes. He looked a little familiar, and he also looked like he was two seconds away from having a full-blown panic attack.

I knew what that was like. I'd been in his shoes before.

She had her hand on his arm and was saying something to him but he was shaking his head, so I went over to them and gently interrupted. "Hi." I stood back enough so as not to crowd him, my tone friendly, and I smiled.

He looked at me with wide eyes and a slightly horrified expression. "Oh God, motherfucking fuck, he's speaking to me." He put his hand to his forehead and glanced at the door.

The woman grabbed his arm but smiled at me. "Hi, I'm Merry. Yes, like the Hobbit. I actually spoke to you on the phone earlier this month." She spoke and smiled like the guy freaking out beside her was an everyday occurrence. "I told you of a friend of mine who could use some encouragement. Well, this is him, this is Jordan."

I remembered the phone call, and I made eye contact with him then and he nodded quickly and shoved out his hand. "Hi. I'm Jordan O'Neill," he blurted. "I'm her weird friend, she should have introduced me as that, if she didn't

already tell you that on the phone. Slash awkward, intro-
verted nerd... Geek also probably fits, though mostly for *Star
Trek: Deep Space Nine*. I mean, the other Star Treks are fine
and I don't disparage anyone for liking them—Janeway and
Picard are credible—but I just prefer Sisko as my captain,
even though his rank was only commander in the beginning
because it wasn't technically a ship, but he was totally a
captain. If we had to choose captains. Unlike literary
captains, such as Dafoe's Singleton. Good fucking Lord
those barbaric times, I wouldn't last a day."

"Breathe, Jordan," Merry said with a kind tone.

He took a breath, then made a face. "Sorry. I tend to
babble when I'm nervous."

"It's fine, Jordan," I said, trying not to smile. Because
wow. "My name is Hennessy. Yes, like the cognac," I said,
mirroring Merry's introduction.

"And I'm Jordan. Like Michael Jordan or the country
Jordan. Or the cute guy from New Kids on the Block.
Depends what you're into, I guess."

"I like all three of those Jordans," I said with a smile.
"And you're allowed to be nervous. It's fine and completely
expected if this is your first time."

"Well, I *am* nervous. Obviously. And I'm not sure if I'm
supposed to be here. Well, not *not supposed* to be here. I'm
not sure I *want* to be here," he said, making a pained face
again. "If I'm *ready* to be here."

Merry put her hand on his arm and looked up to his
face. "Jordan, just one meeting," she said calmly. "If it's not
for you, then we never have to come back."

He nodded again and his eyes set with determination.
"Okay, okay. One meeting."

"Jordan," I said. "You're more than welcome to just sit
and observe. You don't have to talk or say anything. Just

listen, and when and if"—I gave him a pointed look—"*if* you're ready, you can join in. Only if you want to. No pressure, okay?"

He swallowed hard and let out a breath, then he nodded again. He really did look familiar, and I was going to ask him where I knew him from when the sound of a scraping chair behind me caught my attention. People were taking their seats, which was my cue to start the meeting.

I smiled at Jordan and Merry. "For what it's worth, I'm glad you're here." I went back to the table with my clipboard and pulled up a seat while everyone settled into theirs. They all looked at me expectantly, so I began. "Thanks for coming along tonight. We've got some new faces," I said, not really wanting to draw attention to Jordan but not wanting to ignore him either. "So I'd just like to start by saying that this is an open group where we're all free and safe to express what we're feeling and share our experiences without judgement or criticism. This group is aimed at asexual and aromantic people or anyone who might be questioning or curious." I deliberately didn't look at Jordan. "But we're inclusive to everyone on the queer spectrum and their support people, regardless of their sexuality."

Everyone smiled at me, well, except Jordan. He blinked a few times and took some deep breaths. I gave him what I hoped was a reassuring smile. "My name is Hennessy, and I've been attending support meetings for asexuals for a few years. I'm not an expert, by any means, but these meetings are a safe space where we can talk and laugh and gripe and discuss things that are relevant. There are no right and wrong questions or answers here. Outside of these group meetings, I'm actually kind of quiet. My closest friends might disagree," I said with a bit of a laugh. "But for the most part, it's true. I understand it can be daunting to talk about things here in this group, but whatever is said in here, stays in here. Okay?"

Everyone nodded again.

"So, tonight I wanted to talk about sexual identification and social media." That earned me a few smiles and a few sighs. "On one hand, it can be a great source of information and research, and even a platform for acceptance and finding community. If you've googled support groups—such as this one or one like it—you can see you're not alone and there are other people who are going through the same things as you, and that's tremendously important. But then on the other side, you have what might be conceived as an oversexualised society. We see repeatedly, we're told repeatedly, it's shown, it's implied, it's blatant that sex equals love. That we're not complete without it. That sexual intimacy is the pinnacle of all relationship goals."

I leaned back in my chair and took a deep breath. "We're living in an age of dating apps and swiping left or right. Of Twitter and Tinder and Grindr and Instagram, where everything is sexualised to sell. Where beauty is an illusion, Photoshopped, and Botoxed in the name of perfection for one goal: sex. And let's not even start on movies, books, hell, even music film clips are R-rated now. And to 99% of the population, it works. It sells, right? And it's ingrained into each generation that sex equals love. Sex equals marriage fulfilment; I'm pretty sure even most churches say that marriage needs to be consummated and is for the sole purpose of procreation." I shook my head. "I mean, really. Fuck that noise."

That earned me a few chuckles and even Jordan smiled.

"But we know different. Sex doesn't equal love. Sexual physicality is not the finish line; being sexually intimate with someone is not the only expression of our emotions.

Except society thinks it is. Society and, by association, social media tells us sexual intimacy equals love. And the crux of this representation is that sexuality is normalised, mainstream. Which means asexuality is the opposite of that. Stigmatised, and anyone who doesn't want sex, doesn't like it, isn't attracted to it, or is even repulsed by it, is labelled as not normal."

I looked at each of their faces. "When I was sixteen, I told my then-boyfriend, who also happened to be my best friend, I wasn't comfortable fooling around. And I certainly didn't want to have sex. He thought I might have just needed more time or maybe I was scared of being gay. Maybe there were a dozen possibilities but he couldn't fathom that I just..." I sighed. "I just wasn't interested in that aspect of a relationship. And you know what he said?" I smiled sadly. "He laughed at me and asked what was wrong with me. He said he thought about sex *all* the time. He said all normal teenagers thought about sex all the time and that gay guys thought about it even more. He dismissed me, laughed, and made jokes at my expense. And I can tell you, it didn't get much better as I got older and told other people. But there it was, the one word that would haunt me for years."

A few people nodded. I didn't even have to say it.

Normal.

"There's a difference between normal behaviour and normalised behaviour," Nataya said. "Normal is subjective. And by whose definition should we fit anyway? Do we take normality from people like my grandma who is horrified by just about everything we see on the internet, or do we take normality from guys who think it's normal and completely okay to send dick pics to people they've never met?"

"Oh my God, that shit has been so normalised it's

expected," Leah said. "And it shouldn't be. It's just all about sex, sex, sex."

"Exactly," Glenn said. "I tried Tinder and well, I matched with quite a few women, but as soon as I told them I'm not looking for a sexual relationship, it was over. Then I tried the 'asexual equivalent,'" he said, using air quotes. "And there are still people who think you'll change. Or they expect you to change. Or God, Glenn," he said, mimicking a high-pitched voice, "it's just sex. If you were a real man..."

Anwar groaned and rolled his eyes. "It never fails."

"Yes!" Bonny said, throwing her hands up. "Oh my God, I can't tell you how many times I've been told I'm frigid or cold or unreceptive. That something is fundamentally wrong with me. I've had guys from dating apps try to 'convert' me, if you know what I mean. Telling me if I just relaxed, I'd enjoy it." Leah and Sabina both nodded.

"That's not okay," Anwar said, frowning.

"That's never okay," Merry agreed.

"There's nothing wrong with you, Bonny," I said, making direct eye contact. "Nothing needs fixing and most certainly can't be converted. I hope you were able to leave that situation."

"Oh yeah," she reassured. "I was fine, thanks. I mean, we've all had people, men and women, tell us we just haven't found the right person yet, right? Or we're just not ready or we haven't hit our peak yet, but look out when that happens, because sex is awesome!" she said, rolling her eyes.

Most everyone nodded and sighed, because yes. We'd all had those things said to us at some time. "And that, in itself," I continued, "is a form of normalisation of sexualised behaviour. We become normalised to expect to have these views thrown at us. We're becoming normalised to their behaviour."

And so began group discussions on the semantics of the definition of normal, and then online dating sites and forums and the importance of sites they felt safe and comfortable in, where they could talk about their asexual or aromantic orientation. People were busy swapping weblinks and talking about which chat groups they were in when I chanced a look at Jordan.

He had sunk back in his chair, his face half cast in shadow. His expression was sullen, even a little lost. I couldn't tell if he was listening intently or if he was a million miles away, though my guess was on the latter. Merry was fully immersed in the group discussion, laughing with Nataya so Jordan was kind of by himself, and I thought it might be a good time to ask him what he thought of the group meeting, if he thought it was relevant to his needs.

"Jordan," I said, just loud enough for him to hear but without disrupting the group chat.

He turned to face me, like he'd been snapped from a trance, and that's when I saw a tear escape to run down his cheek. He scrubbed it away and shook his head, but I was on my feet already. I pulled up a chair on the other side of him and took his hand, encouraging him to face me, away from the group.

"Jordan," I said gently. "Are you okay? Is there something you need to talk about?"

He shook his head but his eyes welled with fresh tears and he started to cry.

CHAPTER THREE

JORDAN

I DIDN'T EVEN NOTICE that the room had cleared out. Merry had pulled up a chair at my side, but Hennessy sat with his knees between mine, holding my hand while I cried.

I fucking cried.

Through my stupid, traitorous tears, I caught the end of a silent conversation between Merry and him, my Headphones Guy.

Hennessy.

And then Merry rubbed my back before she walked out, and Hennessy squeezed my hand. "She's just gone to get you a drink of water," he said gently.

"I don't know why I'm crying," I said, wiping my face with my free hand.

"Because it can be overwhelming," he said. His voice was calm and soft. "Because it can be life-affirming and scary as hell, all at the same time."

I nodded. "I don't want another label, you know? Because I have enough. I have more than enough. Too many, probably, you know for a geeky book-nerd gay man with so many levels of social awkwardness Freud would need an elevator, but the labels fit. And I hate that they fit. Everything that was said here tonight was like it was said for me, like I was saying those things. I didn't want this to happen," I said, shaking my head, fighting more tears. "I wanted to come here and, well, that's not exactly true. I didn't want to come here at all; it was Merry's idea. She suggested that I look into what being asexual meant. After my 683rd failed attempt at a relationship, she thought maybe I should see if I ticked any boxes on the 'How To See If You Could Be Asexual' questionnaire on *Teen Vogue*, and after I realised that I could almost tick all the boxes, I decided I didn't want or need another label. So then I had to come here tonight to shut her up. I was going to prove her wrong and then I could go on living my best life being not asexual but just a gay man who didn't actually want to have sex. A socially awkward, geeky book-nerd gay man," I amended through more tears, "who doesn't actually want to have sex. I'm sorry for crying. I wasn't expecting the emotional dump, but I wasn't expecting to feel so... lost and found. Like I once was lost but now I'm found, kind of like the song, which is cheesy as fuck and I didn't mean it to sound like that. I just didn't realise how hard I'd been trying to fit in with the real world, trying to be normal, when my normal was here all along. Because I really am asexual and it hit me like a metric fuckton of bricks that there's actually nothing wrong with me."

And then there were more tears.

"Because that's my truth, even if I thought there was something wrong with me, and fuck knows I've been told there was, many times," I said, wiping my face. "But there's not. I'm asexual, and that's my motherfucking truth whether I like it or not."

Hennessy smiled at me. With his perfect lips and perfect teeth, his pretty blue eyes, and three-day scruff. He looked so different without his headphones, like seeing someone who normally wears glasses without them. "There's nothing wrong with you," he said, still smiling, still holding my hand.

"I'm sorry, were you not here for the geeky book-nerd gay man with so many levels of social awkwardness Freud would need an elevator conversation?"

He laughed at that. "I believe I was, yeah."

"Sorry about that. I tend to babble a lot when I'm nervous. And swear. Well, I say fuck a lot even when I'm not nervous. I don't have Tourette's or anything, I just like the word fuck. The noun and adverb, even the adjective, not the verb obviously because I'm asexual. Apparently. So there is definitely no actioning of the word."

Hennessy chuckled. "No actioning of the word, got it." He still had hold of my hand, and I liked it. As in, really liked it. My Headphones Guy was holding my hand, and he was smiling at me, in what I think was not in a bad way. I mean, his smile was kind and his eyes were smiling too, if that was even possible. I mean, no it wasn't possible—eyes could not physically smile, I got that—but damn, they sure looked happy.

"How are you feeling now?" he asked.

"A little weirded out," I answered. "Not gonna lie. I didn't want to admit the asexual thing to myself for a long time, and I'm thinking it will take some getting used to. Like breaking in a pair of Doc Martens, ya know? Like they're uncomfortable and tight and basically kill your feet until they're the most comfortable shoes you'll ever wear. They become like a second skin, and I'm pretty sure this whole asexual thing will be like that."

He made a thoughtful face. "I like that analogy."

"And it's even weirder, because you're my Headphones Guy and I had no idea you'd be here, but here you are and now you're holding my hand and I cried in front of you, which is not how I wanted our first meeting to go. Believe me. I had visions of it involving me not being so... well, so me. And doing all the talking, because I tend to talk a lot when I'm nervous, which I think I've said already—"

"I'm your Headphones Guy?"

Oh fucking fuckity motherfucker. "I said that out loud, didn't I? To your perfect face, and what kind of perfect name is Hennessy, by the way? Because—"

A loud peal of laughter broke through the door when a couple, a guy and girl, stumbled into the backroom, their arms around each other, obviously intoxicated and handsy and half kissing, half laughing, until they realised the room wasn't empty.

I shot to my feet and pulled my hand away from Hennessy's.

"Oh, sorry guys," the girl said.

"Didn't mean to interrupt," the guy said. He took his hand off her arse to wave it. "Keep doing what you're doing. We don't mind. We thought this room was empty."

"We weren't doing anything," I said quickly.

"Excuse me," Merry said, sliding in around the drunk couple. She held three bottles of water. "Sorry, it took forever to get served. They're really busy."

I'd never been happier to see her. "Oh, thank God." I grabbed her arm and turned her back toward the door. "We need to leave. I called him my Headphones Guy to his perfect fucking face."

Merry shot Hennessy a look and held out a bottle of water for him. He took it, still smiling, though somewhat confused. Then Merry looked up at me as I dragged her to the door. "To his face?"

"What was I supposed to do? You left me unsupervised!" I stopped at the couple who were still standing in the doorway, and only just then I realised what the guy had meant when he said they thought the room was empty... "Oh praise baby motherfucking Jesus, I hope you have antibacterial wipes."

Now Merry was hauling me out through the crowded pub. I yelled back at the couple, hoping they'd hear, "At least wipe it down afterwards, we have meetings in there!"

We burst through the crowd onto the street and Merry looked up at me and sighed. "What else did you say?"

"What didn't I say?" I answered. "I was a mess, crying all over him because of the whole asexual thing, thank you very much. Then I was nervous and we both know how well that ends. And I think I might have told him that he was my Headphones Guy, that he had a perfect face and a perfect name, because who the fuck calls their kid Hennessy, and now he thinks I'm a raving lunatic because you. Left. Me. Un. Supervised."

Merry cracked her bottle of water, took a long drink, sighed, then hooked her arm around my elbow. "He really is very good looking," she said as we began the walk back to my flat. "I can see why you've been crushing on him forever."

I took a swig of my water. "Fucking hell, I wish this was wine. Where is Jesus when you need him?"

Merry hummed a happy sound. "I'm proud of you for going tonight. It wasn't easy, but you did it, and you faced it head on."

"I cried like a motherfucking baby."

"Because you realised it's okay," she replied. "And it is."

"Can we not talk about it right now," I mumbled. "I need to get my head around a few things, I think. And see what makes sense when the dust settles."

"Sure thing. Is Angus home tonight?" she asked.

Angus was my flatmate. And if people thought I was weird, then Angus was a one-man what-the-fuck show. Maybe that was why we lived together so well. In three years, there'd never been one issue between us. He worked as a painter, and I think all those fumes had left some irreparable damage because he was dopey as fuck. But he paid his rent, his share of the utilities, bought his own food, didn't eat mine, and he respected boundaries. He was also a shameless bisexual flirt but was so bad at it and so clueless about it that it was almost sad, in a Shakespearean Comedy of Errors kind of way. The easiest way to describe him was as Hugh Grant's flatmate in *Notting Hill*, only Australian instead of Welsh, because everyone replied with "Oh" and a smile and a nod. And it was a true and fair comparison. They looked nothing alike but were still basically the same, and he would even sometimes parade the flat in his tighty-whities while he was waiting on something in the dryer. He'd once harboured great fondness for Merry, in a futile attempt at wooing her. She'd explained to him she was a lesbian, and he said that was perfect because he was bisexual, and she'd then had to explain that wasn't how any of that worked at all. I'd almost needed to draw Angus a diagram to clarify that one, and in the end, I still don't think he understood. So, and this was said with great affection, he wasn't the brightest crayon in the box. But, he was polite and kind and had the biggest heart in the world, and he was possibly one of the greatest guys I'd ever met. I'd even probably call him one of my best friends. I didn't have many, so that was quite a statement.

"Yes, I think so."

"Should we see if he wants some pizza?" Merry asked.

"I think it's safe to assume that'd be a yes."

So, two wood-fired pizzas later, we went back to my flat and met a very enthusiastic and grateful Angus. He was bingeing *Orange is the New Black* on Netflix, so we joined him on the floor, ate pizza, drank a few beers, and I tried really hard to forget my night.

"You'll never guess who was running the meeting," Merry said, throwing me holus-bolus under the bus.

I groaned and Angus' whole face brightened. "Joel Edgerton!"

"What?" Merry asked, somewhat startled. "No. It wasn't Joel Edgerton."

He tried again. "Clover Moore."

Merry squinted at him, then obviously remembered how she phrased it. She'd asked him to guess. "No," she said. "The Mayor of Sydney was busy. It was Jordan's Headphones Guy. You know, the guy on the bus that he's mooned over for six months?"

Angus slow-turned to me, with a comically surprised expression. "Nooooo."

"There was no mooning. I did not participate in any mooning." I was horrified.

Angus' eyeballs almost exploded out of his head. "You mooned him?"

Merry nodded as she bit into another slice. "Not that kind of mooning. He did not show him his naked arse. If you moon over someone, you daydream over them."

"Ohhhh," Angus said, nodding slowly.

"I did not moon him," I said indignantly. "Butthole or daydreaming or any kind of astral body. Jesus, fuck. Where is my dignity?"

Angus looked around the room. "I dunno man. Did you lose it?"

I slow blinked. "No, it's around here somewhere."

Angus smiled. "Cool. So did you speak to him?"

"Yep."

"He did more than that," Merry said, smiling as she shoved the crust of her pizza slice into her mouth.

"Shut up." I grabbed another piece of pizza with as much aggression as I could. "I'll need to find another bus to catch home and possibly move suburbs. Cities even. I haven't decided."

"You'll be fine," Merry said.

Angus frowned. "Jordan, are we moving?"

I wouldn't ever admit it to anyone out loud, but I did like how he assumed if I moved, he'd be moving with me. I patted his leg. "No, mate. We're good."

"Phew," he said, smiling and taking another slice of pizza. "You want another beer?"

"Sure." I smiled up at him as he stood and headed toward the kitchen. "I need all the help I can get with forgetting this clusterfuck of a night."

"Jordan, you'll be fine," Merry said.

She said the same thing to me on Monday at two minutes past five as I was almost hyperventilating at the bus stop. "Jordan, you'll be fine. He's a nice guy. You have nothing to worry about. Unless he's not on the bus..."

"Oh motherfucker, why would you say that?" I took some gulps of air. "What if he's not on the bus? What if he moved suburbs to avoid me? And now he's joined the witness protection program, his name is Hans Solo Gruber and he's an intergalactic German terrorist smuggler, living in the Nakatomi Cantina—"

Merry gave my arm a shake. "Jordan. Stop it. Get on the bus. Say hello to him."

I made a high-pitched sound that surprised even me.

Merry smiled. "I'll call you tonight." She nodded over my shoulder, and I turned to find the bus right fucking there.

Motherfucker.

I had no choice but to get on. I swiped my Opal card and didn't want to scan the faces. I truly didn't, but of course I did. There he was, sitting halfway up, headphones on. And of course I had to walk past him, and just as I made my way through the crowd, he looked up. Then he did a double take, and he smiled and nodded and pointed to his own head. "Headphones Guy."

I nodded. There were no spare seats near him, so I stood there like a loser. It took me forever to get my brain to work, and Hennessy pulled his headphones down to rest around his neck. "Um, yeah. Hi. I'd always wondered what music you listened to. I would guess it's some ultra-cool indie band that no one has ever heard of or some underground jazz-fusion mix that won't hit mainstream for another five years. But then I saw you listening to something that made you upset last Thursday, or maybe it was something completely unrelated to your eclectic music taste. I don't know, that's not really my business and that's not why I'm bringing it up. I just, well, I saw you upset and then the next day you saw me upset, so I guess we're even—"

He stood up, our fronts almost touching, and the bus jerked and we brushed against each other and I thought I might die. He was a fraction taller than me and I could get lost in those eyes and that smile should be a federal offence. "My stop," he said, nodding toward the door. Other people were now lining up to get off the bus, and I was holding them up. He was still impossibly close to me. "And it's not music I listen to. It's audiobooks."

"Audiobooks?" I whispered, like he just announced his undying love for me. My heart, my heart was about to explode. I was sure I had ridiculous cartoon hearts in my eyes.

"*Flowers for Algernon*," he whispered. "It's what I was listening to."

"Daniel Keyes," I breathed, looking right into his eyes, our faces an inch apart. "That book... Ow, my heart."

He let out a quiet gasp. "You know it?"

"I cried like a baby."

"Me too. Every time." He grinned, our gaze broken by the rush of people trying to get off the bus, and Hennessy turned and stepped off, leaving a void in his place. I fell into his now-vacant seat, pretty sure by the way my head spun that I hadn't breathed since I got on. And he stood there on the footpath with his head down, and he pulled his headphones back on and popped his coat collar up around his neck to protect him from the wind, looking seven different realms of handsome. And I thought for sure I'd blown it—again, with the incoherent babbling. But as the bus pulled away, he looked right up at me and smiled, all shy-like and timid, and I breathed the only thing worth saying. "Motherfucker."

The old lady I was sitting next to gaped at me. I shrugged, not even the slightest bit sorry. Okay, well maybe just a little sorry. But he smiled at me. Hennessy goddamned smiled right at me, like I was the reason for his happiness.

"*Flowers for Algernon*," I said to the lady who was now scowling at me. She didn't understand the enormity of this revelation, but I knew who would. I pulled out my phone, hit Merry's number, and didn't even give her time to say hello, though I did try and keep my voice down. "It's not music he listens to in his headphones. It's audiobooks. He reads books, and not just any books, Merry, but classics. Well, modern-day classics and holy fucking shit could he be any more perfect?"

"New phone, who dis?"

"I'm not even kidding right now," I replied. I ignored the daggers Mother Teresa was giving me because of my colourful language. "His grandfather didn't die, and he wasn't heartbroken by some incomparable Adonis that I'd have to track down and kick in the shins. He was crying because of the book. Guess which audiobook he was listening to that puts him in the stratosphere of cool? Guess!"

"*The Social War* by Simon Mohler Landis."

I stopped like I'd teleported to an alternative universe, blinked, then sputtered. "What the actual fuck, Merry. Who hurt you?"

She laughed. "I don't know which book he was listening to, but I can only assume you spoke to him?"

"I made him smile. In a good way. And you haven't guessed the book. You'll never guess but, oh my God, Merry. He just became a twelve on the scale of one to ten on perfection."

"This will be over a whole lot quicker if you just tell me."

I grinned, even just thinking about it. "*Flowers for Algernon.*"

There was a long beat of silence. "Oh."

"I know, right?"

"That explains the tears."

I sighed happily. "It does. It tells me so much about him.

Plus, I spoke to him. Like actual words, in somewhat semi-coherent sentences. Unlike *The Social War* by Mohler Landis. Jesus Christ, Merry. We need to talk about the credibility of your bibliophilism."

She laughed again. "So can we stop calling him Head-phones Guy now he has a name?"

"I think so. His name is kind of perfect, don't you think?"

"Okay look, Jordan, I'm just going to say this at the risk of you having a freak out on the bus, in public, but I don't want you getting way ahead of yourself so here it is. Yes, he's gay. He's even asexual. We know this. He said he was. What we don't know is if he's seeing someone, dating, or married even. Or what he does for a living."

"What difference does his job make?"

"What if he's an undertaker? Or a hitman?"

"Undertakers and hitmen need love too, Merry. Prob-ably more than other people."

She snorted. "We're talking about this tomorrow, okay?"

Hmmm. "Fine." I ended the call, determined once I got home I'd do some social-network stalking. How many guys living in Sydney called Hennessy could there possibly be?

CHAPTER FOUR

HE KNEW who Daniel Keyes was. He knew the author and title of one of my favourite books in the world. Nobody knew who Daniel Keyes was. Well, not guys I'd dated anyway. Some were lucky to know which end of a book to hold. I had nothing against guys who didn't read, per se, but most of them couldn't even pretend to act interested when I told them about books I loved.

But I only had to mention the title and Jordan knew who the author was. And his eyes when I admitted it wasn't music I was listening to... well, his grey-coloured eyes melted like silver, warm amber with hints of blue and green. And he smelt really good, and his nervous rambling was kinda cute.

At the meeting the night before, I thought he'd looked familiar and I wondered where I'd seen him before. And I'd wondered where the hell he'd seen me. What did he call me the other night? He called me Headphones Guy, so it was either to or from work, or maybe the gym. And then I recognised him on the bus. Of course I'd seen him get on the bus before, always at the same stop on Crown Street, but I didn't reconcile him with the guy at the meeting the other night. But now it kind of clicked.

I had to admit, I was intrigued.

I'd been intrigued after the meeting, when he'd broken down the defensive walls he'd put up around his acceptance of being somewhere on the asexual spectrum. He talked a mile a minute, and it was kind of hard to follow at first, but he was clearly very smart and articulate, and he was funny as hell. But he was also vulnerable, and he was there for help on understanding and coming to terms with who he was. Being intrigued by him in a romantic way wasn't on the cards at all. I couldn't and wouldn't abuse his trust in me as a support group leader.

But then he had to go and know who Daniel Keyes was, and he just had to look at me in a way that made my heart squeeze. Eye contact was such a big thing for me, and there was no way he could even know that.

So there I was at work the next day, distracted enough for Michael to notice. "You want to talk about what's got your mind a million miles from home?"

Michael and I had known each other forever—since primary school, then high school, and later on at university where we both studied fields of computer sciences. We were never overly close as kids or at high school, but at uni we had social circles that overlapped like a Venn diagram, with him and me in the middle common element, and we just clicked.

Even before uni was over, he'd put down the foundations of an interactive computer engineering company and needed a network architect, which was my area of expertise, and over the last five years, we'd become inseparable mates.

He had black hair, dark eyes and eyelashes that people paid a fortune for, a smile that won contracts, a jaw that could cut glass, and a stare so intense, it made a competitor fold like a pack of cards.

And while I'd initially helped him set up his business, technically he was my boss, and I was perfectly okay with that. Actually, seeing him stress over corporate taxes and dividends and margins and a tonne of other business-related bullshit, I was more than okay with him being the boss. He paid me well, and sure, we talked business and he asked me for my professional opinion on some business deals, but I was happy without the added responsibilities he had.

And, somehow, we'd managed to maintain our friendship over the course of our careers. Which would explain why he put a fresh coffee in front of me and looked at me with that expectant gaze. I took a sip of the coffee, and it was good. "Thanks. And yeah, I don't even know what I'm thinking about."

He snorted. "So, what's his name?"

I tried not to laugh but rolled my eyes. He knew me too well. "Jordan. But before you say anything, it's not like that. He came to my support meeting last Friday night and he was a bit upset. We spoke afterwards for a while, but then I saw him again yesterday. On the bus," I added before he could assume anything.

"And?"

"And he's funny. He does this flustered, awkward thing, which is cute."

"And he went to your support meeting? So he's..."

"Gay, yes. Asexual, maybe. He's pretty sure it's a fit. But it's early days. I think he needs time to get used to the idea."

"So why are you even thinking about him?" Michael

asked, and it was a fair question. "Is that not a conflict of interest? I don't want to see you get hurt, that's all."

I smiled at him. "I know, and thank you. I do appreciate that. It's just..."

He narrowed his gaze at me. "It's just what?"

"He knows who Daniel Keyes is."

"One of your book guys?"

"They actually have names for them now. They're called authors," I said with a grin. "And yes. But he didn't just know. I said the title, and he knew the author without blinking, and he knew the tone of the book and he did this excited gasping thing when I mentioned it."

Michael stared at me over his coffee cup, mid-sip. "Oh shit."

I pressed my lips together tight, then let out a long sigh. "Crazy, huh?"

"That you found another book-loving asexual gay man under sixty living in Sydney?"

I chuckled. "Well, yes. But I don't know. I've spoken to him twice. The second time for all five seconds on the bus. And like you said, it's a conflict of interest, and he came to the meeting for help. The last thing he needs right now is me messing that up."

Michael shook his head slowly. "All this could have been avoided if you just bought a bloody car."

I snorted at that. "The bus literally takes me from my front door to here, then here to home again. It's less hassle, cheaper, and it's better for the environment."

He rolled his eyes, like he always did when we had this conversation. Then he brightened. "Oh shit, I almost forgot. Vee invited you to come over for dinner on Saturday night." Vee, or Veronica, was Michael's wife, and by association, a dear friend of mine. Since I'd split with Rob, she'd been trying her hand at matchmaking.

"She's not trying to set me up again, is she?"

"She worries about you."

"Worries? What for? I'm doing fine. Happily single."

"I told her you're doing fine. Actually, I told her you're much happier now."

"I am, thanks." I took another sip of coffee. "If it's not a blind date disguised as a dinner date, then yes, I'd love to come over."

"I don't know who she's invited," he replied, hiding that twisted-lip thing he did behind his coffee cup.

"God, you can't lie for shit." I conceded defeat. No, I didn't want a blind date with anyone, but dinner with my best friend and his wife and not another weekend alone sounded pretty bloody good. "Ask her if I need to bring anything."

"I will," he said. Then his smile faded before he added, "So, if this Jordan guy catches your bus, you'll be seeing him again this afternoon..."

"Possibly. But I might not get to speak to him if the bus is crowded or whatever."

Michael nodded slowly. "Right."

I sighed. "It's not like that. It can't be."

"I feel a qualifier coming on. It can't be like that *until*... it can't be like that *while*... it can't be like—"

"Oh shut up," I grumbled, turning back to my screen, trying not to smile. "Piss off and let me get back to work." He smiled and left me to it, thankfully, without another word.

But the truth was, in my mind, I was adding a qualifier. Which wasn't good.

My priority as a support group leader was to offer

support, information, and pathways to resources if required, not to abuse his trust in my hopes of a possible date prospect.

For the rest of the day, I tried not to think about it. I tried not to think about Jordan, and I tried not to think about how he'd looked at me on the bus when I stood up and we were standing almost nose-to-nose, or how he'd blushed, and how he'd smelt. And I told myself I wasn't ready for another failed attempt at a relationship, and I had to keep reminding myself that it was stupid and foolish to be thinking *anything* about a guy I'd only just met.

But later that day on the bus, I smiled when I saw him waiting to get on. His friend Merry was waiting with him and I saw her look into the bus and she smiled when she saw me, so I could only assume they'd been talking about me, and that made me happier than it should have. But the bus was kind of full and he got bustled up toward the back. He was flustered and he almost tripped, and he mumbled, "Motherfu—" before he caught himself and didn't actually swear, but it made me smile.

I resisted turning around to see if he'd found a seat or to see if he was looking at me, but when it was my stop, I looked up toward the back of the bus without really meaning to. He was sitting second from the back with his nose in a book, and he glanced up just as I was stepping off.

I smiled at him; he smiled right back. I waved and he grinned and blushed and held the book up to hide his face. I stepped off the bus, sorry I didn't get to speak to him, but our wordless exchange was perhaps even better. It was shy and almost sweet, which said more than maybe what a full conversation might have, and that was ridiculous.

I was still smiling when I opened the door to my townhouse. I threw my coat onto my couch and tried not to overthink anything. I said hi to my two Siamese fighting fish, Ali and Bruce, and asked Spike how his day was. Spike was a cactus I'd had for years, but I still spoke to him. He sat on the windowsill, ever silent. When Rob and I split, he remarked on the irony of me having two fish who lived in separate tanks, never allowed to touch, and a prickly—very untouchable—cactus. I didn't care what it said about me. It made me love Ali, Bruce, and Spike a little bit more. I sprayed Spike with the water bottle. "Cheer up. It'll be summer soon enough," I told him.

I threw dinner in the oven, pulled on my running gear, and hit the pavement for half an hour while my roast for one cooked, but I couldn't get something out of my head. The book he was reading... It had an unusual cover: red and some vine-looking thing. It was distinctive, and for some strange reason, I couldn't stop thinking about it. So later on, as I sat at the table and ate my dinner, I opened up my laptop and began a search. It took a while, but I was almost certain I'd found it. Well, I found the cover, but the book made no sense.

It was an old book, mid-eighteenth century to be exact, by French Revolutionist author George Sand. It was called *Mauprat*, had won literary acclaim for its time, and was considered a great from anyone who knew anything about French literature.

Was that really what he was reading?

I stared at the cover, and I pictured him smiling and blushing, hiding behind his book, bookmark in hand. *This* book. This book by some old French author almost two hundred years ago.

It was definitely the same. Obviously the book had had dozens of different covers over the years, but this one was distinct and unusual.

And I was distinctly, unusually, very much intrigued.

Most guys I knew didn't read much. Well, they read about keto diets and shredding, or the financial review or sports pages of the paper, but never literature. Let alone literature in a different language from a different century.

Yes, I was intrigued.

The next day, the bus was full again. The weather was drizzly and the wind was cold, and someone had already taken the seat next to me. When Jordan got on the bus, he appeared hopeful and he smiled as soon as he saw me, but when he realised the bus was full, he let out a visible sigh and trudged up the back.

When it was my stop, I stood up, edged out of my seat, and when I was standing at my full height in the aisle, I pulled my headphones off. I turned to say something, but he had his book open, though he was frowning out the window. Only when he seemed to realise where we were, he glanced up, and finding me looking right at him, his smile was instantaneous and he clutched his book to his chest and watched me as I got off the bus.

It made me so happy, I didn't even try to hide my smile as the bus pulled away.

I went for my usual jog, ate my usual dinner for one, and the next day I went to work with my smile still in place.

Michael took one look at me. "You spoke to him again," he said, not a question at all. "To that book guy."

I chuckled. "No." My grin widened. "But I'm going to."

Michael had nodded slowly and frowned. It was a look I knew well. He had something to bring up but he wasn't quite sure how. "Just ask," I said, pushing away from my desk and giving him my full attention.

"Oh, it's nothing," he said dismissively, but from the look on his face, it was clearly something. "It's stupid and

I'm probably speaking out of turn, but can I ask you something?"

I'd always been very honest with Michael, and I had no problem in answering any questions he might have about what asexuality meant for me. But this felt different, and I tried not to be defensive. "Yeah?"

"It's just." He laughed and shook his head at himself, then stared out at the Sydney city view from my window. For a moment I didn't think he was going to say anything else, but then, still without looking at me, he frowned again. "Do you think it's possible to love two people?"

Wait. What? "Michael, what are you saying?" I whispered. "Are you cheating on Vee? Because that's not cool, and that's not like you. Man, I thought you were happy? I thought you were both so happy it was vomit-inducing."

He laughed. "No, it's not like that. Of course I'm not cheating on Vee. I would never..."

"Then what is it?"

He shook it off with a bit of a laugh. "Nah, it's nothing. I'm just thinking about something else." He grinned at me and laughed it off again. "So, how's working with Rob?"

If his change in subject was a distraction, it worked. Because yes, one of the biggest contracts we had right now was with my ex-live-in boyfriend, Rob. He'd wanted a new website for his fire-safety company, which was growing exponentially. Sure, he was successful, but he was also a jerk. And he wanted the best corporate website engineer company, which was us. "Ugh. Getting there. The port parameters need work but, it's just time consuming."

"We have a month till the relaunch," Michael said.

"Easy." And so began a more in-depth conversation about the job, and I didn't give Michael's question about loving two people any more thought.

Later that afternoon, I snagged an empty double seat and sat in the aisle, giving my messenger bag the window. I felt bad for hogging a seat, and truthfully if someone needed it, I would have gladly given it to them. Or mine, if needed. But thankfully the bus wasn't completely full, and when Jordan stepped on and swiped his Opal card, he looked up and saw me. I lifted my bag and slid over and he grinned, then totally tried to rein it in, but failed.

He sat beside me, his messenger bag on his lap. "Uh, thank you."

"You're welcome," I replied. "I thought you might need a seat."

"Oh yeah, I really did. The other day, I sat next to a lady who was like, I don't know, eighty something, and of course I said motherfucker—" He froze. "I didn't call her that. I just said it in general, but she heard it and I'm convinced she thinks I'm possessed by Satan. Pretty sure there was a string of Hail Marys mumbled under her breath. You know, to save my soul. Or whatever people pray for. I wouldn't know. I'm not inclined to pray. Unless it's to the bean god, Java."

"Java?"

"Yeah, you know coffee," he said without missing a beat. "But thank you for the seat. Were you waiting for me? I mean, it's totally cool if it was just a coincidence and all, I appreciate it at any rate."

"I uh, I did save it for you," I said. "If that's okay..."

"Oh sure. But if someone else needed it, you should have absolutely given it to them." He looked around behind us and made a face. "Except for the lady three rows back. She's the one who prayed for me."

That made me laugh.

"Was there any reason?" he asked. "That is, for saving me a seat. I'm glad you did, don't get me wrong."

"Actually, I wanted to ask you about your book."

"My book?"

"The one you were reading, with the red cover."

"Oh." He opened his bag and took out the book in question. "This?"

There it was. He was definitely reading old French literature. The jolting of the bus made me look up and I realised we were almost at my stop. "Shit." I stood up, holding my bag, and Jordan had to move his legs so I could get out. Once in the aisle, I stopped to say goodbye but noticed he was frowning.

"Is there something wrong with my book?" he asked, looking up at me from his seat.

I grinned and shook my head. "Absolutely not. It's perfect."

He blinked and smiled slowly. "Oh."

Then the doors beeped to signal they were about to close, and I realised that everyone who had been waiting to get on were taking their seats, and I had to dash off the bus. I looked up as the bus pulled away and saw him grinning.

The next day I saved him a seat again, and I slid my headphones off so they were around my neck as he sat down. Today's scarf was green to match his shoes. "This is becoming a habit," he said shyly. His cheeks were slightly pink. If it was from the cold or if he was blushing, I wasn't sure.

"If you'd rather I didn't," I hedged.

"Oh no," he shot back quickly. "It's fine. I didn't mean to sound ungrateful."

"You didn't sound ungrateful." I pulled my headphones off from around my neck and shoved them into my messenger bag.

"Which audiobook are you listening to now?" he asked.

"Oh, it's called *Death's End*. It's um..."

"It's good, apparently. I haven't read the trilogy myself, but I've heard good things."

"You know a lot about books."

"I do." He swallowed hard, and that was apparently all he was going to say on that subject.

"I like your scarf today," I said.

He laughed and looked down at the ends of the scarf and ran it through his fingers. "Thanks. I like to add a little colour to an otherwise drab uniform."

"It matches, every day," I said.

"Of course it does." He leaned in and whispered conspiratorially, "I'm gay. Of course it fucking matches."

I snorted out a laugh. "I like it. That it matches, that is."

"I like that you have such eclectic taste in books, and I like that you save me a seat." He shook his head like he couldn't believe he'd just said that.

The bus turned onto Cleveland. "Um. This is my stop." He turned his knees to the aisle, giving me room to get out. I stood and fixed my messenger bag over my shoulder. "I like that you like those things."

"Tomorrow then," he said, his cheeks pinking up nicely.

"Tomorrow."

MICHAEL TOOK one look at me, handed me my coffee, and narrowed his eyes. "Okay, spill the deets. What happened?"

"What do you mean?" I feigned ignorance.

He held out his hand, counting off his fingers. "You're happy, for one. Two, I know that smile. That smile tells me something happened with, I'm assuming, your bus guy. And three, you can't lie for shit."

There was no point denying it. "We've been talking. On the bus. But just for five minutes, each day. That's it. Nothing too exciting. But..."

"But?"

"But he's interesting. And he's cute."

"And he's asexual?"

I frowned up at him. "Not that it matters, but yes. Well, we haven't discussed it since the meeting, but he went to a support group for asexuals and he had a bit of a freak-out because he realised it was his truth, so yes. I'm thinking he is."

"I just don't want to see you go through all that shit again, that's all."

"I know. And I appreciate that. But it shouldn't matter."

"But it kind of does."

I sighed and let my agreement go unsaid. We both knew he was right.

"Maybe you should ask him," Michael said before sipping his coffee. He left me alone with that, and I knew he had a point.

"Maybe I should."

───────────

I LIFTED my bag onto my lap and Jordan smiled as he sat next to me. He wore a red scarf today, matching his red shoes, and the colour complemented the pink of his cheeks perfectly.

"Good afternoon," I said, unable to hide my smile. I ignored the feeling in my belly that felt a lot like butterflies.

"Hi," he replied. "Thanks again for the seat. It's cold out there today."

"It is," I said, nodding to the dark and gloomy Sydney sky. "Makes running in the evenings a bit brisk."

"You run?" he asked. "Like, willingly? For fun?"

"Well, I don't know if fun is the right word. Exercise, mostly. It helps to clear my head, and I do enjoy it, so maybe a little bit of fun. I take it you're not a fan."

"Hmm, running," he pondered. "Actually, I run late for most things. I run my mouth off all the time. I have a run-in with some arsehole customers on the regular. I run errands. Oh, and I have actually had to run to the bathroom a few times, which is why I now no longer eat dairy."

I laughed at that.

Smiling, he added, "Wasn't pretty. But general running for cardiovascular exercise, not so much."

The bus stopped at the lights at Cleveland Street and my stop was up next, so if I wanted to ask him about the asexual thing, I needed to do it now.

"Can I ask you something?"

"Uh, sure," he said, making it sound like a question. "I have soy in my coffee, if you're wondering about the dairy thing. Sometimes almond milk if I want to live dangerously."

I snorted. "That wasn't my question, but it's good to know, thanks."

He looked at me and I suddenly found the stitching on my messenger bag really interesting. The traffic lights turned green and we rumbled around the corner. Dammit, I needed more time...

"Your question?" he prompted. "I mean, it's no big deal. I get asked questions all the time. Like just today, I got asked why *Sun-Beams May Be Extracted From Cucumbers, But*

The Process Is Tedious wasn't included in all state libraries. Not completely random, but throw in the fact it was a guy literally wearing a tin foil hat who asked... And they look at me like I'm the one with a problem."

I blinked at that and considered asking *what the fuck* because how was that, in anyone's definition, not random, but the bus was pulling up at the kerb. "Well, damn. That was my question. Now I feel stupid."

He gawped at me until he realised I was smiling. "Your question was about *Sun-Beams May Be Extracted From Cucumbers, But The Process Is Tedious*?"

"Yes. How uncanny that someone should think to ask it before me."

"You are joking, right?"

"Yes."

"Sarcasm is in the self-help section, by the way."

"Self-help?"

"Yes, so you can pull your head out of your own arse."

I barked out a laugh. "Are you always so funny?"

He shrugged. "I don't know. There's a fine line between comedy and horror. It could go either way."

The doors opened and I had to get up. "Sorry, this is my stop."

"Oh, sure." He swung his legs out so I could slip past. "Was the 'are you always so funny' question your actual question?"

I stopped in the aisle. "No." I had two seconds to move or I'd be walking back to my place from wherever the next stop was. "It can wait till tomorrow."

He looked suddenly horrified. "No, it can't. Do you know what that kind of waiting will do to me? I'll be like the critter in *Ice Age* who chases that damn acorn for four movies."

I laughed, but I really did have to get off. I climbed off before the bus driver could shut me in, and when I looked up at the window where he was sitting, his face was priceless.

"Tomorrow," I called out.

He narrowed his eyes, his mouth open. I didn't have to hear what he said. I could read his lips just fine.

Motherfucker.

CHAPTER FIVE

JORDAN

"DO you know what kind of torture that is?" I asked Merry as I slid a pile of books onto the trolley. I'd barely slept a wink, and I'd let every possible conceivable question he might want to ask me run through my mind. I'd also talked pretty much non-stop at Merry since she arrived at work. By the way she'd stopped trying not to roll her eyes and sigh, I gathered she was over hearing about it. But this was driving me insane.

So as my best friend, it was only right she was driven up the wall too.

"Well, it's not like waterboarding or the old bamboo under the fingernail kind of torture," I allowed. "It's more like a dripping tap that you can't shut off. Like a constant *drip, drip, drip.* Or when you're trying to think of the name of a song but you can't because you can't remember who sang it or any of the lyrics, only that you think it was in a movie where some guy holds up a stereo or fist pumps the air or something. Like that Simple Minds song and you could have sworn it was John Cusack in *Say Anything,* and you can't think of it for days—it drives you motherfucking crazy—only to find out it was really Judd Nelson at the end of *The Breakfast Club*."

Merry held up a book like it was a shield. "Do you know what my favourite part of a book is?" she asked, her face stoic. She didn't give me time to change gears in the conversation.

"Huh?"

"My favourite part of any well-written book is that it will have a beginning," she said. "And a middle, and a goddamn end, Jordan. An ending! Which is what this conversation is lacking. They're magical. Maybe you can try it."

"I hate you. And I take back what I said about your cardigan. It's not cute. It's hideous."

"Of course it is."

"Anyway, as I was saying, and this is the end so you can shut your taco-hole. He's going to ask me something, and he's given me twenty-four hours to think about all the possible scenarios. What if it's something revoltingly embarrassing? I'll need to change buses and possibly wear a disguise. Which brings me right back to his lack of social media presence. No one under the age of thirty doesn't have some kind of social media thing. And Hennessy, the name. It sounds made up, doesn't it? I'm convinced he's in the witness protection program, in which case I'll probably blow his cover. Or what if he's actually an undercover cop? No," I said, answering my own question. "They would have set up fake profiles as part of his new persona, surely."

Merry took a long breath and sagged. "For the love of everything that is good in this world, Jordan, he's not in the witness protection program. He's not an undercover cop. He's just a guy. A normal guy with an unusual name, who happens to catch the same bus you do. Who happened to be at the same local support group meeting as you. You're over-thinking this, and you're going to give yourself an ulcer. For all you know, the grand and mysterious question he's going to ask you is where you bought your shoes from. Or which restaurant you'd recommend for a date night with his husband. Or—"

"His husband? Why is he married? And why am I going out on a date night with his husband?"

Merry closed her eyes slowly and bowed her head, taking in a deep breath before she looked up at me. "You're not going on the date night with his husband."

"How do you know he's married?"

"I don't," she replied. "But you don't either. That's my point. Stop overthinking this. For all you know, he won't even be on the bus this afternoon and you'll never see him again and this burning question will remain a mystery forever and you'll die of old age still wondering what he was going to ask you."

My mouth fell open and it took me a good ten seconds before I could speak. "Why would you say that?! Was it your mission today to come to work and inflict physical pain on me like that?"

She deflated. "Yes. It was my sole mission. It's my life mission, actually. My cover's blown. I've been recruited to infiltrate your social circle, just like Hennessy the Head-phone Guy, to ensure harm is inflicted upon you daily."

I narrowed my eyes at her. "I knew it."

She dumped her pile of returns onto my trolley. "You can put these away. I'm exhausted from this conversation."

Then I felt bad. "I was just joking. I really do like your cardigan."

She sighed the mother of all sighs. "Jordan, no matter what he asks you and no matter what comes from it, I can tell you're already hopeful and invested, and I don't want to see you get hurt, but even if he's not interested in you like that, I think you could have a real good friend in him. Someone who understands you, who understands your relationship problems because chances are, he's been through the same."

"What are you saying?"

"If he plays the 'just-friends' card, that is still a good thing."

"Well, yeah..." I made a face. "Of course. I can see that."

She pursed her lips. "Jordan."

"No, I get it. I do. I can be friends with an undercover, asexual cop in the witness protection program." Then something occurred to me. "Oh God, what if he's not really asexual?"

"If he said he is, then he is. It's not something people lie about. And if he did lie about it—" She gave a serious nod. "—then we'll kneecap that motherfucker."

"Merry!" Mrs Mullhearn said from behind us. "Language!"

I burst out laughing and quickly pushed the trolley of returns away, abandoning Merry to cop a lecture about appropriate language and acceptable vernacular in the workplace. I smiled the entire time, though my ears burned. Like a motherfucker.

WAITING for the bus was like waiting for Christmas morning to see if Santa Claus either delivered the best present ever or if he merrily burst your bubble, depending on whether you've been naughty or nice, and Lord knows that could go either way. At any rate, I was either going to be thrilled or disappointed. I doubted there was a middle ground even if what Merry said made sense—and it did. My brain was the studious, logical type that could see very rationally that gaining a new friend who was also asexual and gay could be like the best thing ever. But my heart, on the other hand, was the blind drunk one, stumbling around in the dark, belting out 80s hits like "What About Me" and "Wake Me Up Before You Go-Go".

My brain and my heart very rarely saw eye to eye, which explained my string of failed relationships well enough. Well, that and the fact that me being asexual was an issue. It never started out as an issue, but as things progressed and time went on, it sure as hell became one.

But Hennessy wasn't like them.

So, as the bus pulled in, my heart was dressed in neon Lycra, a bottle in one hand and a microphone in the other, singing Deniece Williams' "Let's Hear It For The Boy" while my brain was stoic, arms crossed, working on some algorithm or genius equation that would determine indisputably, unequivocally, that I was the dumbest motherfucker on the planet for even entertaining the idea that Hennessy would be one, single. And two, remotely interested in me.

Taking a deep breath, I stepped onto the bus and couldn't even bring myself to scan the faces. Because what if Merry had jinxed me and he wasn't on the bus at all, and I'd have to somehow survive the weekend—or God forbid, the rest of my miserable existence—without knowing what he wanted to ask me.

But then my stupid heart broke out with Bonnie Tyler's "Turn Around Bright Eyes" so of course I turned around and there he was... smiling at me.

But the bus was full and he had a window seat. The

lady sitting next to him was the sweet old dear that I had to apologise to for dropping the mofo-bomb, though by the way she shot me a look of disdain, I was sure she thought I was evil, and I didn't fancy standing right next to her while I attempted to talk to Hennessy. It was going to be embarrassing enough without the judgemental audience mumbling ten Hail Marys under her breath.

So I gave Hennessy an apologetic smile and had to stand toward the front, holding onto the railing. And I put my head down and did some deep breathing, because as it turned out, the worst possible scenario did occur. I thought him not being on the bus would be the worst, but oh no, him being right fucking there but not being able to speak to him, that was the worst.

"Excuse me, excuse me," someone said, as they tried to weave their way through the people standing up. Keeping my head down, I shuffled forward a little, not that I could really go anywhere. I apologised to the poor woman sitting in front of me for the almost lap dance, but a warm hand on my back made me spin around.

And sweet baby Jesus in a manger, those eyes. "Hey," Hennessy said, really close and really sweet.

Every suave line I'd ever read evaporated from my mind. My traitorous brain had taken the bottle of vodka from my heart and was chugging away, leaving me to my own devices. "Hi," I said. Not even remotely manly, but more of a breathy, smiley, nervous sound which wasn't embarrassing at all. He was so close, and as the bus jostled, he bumped into me and put his hand on my arm to steady himself.

"I uh, I was hoping," he said, then broke out in a grin, like he was embarrassed or nervous or something that didn't make sense. "I had to offer your seat to that lady."

Why the hell was he nervous and flustered, and why was he blushing a little, and his hand was still on my arm? Nothing made sense, because my brain was now doing the drunken hula dance with a Mai Tai in each hand on a tropical beach singing the words horribly wrong to the Beach Boys' "Kokomo", a million miles away from where I needed it to be.

This was going to be a disaster.

"Are you okay?" he asked.

"Oh sure. I'm just... I was going to stand by your seat, but the lady who you were sitting next to thinks I'm the antichrist and it's Bonnie Tyler's fault I even looked for you, but now the Beach Boys are involved. God, I need to stop talking."

He stared at me and I shook my head, internally kicking myself. And you just wait, brain. I'll give you fucking "Aruba, Jamaica, oh I wanna take ya."

He was now looking at me like he had serious concerns for my mental health. "Sorry," I mumbled. "I'm just really nervous and you were going to ask me something yesterday but you didn't and I've spent the last twenty-four hours freaking out and I'm pretty sure Merry is—" His expression was growing more concerned so I stopped talking. "Not relevant to this conversation, sorry. You were going to ask me something. Please put me out of my misery."

He smiled and the bus came to a stop and he brushed up against me again. He didn't apologise, which could either mean he wasn't sorry for the physical contact or he was a mannerless jerk, and I hoped to all the gods it was the first.

"Yes, I did want to ask you something," he said. "And there's no right or wrong answer. You need to do what you're comfortable in doing. I don't want to influence your decision."

The bus jolted forward again as we took a right at Cleveland. Shit his stop was next. "If you don't just spit it out, I'm pretty sure Merry will hunt you down. Not sure she can take much more of me not knowing what you were going to ask me."

"You told her?"

"Of course. I might have mentioned it once. Or eighty-seven times."

He looked out the window and made a face when he saw his stop was coming up. "I just wanted to know," he said. "You know, the support group I run?"

"Yes."

An amazing explosion of blush coloured his cheeks. "Well, I was just wondering if you were thinking of coming back."

"Oh." I couldn't have hidden my disappointment if I tried. Of course it was about his meeting. It wasn't about me at all. "I was planning to, yeah. Do you like need to know for numbers or something? Because that's fair. Or if you need to change venues because we got interrupted by the drunk, horny couple. Oh God, did I make someone feel uncomfortable with all my crying and you need to tell me that it's probably for the best if I don't come back? Because you can just tell me. I'll understand."

"No, no. Nothing like that," he replied and the bus slowed to a stop. "Shit. I wish we had more time than five minutes a day."

Wait, what? He wants more time with me?

"Um, me too," I replied in that traitorous breathy voice. "I mean, what even is five minutes?"

The doors opened and people started to pile off the bus.

He looked a little panicked. "Tomorrow's Saturday. Are you free tomorrow? For a coffee, say two pm? I have more questions and—"

"Yes!" I all but yelled, then tried to play it all cool. "I mean, sure. I think I can squeeze that in. I have questions too." Yeah right, because my plans to do absolutely fucking nothing all day needed scheduling.

"Awesome. So, Alberto's at two?" He asked. I nodded; he grinned and, still facing me, took a step backwards to the door. Now some people were trying to get on the bus and he was kind of in their way, but he didn't even seem to notice. He was too busy smiling at me. "Oh, Alberto's is just around the corner."

I nodded. "Yep. Alberto's at two."

He bounced down the steps and onto the footpath. He pulled his headphones back on. Still smiling, he peered back up at me. The wind tousled his hair under his headphones and he bit on his bottom lip, like he was trying not to smile, and for one split second, for one perfect moment, he was the most beautiful thing I'd ever seen.

If this was a movie, this shot right here would be deemed a goddamned cinematic masterpiece.

I all but collapsed into a seat, sighing with relief that I'd spoken to him and he'd asked me his question, which I would no doubt overthink later. But yes, I was so relieved and even more excited because I had a motherfucking coffee date with him tomorrow.

I fished my phone out and hit Merry's number. She answered on the third ring with, "So help me Jordan, if he was a no-show and there was no resolution to this freakin' life-altering question, I'll be changing my name to River Blossom and moving to Nimbin where I can make hemp-infused soaps, and I'll grow carrots and smoke purple weed, and you'll never find me."

"Well, it won't be hard to find you because you just told me where you'd move to and your new name," I replied. "And you'd be so high from the weed and vegan pot brownies, I'd only have to follow the pizza delivery guy and he'd lead me straight to you. You'd also probably be glowing orange from all the beta-carotene from living on carrots too. You really need to work on your witness protection schemes, Merry. If this was in the *Bourne Supremacy* universe, you would have died in the first book."

She laughed and made a contented sound and I pictured her plonking herself on her couch.

"Are you home?" I asked.

"Yes, thank God. And I have no intention of moving from in front of Netflix all night." Then she groaned. "I should have got myself a drink before I sat down. Jordan, be a darling and come over and bring me a glass of wine so I don't have to move. And pizza."

I sighed dramatically. "I'm sorry, beautiful. I'm far too busy. I need to spend my entire night planning my coffee date tomorrow at two o'clock with one totally gorgeous Hennessy... Hennessy... Mister Hennessy who has no last name because he has no social media presence and he's too cute for a surname."

"Wait, what?"

"He has no surname," I answered. "Like Adele and Rihanna. Not that I've found anyway. I told you that before."

"Not his name," she cried. "You said coffee date. You said coffee date at two o'clock!"

I barely refrained from squealing. "I know!"

"Jordan O'Neill you tell me everything this second! All the details. Who asked whom?"

I snorted. "Really, Merry. Do you think I'd be capable of asking him?"

"Well, you could have blurted it out or asked him without meaning to or something. I don't know," she said. "So he asked you? Oh my God, Jordan, this is huge!"

That time I did actually squeal and I might have done a little happy dance in my seat. I did try to keep my voice down, but I was so used to people glaring at me for dropping a motherfucker every now and then, I figured a bit of volume was the least of my worries. "I know! He said he had questions and he wished we had more than just five minutes on the bus each day, and the bus was full so I couldn't sit next to him. I had to stand and he got up before his stop to talk to me."

"Aww, that's so cute. So, did he ask you the question?"

"Well, kind of. I mean, he did, but it was weird."

"Weird, how?"

"Well, he wanted to know if I had any intention of going back to the next support meeting. That was his question. The one burning question that drove me crazy."

"Hmm," she said.

"What does that mean? What does *hmm* mean? Is that the *hmm* of judgement? Or the *hmm* of disdain? The *hmm* of death? Merry..."

"Well, it's just interesting, that's all. It could mean a few things."

"Such as? I haven't had time to think about anything. He got off the bus and I called you."

"Aw, you're so sweet."

"What do you think it means? Should I be worried? Because I asked him if he didn't want me to come back or if

I'd made someone uncomfortable and he looked kinda horrified and said no, it was nothing like that. Just that he had
other questions as well, so he wanted to know if I was free
tomorrow."

"I think maybe he asked you if you were going to the
next meeting as a way to ask if you'd felt more comfortable
with the asexual revelation you had."

I replayed what she said in my head. "Do you think?"

"Well, it's better than asking outright where your head's
at, know what I mean?"

"I guess..."

"Or maybe he asked you as a way to determine how
successful his meetings are."

"Oh."

"But I think it's Option A, Jordan. Look at the bigger
picture. He's been saving you a seat, and he asked you out
for coffee. I think he's interested. I think he likes you."

My heart pounded and I began to sweat. "Oh God."

"Breathe, Jordan. It's a good thing."

I exhaled slowly then inhaled, rinse and repeat. Jesus.
"Until I fuck it up."

"How will you fuck this up?"

"You've met me. I open my mouth and all there is is
explosive verbal diarrhoea. No one is safe."

She snorted. "Jordan, he's not like the other guys. He's
not going to dump you because you don't want to get into
bed with him. Remember where you met him. At a meeting
for asexual and aromantic people."

There was more heart pounding, more sweating, and
now my forehead felt cold and somehow hot at the same
time. Or was that my palms? I couldn't tell.

"Jordan, you'll be fine. Don't overthink it and just be
yourself. Be honest with him. And remember, if dating isn't

on the cards, he'd be a kick-arse guy to call a friend, yeah? He likes books, he's funny, and he's a decent human being, which we all know is a fucking rarity these days. For all we know, he might need a friend. So how about meeting him for coffee tomorrow with the premise of friends-only? Then there's no pressure. Let him get to know you. You can get to know him too. Maybe ask him his surname, and start from there."

I felt better already. "You know exactly how to talk me down."

"Because I know you."

"I'm sorry I drove you crazy today at work."

"That's okay. You can repay me by coming into the city with me on Sunday. I need to buy my mother a birthday present."

"Ugh. Jeez. I said I was sorry already. No need to be mean."

She laughed. "See? And you understand me."

It was true. Merry's mother was one impossible woman. "I will take my punishment for being an arse to you today. How old is Satan turning anyway?"

"666."

"Sounds about right," I said, feeling so much better. "I'll be at your place at about ten on Sunday morning, yeah?"

"Perfect. And you'll bring coffee?"

"Of course."

"You're a lad. Though I fully expect a phone call tomorrow at about twelve as you spiral into freak-out mode."

I considered objecting, but we both knew a spiral into freak-out mode was highly likely. If I put pressure on myself, then I would freak out for sure. But to think of him as just a friend was almost calming. Huh. So weird. "No, I think I like the idea of being friends with him. I mean, I need to know him first, right? Regardless of the fact he's gorgeous and his smile gives me butterflies and he loves audiobooks, I mean let's not pretend the man isn't perfect boyfriend material. But it'd be pretty damn cool to have a friend who's more like me than not, ya know?"

"Absolutely. Friends is good too."

I sighed. "It is. And I would be happy with him just as a friend. I'm not even kidding." I took a second to internalise that, and I nodded to myself. "I'm actually really okay with that. To the point where I'm starting to wonder if that's what I need right now. A friend, nothing more."

CHAPTER SIX

I WAS NERVOUS. Probably more nervous than I should have been, and I tried to tell myself that I should treat this like any and all of my asexual support group meetings. But something felt different.

Jordan was different.

I'd spent most of the morning at work, which was a great distraction, and it allowed me to get a lot done. Except my mind was all over the place.

I couldn't even believe I'd asked him for coffee. I had everything planned in my head for our brief encounter on the bus yesterday, but that all went to hell when the bus was full and that sweet little old lady asked if she could take the seat. There was no way I was saying no to her, but then Jordan got on the bus, all flustered and clearly disappointed that this new seat-saving thing we'd started had been thwarted.

And the idea of being robbed of my daily five-minute conversation with him just wasn't going to fly, so I gave up my seat and squeezed through the crowd just for the chance of saying hello. I'd wondered what on earth had possessed me and had visions of it being a disaster, but then he'd looked up at me and smiled.

And I knew then I'd totally made the right decision.

But five minutes wasn't enough. Not even close. I had the feeling that he and I could talk for hours. Okay, correction. I had the feeling that Jordan could talk for hours. But I also had the feeling that he'd be interesting and smart, and coupled with his sense of humour, it was refreshing.

So I asked him to meet me for coffee, which was why I sat in Alberto's at ten to two, trying to not watch the clock and trying not to get my hopes up that he would even show.

It was cold outside, the wind was biting and blustery, but it didn't stop the good people of Surry Hills from being out in it. They walked dogs and pushed prams, holding takeaway coffee cups as they went. Once a not-so-great suburb, Surry Hills was now the hub of trendy coffee houses, cool clothes, and eclectic homewares stores. I liked it here, and although the move had seemed rather daunting six months before, I knew I'd made the right decision. I'd found a home here. The baristas at Alberto's called me by name. The lady in the fresh produce store always kept a bag of organic pumpkin pasta behind the counter for me because it sold out so fast. My neighbours were nice, not that I spoke to them much, but the move here had been a positive one.

Leaving Rob and being true to myself was the best thing I could have done.

And then there was my new support group meetings, which I was incredibly proud of. And then there was Jordan, and something sparked inside me. I didn't know if it would lead to anything, but it was nice to feel that flicker of hope.

At exactly five to two, said flicker of hope walked up to

the café door. Jordan, wearing blue jeans, a white sweater with a brown jacket, and boots. I was almost a little disappointed that he wasn't wearing a bright scarf to match equally bright shoes, but he still looked great.

He put his hand on the door, let out a long breath, and pushed his way in. He scanned the coffee shop, so I stood up and he smiled when he saw me before walking over. "Hi," he said, breathily.

"Let me order you a coffee," I suggested. "You don't have dairy, right?"

"Believe me," he said. "Nobody wants me to have dairy."

I laughed. "Duly noted."

"Soy latte is fine, no sugar. Thank you."

I went to the counter, ordered and paid, and the barista said she'd bring our coffees over. I went back to Jordan and smiled as I sat opposite him. "You found the place okay?"

He nodded. "I work not far from here."

"Where is that exactly?" I asked. "I mean, we haven't really even got that far in a conversation, have we?"

"Five minutes a day doesn't leave time for much discussion, especially when I tend to talk a lot."

I grinned at him. "You do. But there's been no nervous rambling yet today."

"Well, I'm not so nervous today. I mean, I was yesterday. After you got off the bus, I kind of had a freak-out so I called Merry and she talked me down."

"She's a good friend," I prompted, hoping he'd say more but not wanting to push.

"She's the best. She knows how to deal with me."

"Which is...?"

"Well, that depends. She either tells me to pull my head out of my arse and stop being such a dick, or she talks me back from the ledge. It totally depends on what I need more, which she seems to know better than me. And I work at the library."

I nodded slowly. "That would explain the knowledge of books."

He smiled. "It would."

"I've never been to the library here. I have no excuse. I've been here for six months."

"You should come by one day," he said, blushing a little. "I could show you around. It's really so much more than just a library."

"I'd like that."

The barista delivered our drinks, and Jordan thanked her with a grin, his unrestrained grin. I kinda got the feeling that Jordan had two settings for nervous. One being where he was nervous, yes, but felt comfortable enough to ramble wildly. The second kind was him being nervous but not comfortable enough to ramble. He had his guard up today, and that saddened me a little. I wanted the relaxed, comfortable, rambling Jordan. Not someone who felt they couldn't be themselves.

I was going to ask if he wanted to leave, but he narrowed his eyes at me, a puzzled, thoughtful look to his face. "Can I ask what you do for a living? I mean if you can tell me."

"If I can tell you?"

"Well, yes. I might have searched online for you," he said, cringing. "For my safety, of course. I mean, I don't just meet anyone for coffee without at least trying to find out something. I don't even know your last name let alone what you do for a living. But I searched the name Hennessy because seriously, just how common a first name is it? So I googled, and I have to admit, I have admirable internet skills."

I smiled at him because here was the nervous rambling. "Admirable internet skills?"

"To rival most," he added. "So I refined the search to your name and the support group meetings, because that's all I know about you. And I got nothing. Not even a hit on Facebook, and that place is stalker central. So, my official findings are that you're either in the witness protection program or you're a spy. In which case you will admit to neither—well, not out loud anyway—so maybe you can wink or something to let me know I'm on the right path. Or if it's the cliché line of 'I could tell you but then I'd have to kill you,' well, I'd rather you didn't tell me at all and I can just pretend this conversation never happened. I'll admit I'd be disappointed. The seat-saving thing on the bus was kinda sweet, but I'd survive. And Merry suggested I come here with no expectations of anything more than friendship because for all we know, you're married or a spy. Or in the witness protection program. And so much for no rambling. I promised myself there would be no senseless rambling, but clearly that's not going so well."

I laughed and he stopped talking. "I'm not sure what to answer first. My last name is Lang. I'm not familiar with the statistics, but no, Hennessy isn't a common first name. I'm not in a witness protection program, and I'm not a spy, but there's a reason you won't find me on social media, and that's because I'm a network computer security expert, and believe me, I know the ramifications of having personal details on the internet. And for what it's worth, I like the rambling. I thought for a second you might not have wanted to be here, but when you do your rambling thing, I get an insight to the real you."

"You like my incessant rambling?" he asked. "Okay, sure. Five minutes a day of it might be considered cute, but all day every day is a lot to take. Believe me. Ask Merry. She'll tell you. And Mrs Mullhearn. She's our supervisor at work, and she's like two hundred years old, and I swear she turns her hearing aids off when I get there. Though she can hear me drop a *motherfucker* at fifty yards, or maybe she reads lips. I don't know." He frowned. "Wait. What the hell is a network computer security expert, and why does that explain not having a Facebook account?"

"It's a fancy name for professional hacker. I'm paid by large corporations to legally hack into their companies and tell them where their target areas are."

"You are not," he said, his face incredulous. "There is no such thing and you totally just made that up."

I snorted. "It's true."

He sipped his coffee. "Well, please kindly disregard my earlier comment about having mad internet skills, because that'd be terribly embarrassing if I'd said that. Which I absolutely didn't."

I smiled into my coffee. "Of course not. But knowing what personal information people put online, and what corporations do with that information, is the reason I'm not on any social media."

He nodded thoughtfully, then eyed me for a minute. "It's kind of fitting, I guess." I gave him a questioning look, so he added, "I'd wondered what you did for a job. You never wore a suit, but you clearly get paid well because you have more style than I could dream of."

"A suit? Me? Never. And I don't know about more style than you because I've seen your outfits with matching shoes."

He blushed. "Well, I have to do something with a drab work uniform."

"I like it," I replied. "I wondered what colour you'd wear

today. I have to say, I wasn't expecting brown."

He looked down at his brown jacket and stuck his booted foot out. "Do you not like it?"

"I do," I said quickly.

"I just thought I should tone it down a little."

"You don't need to censor yourself for me. I mean, that's the point, isn't it? Finding friends—" I stopped and tried again. "People to be around who we don't have to censor ourselves?"

He smiled and made a thoughtful face. "Can I be honest with you?"

Oh God. "Yes, of course."

"You look worried."

"I'd suck at poker. My face gives me away every time."

"That's not a bad thing." He smiled and took a deep breath. "You mentioned us being friends."

"I did. I dropped the F-bomb. But I did amend it..." It felt like my face was on fire.

"Yeah, about that. Merry suggested I meet you with being friends in mind. I tend to put pressure on myself and freak out and make an arse of myself." He chewed on his bottom lip, but I could tell he wasn't done talking. "I'd said to her we had a coffee date and I was like oh my God, he's kind of perfect. I mean, he cried during *Flowers for Algernon* and that kind of puts him perfect territory, and he's asexual, so..." He let out a slow breath, fixated on his coffee. I guessed it was easier not to look at me. "But Merry was probably right. I do need a friend who might understand where I'm at with this whole asexual thing."

"Friends is good," I managed to say, though my mouth was suddenly dry.

"Jesus, don't ever take up poker."

I chuckled. "Being transparent is a curse."

"No it's not," he replied, looking at me now. "I'd take it any day over the opposite. I like it."

I kind of felt a little scrutinised under his gaze, but he'd been honest with me so I figured cutting to the chase wouldn't hurt. "So where are you at with the asexual thing? How are you feeling with that realisation that it might be a good fit for you?"

"I'm terrified and relieved. I don't know."

"That sounds about right." Fuck. Fuck, fuck. "Can I be honest with you?"

He nodded.

I took a fortifying breath. "On the bus, I asked if you were thinking of going to the next support meeting as a way of gauging if you'd thought more on whether asexual was a fit for you or not. Because I could be interested in seeing where things go with you, but I can't be with someone who doesn't understand the whole no-sex thing."

"Interested in me?" he breathed. "Really? Me? Are you drunk?"

I laughed. "No, I'm not drunk. But uh, yes. You. You're incredibly interesting and funny. And you know who Daniel Keyes is, which kind of puts you into perfect territory." I smiled at him. "But I'm happy with friends, Jordan. I think it's a really good place to start, and if you want to catch up for coffee and a chat any time, I'm up for that. We can talk about books and canonical and classic literature."

Jordan stared at me. "You know what that is?"

"I studied a unit or two of English literature at uni."

"To be an internet security expert?"

"Well, no," I admitted. I cringed a little. "I took it for fun."

He blinked. "Are you even real? Or are you some interactive holographic program with all the right things to say?"

I chuckled. "No. I don't think the field of digital physics or plasmon, for that matter, is that advanced."

He side-eyed me. "That's something a hologram would say. Or someone who knows his sci-fi."

I laughed. "Are you avoiding what I said before?"

"That you're interested in me?" He blanched. "Well, yes. Because you seem to have full faculties, so maybe just a lapse in judgement...?"

I probably would have laughed if he didn't look two seconds from freaking out.

"Jordan?" I said, getting his attention this time. His eyes snapped to mine. "Want to go for a walk. We can walk up to the park? Get some fresh air."

He nodded woodenly. "Yes please."

I thought the walk, burning energy, or focusing his output somewhere else might help. Sitting in a coffee shop could feel a little confined. I waved goodbye to the barista, and Jordan and I stepped out of the shop to the footpath, coffees in hand. The cold wind was like getting in an ice bath. He shook his head and held his coffee like it was his own personal heater, but he seemed focused, sober now.

"This way," I said, nodding up Crown Street. We fell into step beside each other as we walked. "So, I didn't even ask. Do you live close by? Please don't tell me you live at Penrith and I made you come all this way."

He smiled. "No. Newtown. Twenty minutes from here on the 353."

"You like it there?"

"Newtown? Yeah, sure. It's like Surry Hills just minus the price tag and some of the pretentious kale-smoothie types." He shot me an oh-shit look. "You're not the pretentious kale-smoothie type, are you?"

I laughed at that. "No. Coffee, water, sometimes a juice

if I need sugar. A wine or a beer maybe, depends what I'm in the mood for. Nothing overly pretentious."

"Phew. That was lucky. It could have been super awkward." He grinned at me. "So what about you? Have you lived around here long?"

I was right. Getting him out and changing the subject had him more relaxed already. "Six months. I moved from the North Shore, so not too far. Surry Hills was close to work and I needed a change of scene, and at first I was like, what the hell have I done? But now I like it."

"You needed a change of scene?"

"Relationship breakdown," I said. "It was over months before that, but I just don't think I wanted to admit it, ya know? Anyway, it was kind of a mess. Nothing horrible, but every time I left my place, it felt like I ran into him. Or him and his new boyfriend. Or his friends. At the supermarket, at the café, restaurants. So I just thought a move sounded exactly like what I needed." Our walking pace had slowed to a leisurely stroll. "Is that too much information?"

"Not at all. As I said, I like transparency."

We passed the Clock Hotel and crossed over to the park. It was busy for a cold wintery day; there was a kid's birthday party or playgroup or parents' group with an army of three-year-olds in the middle of the park and a Tai Chi group at the other end. I was kind of disappointed that we didn't have somewhere to sit.

"That reminds me," I said. "The other day when I asked you if you were still interested in attending my support meetings, you asked if there would be a venue change. What did you mean by that?"

"Was that during one of my nervous ramblings, because you can probably disregard anything and all I ever say when I'm like that."

I chuckled. "I think it might be the opposite. I think the filter comes off and you say what's really on your mind."

His bottom lip pulled down. "Well, I just thought it was weird and I understand finding a venue open at night and one that's free isn't easy, but there I was freaking out about finding other people who were like me, who have no interest in sex, when that couple burst in dry humping each other. It was kind of like a paradox of horrors."

I put my hand on his arm. "Yeah, I really am sorry about that, and I feel bad. But finding somewhere else isn't easy. Like you said, open at night and free. The group meetings aren't part of a national group or anything. There isn't an advisory board to source anything; it's just me trying to get a group up and running. When I was younger, the support group I was in kind of saved my sanity. I just wanted to return the favour, ya know?"

Jordan stared at me, a lazy smile on his lips. "I can get you somewhere. A room that's open to the public but private, and it's free." He nodded over my shoulder. "I can show you right now."

I turned and found him looking at the library, his place of employment. "You can do that?"

"Of course I can. It's not a super power or anything. Come on, I'll give you the grand tour." When we got to the door, he stopped, looked at his coffee, then mine, and made a face. There was a big sign that said no food or drink. "I'll buy you another one if you're not done."

"I'm almost done," I replied, dropping my coffee into the bin, "but I'll let you buy me another one."

We went inside and I was truly surprised. It was all high ceilings, open spaces, natural light, the front wall completely made of glass. There were interactive stations and reading nooks and seating like a trendy café. "Okay, so you're probably going to hate me, but I was not expecting this."

He stopped. "Expecting what?"

I gestured broadly around us. "This. How cool it is. Admittedly, I haven't been in a library since university, but it sure as hell didn't look like this."

"Wait till you see upstairs," he said with a smile, leading me toward a staircase that ascended the glass wall, and my God, it was even cooler up there! The trees planted at the second level glass wall gave the entire floor a magical feel. There were seats and tables and comfy lounges, and the people using the space looked so at home.

"It's like a treehouse," I whispered.

Jordan grinned. "Isn't it awesome?"

"Pretty sure whoever designed this was a reader or someone who really loved books."

This seemed to make him happy because that carefree smile was back. "I'll show you the rooms we hire out," he said, now leading me past the stacks to a hall with natural lighting from long narrow windows near the tall ceiling. There were several rooms, each of them big enough for my support group meeting, with chairs and tables.

"And it's free?"

"It is if I make it free," he said with a wink. "We're allowed to make a discretionary call on hiring fees. If it's a community-based meeting, then yes, definitely. If you were making money or profiting from the meetings, I'd totally charge you."

I chuckled. "Just as well I do it for the love of it then, isn't it?"

"We can go downstairs and I'll check the schedule and availability."

"Perfect. And thank you. I'm impressed."

He rolled his eyes but he blushed and held the door open for me, waiting for me to walk through first. "And a gentleman?"

He rolled his eyes again and mumbled something under his breath, and as we walked out, there was an older woman at the top of the stairs with her arms full of books.

"Mrs Alvarez," Jordan called out, rushing to her side. "How many times have we had the 'there is an elevator' conversation?"

"Ah, Jordan," Mrs Alvarez said, looking up at him and smiling. "What are you in for today? It's your day off."

"Oh, I was just showing my friend here the meeting rooms we hire out," he said. "Here, give me your books. Let me carry them for you." He took her books under one arm and offered her his elbow, and they slowly descended the stairs. She held the handrail, and how on earth she ever thought she was going to manage those stairs carrying that pile books on her own, I'd never know. But I walked behind them and listened to their idle chitchat, and I was sure of one thing. Jordan was a really, really decent guy.

He walked her over to the service counter and said hi to the woman who was working and handed Mrs Alvarez's books over, then asked if she minded if he had a quick look at the reservation listings for the rooms upstairs.

Two minutes later, Jordan had a booking screen up on one of the computers and was scrolling through dates and times. "How often do you meet?" He looked up then, and I hadn't realised we were standing so close together. His eyes really were the prettiest greyish-blue.

"Oh, uh, the last Friday of the month. Six thirty till required. We never go past eight."

He looked at my lips and blushed again, then turned back to the computer. "Easy. One room free, if you want it.

You might need to send everyone a text alert about the venue change."

"Okay, yeah, that's a good idea."

"I'll just need to enter a contact phone number in," he said. "That way if anything changes, we can let you know."

I rattled off my mobile number. "And um, if you wanted to add that number into your mobile, you know, if anything changes, you can let me know."

I wasn't talking about hiring the room.

He looked right at me, into me. His eyes were intent, searching, questioning, a little wary, but maybe there was a spark of something else there too. Something that looked like hope. He let out a sharp breath and took out his phone. "I guess. You know, in case something changes." He thumbed the number into his contacts; then he put his hand to his forehead, to his cheek, through his hair, to his heart. "Um..."

"Wanna get out of here?" I asked.

"Yes," he squeaked.

He turned around toward the front door, but Mrs Alvarez spotted him. "Oh, thank you again, Jordan."

"Anytime," he said. "Tell Mr Alvarez the book he ordered will be here next week. And say hello to Catalina for me, won't you?"

She beamed at him, and he made it to the door and someone else called out goodbye to him, and he waved and tripped and almost fell through the glass door. "Mother-fucker," he cried.

A young woman close by laughed and said, "Bye Jordan."

He righted himself and patted down his shirt and fixed his hair. "Oh hi, Olivia. How are the exams going?" he asked.

"Good thanks, almost done."

"That's good, good. No need to tell Mrs Mullhearn I dropped another mofo-bomb." He made a face, shaking his head.

She laughed again. "Hell no. I got you. Don't you worry."

He let out a sigh of relief. "I was just... we're just..." He looked at me, found me grinning at him, so he grabbed my hand and dragged me out the door and up the street where he stopped, dropped my hand, and sighed. "Just one day. One day would be great where I don't make an arse of myself."

"I think you're kind of great."

He stared, blinked, then blushed a dozen shades of pink and red. "Oh look," he said, as if suddenly realising where we were. "You need to try these," he said, walking into the Thai restaurant we were outside of. "Hey, Sunan!"

"Hey, Jordan," the guy behind the counter said. "The usual?"

He held up two fingers. "Two today, please."

Sunan's face lit up. "Oh, two," he said, looking between us suggestively. "Special treat for special friend?"

Jordan didn't miss a beat. "Without the side serving of innuendo and embarrassment, that'd be great."

Sunan laughed and disappeared out the swinging door to what I assumed was a kitchen. "Come here often?" I asked.

"Shut up. When you taste these, you'll understand." Then he let his head fall back and he sighed. "Sorry. I didn't actually mean to tell you to shut up."

I laughed, making him look at me. "It's fine, Jordan. I like seeing this side of you. Everyone knows you by name, and it's pretty evident you have a lot of friends here."

"I'm considering changing my name and joining the bird watching fraternity where I can get a grant and permit to go live in the wilderness and pretend to look for some kind of bird that I totally made up, but really it's just so I can't die of embarrassment in front of every single person I meet. And you might call them my friends, but I'm sure they've just been planted to make me look like an idiot. Like *The Truman Show*. Is that what you're doing? How much are they paying you? I hope it's a lot."

"No payment," I said with a laugh. "If they asked, I'd totally do it for free. And about the breed of bird you made up, do they look like puffins? Because they're the cutest bird I've ever seen. You know, if one was curious."

"If one was curious, they'd be pleased to know the Australian Pygmy Puffin is far cuter than the Atlantic Puffin. Like all Australian animals, they look adorable but are either venomous, poisonous, or just total jerks."

"The Pygmy Puffin?" I asked, smiling.

"Yes. Small fluff balls, incredibly rare. There are three rules when handling them: One, no bright light. Two, don't get them wet. And three, never feed them after midnight, no matter how much they beg."

I laughed. "Must be related to the Gremlin."

He nodded and tried not to smile. "The genus name is the *Mogwai*."

"You're an expert on birds *and* eighties movies. I'm impressed."

"You got the reference. I am also impressed."

"I'm impressed that this is a serious conversation," Sunan said from behind the counter. He was holding two white takeout bags. "You lost me at small fluffy puffin balls."

Jordan turned to Sunan and sighed, then spoke in a voice that sounded a lot like Deadpool's. "Thank you,

Sunan. Thank you for your valued input. Please know your hard work and dedication to the team hasn't gone unnoticed, and accept this expression of my gratitude." He slid a tenner across the counter and Sunan laughed and handed him the bags.

"Always a pleasure, Jordan." Then Sunan looked at me and winked. "And Jordan's special friend."

Jordan groaned comically and walked out without another word. We crossed the street back to the park, which was now, thankfully, a lot less busy. I laughed when I said, "I think that might have been the weirdest experience ordering food in a Thai restaurant I've ever had. Actually, in any restaurant."

He sat on a bench seat and I sat beside him. "That." He nodded to the restaurant, to his work. "That madness is just a day in the life of Jordan O'Neill."

I chuckled and he handed me one of the takeout bags and a pair of wooden chopsticks. "Thanks. What exactly is this we're eating?"

"Deep fried heaven."

I snorted. "Is that a thing?"

"Try it and you can tell me."

In the bag were thin strips of something that looked like fries but thinner and wispier and a browny-orange colour. There was a light drizzle of some kind of sauce. It looked interesting, to say the least. "Heaven, you say?"

He used the chopsticks deftly and shoved a few strands of whatever it was in his mouth. He hummed and did a little happy wiggle in his seat, then pointed his chopsticks at my takeout bag. "Try it."

So I did. And, oh my God. It was sweet and salty, rich and acidic, yet soft and crunchy, and... and... and it was freaking heaven.

He grinned at me. "Told you!"

"What the hell is it? It has every taste and every texture, and where has this been all my life?"

Jordan laughed. "Mango fries with some kind of salt and chili seasoning and a dressing I'm too scared to ask what's in it because what if he says it's some kind of mayonnaise with a dash of fish sauce and buffalo testicles, I'll never be able to eat them again and that would be a tragedy."

I laughed again, something I'd done more today than I had in a long while. "Mango fries?"

"Well, it's dried and sliced really thin, then Sunan does some gastronomical wizardry."

I ate another mouthful, then another. "And he does it well."

"You're welcome."

We ate in a companionable silence, savouring every mouthful. It was then I noticed the clock on the very aptly named Clock Hotel. "Oh crap. I didn't realise the time."

"Need to get ready for a hot date?" he asked, then baulked. "I mean... it's not my business if you are, because if we're doing this only-friends thing, then—" He waved his chopsticks. "—go forth and date at will."

I stabbed another mouthful of heaven and shoved in it my mouth. It gave me a second to get my thoughts in order. "No date tonight. Unless dinner with my best mate and his wife counts? Although Veronica has been trying to set me up with every not-straight man she knows. It's painful, if I'm being honest."

He looked genuinely stricken. "Ugh. You have my sympathies."

"Apparently it's not a blind date. Not this time, anyway. Just dinner, probably wine, and some laughs. I don't want to date just anyone," I said, eating another mouthful.

His lips twisted in some kind of pout, but he didn't say anything.

"And I'm completely okay with the friends-only thing," I added. "And I mean it."

He nodded quickly. "Yeah, me too. But I do owe you another coffee, and it's completely normal for friends to meet for coffee."

"It totally is."

He stared at me and I tried to ignore the rise and fall of his chest, his pink lips, or the grey clarity of his eyes. "Uh, yeah coffee... I was thinking maybe next weekend or before a movie or something. Because that's what friends do, right?"

My smile widened. "Absolutely. So? Next weekend?"

"And every afternoon on the bus," he said. "Well, not coffee. But if you can save me a seat, we can talk at least. It's okay if you can't. Don't go kicking some old lady out of a seat on my behalf."

"I won't. But I do have a lot more questions, and there's so much we didn't get around to talking about."

He smirked. "A question a day? Will five minutes be long enough?"

"Probably not. But you do have my number if you'd rather text."

He blushed again. "I do."

"I better get going." God, leaving him was the last thing I felt like doing. "But Monday, yeah? On the bus?"

"On the 353 at 5:06. I'll be the one with the matching shoes and scarf."

"I'll be the one... well, I'll just be the one on the bus that's probably smiling at you."

Jordan's smile became more of a grin and his cheeks tinted pink. "There's a good chance I'll also be the one who trips over, takes out some poor guy in his fall, and yells out motherfucker really loudly, horrifying just about everyone on the bus."

I chuckled and met his gaze. "I've really enjoyed spending time with you today," I admitted, ignoring my thumping heart. "And I really love these Thai mango fries, and I'm certain I'll need to have them again soon. And I think I've laughed more today than I have in a long time, and I'd really like to see you again."

He swallowed hard and nodded. "I'd really like that too."

I licked my lips and my hands itched to touch him, just a palm on his arm, or maybe squeeze his hand, but we weren't there yet. I didn't even know if he was comfortable with that...

"In case you didn't know, you're kind of great, Jordan," I said before I lost my nerve. I stood up in a vain attempt to try and leave, but I turned around to face him. "And well, I'll look forward to Monday. Unless you wanted to text me tomorrow sometime. Or later tonight when I get home. Or I could text you, which would probably be better."

"Hey," he said, smirking. "Nervous rambling is *my* thing."

"Shut up, you make me nervous."

He burst out laughing and it was a good time for me to make my leave. "See you Monday," I said, walking away. And of course I only made it halfway across the park before I turned back around to get one last look. And he was smiling, biting on his bottom lip, and my heart banged against my ribs.

Waiting until Monday just might kill me.

CHAPTER SEVEN

JORDAN

"I SWOONED. I FUCKING SWOONED."

"I thought you were going to say it was a friends-only thing?" Merry asked. She was wearing a blue knee-length skirt, a yellow cardigan, white tights, and red shoes. The ensemble could be described as a dropped Rubik's cube, but she managed to look adorable. She had her hair done in two braids, her dark fringe framed her face perfectly, and her bright red lipstick was warning enough for all to beware.

I handed her the berry iced tea and kept the lemon one for myself. "I did! I told him that meeting him with the boundary of friends-only would eliminate the chances of me having a major meltdown if I thought it was an actual *date* date."

"But you ended up with his number, another date, and you swooned."

"He said I was great and he'd had a great day, and he did that thing."

"What thing?"

"You know, when they're walking away and if they look over their shoulder?"

"Lemme guess. He looked over his shoulder?"

"He totally did. And throughout the day he kept looking at my lips, and he said he has so many more questions, and he was fun, and he's smart. And he's not an undercover cop or in the witness protection program. He's some internet ninja who gets paid a shitload of money to be an internet ninja."

Merry tilted her head and squinted at me. "What the hell is an internet ninja?"

"I don't know. Big corporations pay him to hack into their business websites and tell them their weak spots."

"How is that even a thing?"

I shrugged. "Fucked if I know, really. But I accused him of making it up and he promised me it was actually a thing."

"So have you texted him yet?"

"No." I tried not to look so horrified.

"How many times have you thought about texting him."

"Shut up."

"Jordan, I'm pretty sure if he gave you his number and told you to text him, he wants you to text him. And if he doesn't give out personal information as a general rule, that would make you the exception."

"What would I say to him?"

"That you had a good time yesterday," she suggested. "I don't know. Just be yourself. Remember, if he doesn't like the real you, he's not good enough."

"You could totally get a job writing messages in fortune cookies."

"Where do you think I got that from?" She sipped her iced tea. "And he's probably at home checking his phone every five minutes and wondering why you haven't texted him already. He's probably driving himself crazy overanalysing everything he said yesterday that might explain why you haven't texted him yet."

"Are you trying to guilt me into it? Because I will remain strong. Oh my God, that is a new low, even for you." I stared at her; then I blinked. "Fucking fuck. Now I've left it too late. What if he *is* wondering if he did something wrong, and what if he thinks I don't like him?" I started to sweat, and it was a bit harder to breathe. "Good God, Merry, what have you done?"

"I didn't do anything," she replied. We had somehow walked into a clothes store without me realising it. She held up a floral blouse. "Do you like this?"

"Yes. My Nan had curtains just like it."

She grumbled and put it back on the rack, choosing a yellow one instead. "What about this one?"

"You look like a banana Paddle Pop."

"I like banana Paddle Pops."

"Then buy it, but if random strangers walk up to you on the street to try and lick you, don't complain to me about it."

She put the yellow one back and opted for a dark red one. She read the label, then held it up against her chest. "The tag says it's merlot."

"You look like you bathed in the blood of your enemies," I answered honestly. "I like it. And it would go really well with your brown or navy tunic."

She nodded thoughtfully and took the shirt to the counter. "I knew there was a reason I brought you."

"Merry," I whined. "What do I do?"

"Text him."

I whined and stopped short of stomping my foot. "But what if—"

Merry turned to the young lady behind the counter who was ringing up the sale. "If you spent the day with someone and had a wonderful time and they gave you their number and asked you to text them, what would you do?"

The young girl shrugged. "Text them."

Merry turned to me. "See? It's two to one. You're outvoted. Either text him or stop the whining."

This was Merry's 'I'm so sick of your bullshit' tone, so I was pretty sure I'd whined long enough. "Okay, okay." I pulled my phone from my pocket, found his number, and sent him a text.

Hey, Hennessy, this is Jordan. Hope you survived the dinner party last night. I had a really good time yesterday, just thought you should know.

I pressed Send before I could change my mind. Then I cringed at myself, and then I cringed at Merry. "God, this is all your fault. He's going to think I'm an idiot, and even worse than that, he's going to think I'm a clingy idiot. And what if his friends did try hooking him up again with another blind date? And what if he was an asexual Matt Bomer, and then Hennessy will be all like 'Jordan who? That really weird guy that has verbal diarrhoea and yells out *motherfucker* to little old ladies on the bus?'"

The girl behind the counter stared at me, and Merry did that head-tilting thing again. "You called a little old lady on the bus a motherfucker?"

"Not directly. Also said it to the sliding door at work when I tripped over the chair. That was the only time I said it yesterday for the entire time we were together, which is like a record for me."

Merry nodded. "That is pretty good for you."

"I'm trying to find a new word, but there just aren't any that are as versatile as motherfucker."

Merry gave that a thought. "True."

"I know. But I'm trying to stop saying it. I need something cutesy to say instead."

"Yikes is pretty good," the girl behind the counter said.

"Yikes?" I asked and took Merry's shopping bag, giving the now-creepy sales lady the eye, because honestly, who the fuck says yikes? I gave Merry a wide-eyed stare. "Come on, Velma. Let's go see what Scooby Doo is up to."

I dragged Merry out of the store, we dumped our empty drinks in a bin, and I told her very seriously, "If I ever say yikes in lieu of motherfucker, it means I've been kidnapped by aliens or some shady government agency, and yikes is my distress beacon and you should drop everything and call Jason Bourne or Idris Elba or someone."

Merry laughed. "Duly noted."

My phone beeped in my hand and I tripped over my own feet, almost falling to the ground but catching myself just in time. "Motherfucker."

Merry grabbed my arm. "Jordan, be careful!"

"This is entirely your fault," I told her. "You made me go to the support meeting, and you made me speak to him on the bus, and you made me text him."

"Well, hurry up and read his reply!" she said, ignoring my place of blame and waving her hand in a hurry up fashion. "Don't leave me hanging! What did he say?"

I held my phone out with my hand over the screen. "What if it's not good?"

"Oh Jesus H Christ, Jordan. So help me, read the motherfucking message."

An elderly man who happened to be walking past, gasped at Merry, frowning. "Well, I've never...," he said, hand to his heart as he scurried away.

I grinned at her. "Yeah, Merry, you really shouldn't swear."

She inhaled deeply, her eyes shooting daggers at me. "Siri, what's the average prison time for grievous bodily harm?"

"Siri, where can I find myself a new best friend?"

Merry glared. "Jordan. Read the goddamn text."

I peeked at my screen, my stomach in knots, my heart in my throat.

Hey, Jordan, so good to hear from you. No blind date set-up, thank God. I had a great time yesterday too, and I'm thinking of all the questions I'm going to ask you on the bus. One for each day, right?

I grinned at Merry. "Every day on the bus, he's going to ask me those questions he mentioned. And it's good to hear from me and he had a great time too."

Merry rolled her eyes but smiled. "I think it's safe to say next weekend is a date."

I made a crazy face and did a happy dance, then stopped. "Oh my God, what do I reply?"

"Just be yourself."

I cringed. "God, I don't want him to run away screaming."

"Well, say something that's fun and flirty, in an asexual way."

I stared at her. "What does that even mean?"

"Well, nothing too flirty or sexy."

My stare became a squint. "Uh, have you met me? Any attempt at me being flirty has either ended in mortification for everyone involved, including innocent bystanders, or the guy asking if I'm feeling okay or if I'm allowed out unsupervised. It's not good. It's horrendous, actually. And as for sexy? All I want really big and rock-hard on a guy is his IQ, and what I consider to be hardcore porn is a picture of a guy reading a book with a hard cover. Soft-core porn is a paperback, and browsing Amazon is my version of PornHub, okay?"

Merry snorted. "Well, let's just hope Mr Amazing is on the same page."

"God, I hope that too. You have no idea." I quickly thumbed out a reply.

I'm looking forward to it. I hit Send, then added another. *And I'll try not to disappoint.*

My phone beeped almost immediately with his reply. *That's highly unlikely.*

I made a high-pitched sound and clutched my phone to my chest and tried to gather my thoughts enough to reply with something half-intelligent.

It's only fair if I have questions for you too, I replied.

And I'll be only too happy to answer.

I almost swooned again, right there on Pitt Street. *Can I apologise in advance?*

For what?

The questions I ask and the answers I give.

Ha! I don't think so. Don't ever apologise for being you, Jordan. JSYK, I wouldn't be thinking of questions to ask you if I wasn't interested in your uncensored answers.

Uncensored is risky. You might want to reset your hologram program back a day or two.

"I can't go back to yesterday because I was a different person then."

The air left my lungs, my world tilted, and I had to lean against the building wall. "Jesus, Jordan," Merry said, alarmed. She grabbed my arm. "What's wrong?"

I handed her my phone. "He quoted Lewis Carroll," I tried to say, but it was barely a squeaky breath.

"Oh, Jesus," she whispered. Her eyes went from my

phone to me, then back again. "So that's it then. I'll start planning the wedding."

I ignored that and concentrated on breathing. Breathing seemed important.

Merry handed me back my phone just as it rang. It was Hennessy's number. I hit Answer, and his smooth voice met my ear. "I thought it'd be just easier to talk rather than text. Is that okay?"

"You can't just quote Lewis Carroll to me," I said into the phone. "You can't quote literary giants like Alice in mother-fucking Wonderland to me while I'm in public. That's not fair. You say stuff like that and I forget what oxygen is. You can probably watch the six o'clock news and there'll be the headline Asexual Gay Man Forgets How To Breathe, and there'll be video footage of me freaking the fuck out in the Pitt Street mall."

He laughed. "I should have sent a warning first?"

"Yes, you should have."

"You called yourself asexual," he said, ever so casually. "So I take it that revelation is going well?"

"Did I? I don't think I said that."

He hummed a noncommittal sound. "So what's happening in Pitt Street?"

"I'm with Merry. We're shopping while we wait for Merry's mother. She's getting her talons done."

Merry laughed and leaned up close to the phone. "Accurate description is accurate."

Hennessy snorted. "Talons, huh?"

I chuckled. "Yes, the finger-knives of the velociraptor are its weapon of choice."

Merry gave me a shove. "Come on, or she'll come looking for us. Can you walk and talk at the same time? Are you good with the whole air thing now?"

I nodded. "Yes, air in, air out. Got it, thanks."

"I'm sure she's not that bad," Hennessy said.

"Well, I can tell you this. 'Hell is empty, all the devils are here'," I replied.

He barked out a laugh. "So I can't quote Lewis but you can quote Shakespeare?"

My smile became a grin. "I don't make the rules." Then I sighed. "You knew who said that?"

"I can't say for certain that he *said* it, but he most certainly wrote it."

I did that swoon thing again and quite possibly hugged my phone. "Touché."

"Hey, I'll let you go," Hennessy said, sounding happy. "Be wary of the velociraptors. I hear their talons are fierce."

"Not as bad as their bite, I can tell you that much. Hennessy, I'm, um, I'm..." I put my free hand over my eyes, which was stupid because he couldn't see me, but it was hard for me to say out loud. "I'm glad you called."

"So am I." After a moment, he added, "So, the bus, tomorrow..."

"Tomorrow."

I clicked off the call and Merry hooked her arm around mine and, both of us smiling like loons, went off to find the velociraptor with the pretty nails.

MERRY HELD both my hands and looked me sternly in the eye. "What are the rules, Jordan?"

I gave a hard nod. "No freaking out. No calling anyone a motherfucker. And I have to call you as soon as practicably possible and let you know what his question was."

"Good." She glanced up the road. "Okay, here comes

the bus. You got this Jordan. And just remember, he likes the real you. Not some pretence of who you think he likes. You, in all your motherfucking awkward glory."

"Right. Me, in all my awkward motherfucking glory. Got it."

The bus door opened and there weren't nearly as many people on the bus as normal. There were a few empty seats dotted up and down the bus, but there he was, grinning at me like for some strange reason the sight of me made him happy. He slid his bag into his lap and I fell into the seat beside him.

"Hey," he said.

"Hi."

"Love the yellow." He blushed a little.

"Oh, thanks. It's like wearing a little bit of sunshine during shitty Sydney winter weather."

"So do you have twenty different pairs of shoes for whatever colour you're feeling?"

"Basically. Is that your daily question?"

He grinned. "Well, it wasn't what I had planned, but it can be."

"I'm not opposed to two questions."

"How did your shopping go with the velociraptor yesterday?"

"It was fine. If you throw coffee and cake at it, it simmers down. She's just super judgey and condescending, and whatever Merry does is never good enough, and then, of course, that includes her friendship with me. And basically everything about me, really."

"Is she that horrible?"

"She's all pomp and no ceremony, if you get my drift. Thinks she's above everyone else. No one takes it personally with her though. I mean, she was even critical of Princess

Diana, which is probably why she hates me. Because I called her on that shit. No one says a bad word about Princess Diana and remains unscathed."

Hennessy smiled. "Absolutely. Now, Camilla on the other hand."

I gasped and put my hand to my heart. "Oh my God, you get me."

He laughed. "And you can pick Charles apart if you want, but you must leave William and Harry out of it."

I sighed happily. "I feel validated."

He chuckled and gave me a nudge. "So, do you want to know your real question? It's my stop soon." He peered up the front of the bus.

"I do, yes. Ask away." Then I put my hand on his arm. "Wait!" I relaxed my shoulders a little and let out a breath. "Okay, now I'm ready."

He smiled at me. "If you could live with one family on TV, which would it be?"

I stared at him, then blinked twice. "What kind of motherfucking question is that?"

He burst out laughing. "Come on, hurry up. This is my stop."

We rounded the corner and the bus was slowing down to pull in at the kerb. "Um, well, it's a no brainer, really. There is only one family where I would fit in, where I could be myself and be truly appreciated."

"And that is?"

"*The Golden Girls.*"

His grin widened, pressing a dimple into his cheek I hadn't noticed before. It was hidden in his scruff. "That's actually a perfect answer."

I sighed with relief. "Oh my God, I survived the first one."

He picked his bag up from his lap and stood up, squeezing past me to stand in the aisle, just as the bus came to a stop. "Did you have a question for me?"

"Um, shit! Uh, oh God. Yes, of course!" So what did my brain do? It leapt merrily back into familiar territory, with my stupid mouth written all over it. "'If Winter comes, can Spring be far behind?'"

Hennessy did a double take, opened his mouth, but quickly shut it again.

I cringed. "I panicked."

He laughed and hopped off the bus, still smiling as we pulled away and he put his headphones back on.

"I'm such an idiot," I said to myself. The lady sitting across the aisle was looking at me like she very much agreed with me. "I panicked," I told her.

She smirked and nodded, which was great. Even the general public thought I was an idiot. I took out my phone and hit Merry's number.

"Jordan," she answered. "Tell me, did he ask you a life-altering question?"

"Probably not life-altering, but it was cute and gave him an insight to who I saw myself identifying with, without really asking. So yes, clever and insightful."

"And? What was it?"

"That I'm the fifth fucking Golden Girl, which, mind you, was a brilliant answer. But then I had to go ruin it by asking him one back. I had one question to get right, to show him I can be just as smart and funny and as insightful as him."

"Oh dear."

I nodded. "I not only asked him a rhetorical question, but I quoted 'Ode to the West Wind.'"

"You quoted Shelley?"

"I panicked!"

"Jesus, Jordan."

"I. Panicked."

She laughed. "Well, I guess he now knows what he's getting himself into."

"What's that supposed to mean?"

She ignored me. "You need to go home tonight and write a list of the questions you want to ask him each day. Memorise them, Jordan. So you're not caught off guard again."

I sighed. "Good idea. That's even if he decides to keep talking to me." Then I had a great idea. "Or you could think of some questions for me!"

"Or not," she replied. "He's playing this game to get to know you, Jordan. Not me."

"Oh my God, you suck. How are we even friends?"

She laughed. "See you tomorrow morning." And the line went dead in my ear.

I TRUDGED off the bus and into the blustery cold, thankful to get inside the entry hall of our apartment block and out of the wind. I marched up the two flights of stairs, unlocked my door, and dumped my satchel on the couch. Angus was in the kitchen, and something was smelling pretty good.

"Oh hey," he said, giving me a bright, lazy smile. "How was your bus dude?"

My bus dude. I smiled despite my mood. I'd told Angus about these stupid questions that Hennessy was going to ask me. "He was fine. I, on the other hand, was an idiot."

He frowned at me. "Did he ask a maths question?"

I snorted. "No, his question was fine. I had to ask him one question in return and completely muffed it."

Angus stared at me. "Did you ask him a maths question?"

I shook my head. I wasn't explaining rhetorical questions or seventeenth-century English poetry to him. "Nah. No maths. Whatcha cooking? Smells great."

He turned back to the stove and stirred a huge pot. "Oh. It's a stew thing. My mum used to make it and just throw a bunch of stuff in it, like minced meat, veggies, and pasta. I rang her to make sure I got it right. It's nearly done. Wanna grab two bowls?"

"Absolutely." I felt better already. Something about Angus was comforting; he was like a brother. And considering my family and I weren't close, it made me appreciate Angus all the more. Just easy going, well-meaning, and a joy to be around.

We sat in front of the TV, ate his delicious stew thing, and watched *Family Feud*. Angus nodded toward the television. "You should take notes. Ask him these questions."

"Name something you'd find in a doctor's waiting room?" I echoed the question of the game show. "Not sure it's what I'm going for."

He nodded and chewed his next mouthful thoughtfully before a slow grin spread across his face. "I know what you can ask him," he said.

And I'll be damned, but he had some great suggestions.

I WAITED for the bus with my stomach in knots. Merry shoved me onto it with a wish of good luck, and as soon as I saw Hennessy smiling at me, it all kind of fell away. He had a seat saved for me and I clutched my messenger bag and slid in beside him. "Hey," he said, all smooth and charming.

"Hey." I swallowed hard. "Can I just start by saying I'm sorry about yesterday's question? I kind of panicked and made a mess of it. Oh, and thank you for the seat. I should have said that first, but I see you and my brain circuitry fries and I struggle with a filter on a good day."

"Is it?"

"Is it what?"

"A good day?"

I nodded and tried not to smile but failed. "Uh yeah, it's like a hundred per cent better now. Work was busy as hell today and we had a special community meeting for people who are learning or new to English, so I spent most of the day with them, helping and making sure they had all they needed."

"You do that? At the library, I mean?"

"Oh sure. We run all kinds of outreach programs, including secondary languages and introductions and that kind of thing. I get a real kick out of it. I like helping people, and I can't get myself into too much trouble. Although there was that time I tripped over someone's chair and let out a motherfucker to end all motherfuckers and then spent the rest of the day trying to convince the whole class that it wasn't appropriate when they all took it in turns to break it down into more manageable syllables in front of my boss."

Hennessy laughed.

"I'm glad you think it was funny," I said flatly. "My boss didn't."

He was still grinning. "So today's question," he said. "Are you ready?"

I nodded. "No, but yes."

"It's an easy one today," he said. "Unlimited sushi for life or unlimited tacos?"

I gasped. "That is *not* easy. That is... well, that just might be an unanswerable question."

He nodded toward the front of the bus. "My stop is coming up."

"Argh! Oh, the pressure. Okay, I would say... sushi tacos."

"Are sushi tacos a thing?"

"They are now." I couldn't help but grin. "But in all seriousness, I'd have to say tacos probably, because there are all different kinds, like beef, chicken, fish, even veggie tacos. Whereas sushi tends to be more limited. So if it was for life, I think I'd want the variety."

He made a thoughtful face. "I'm not sure how to dissect that."

"Dissect what?" Oh God. "What are you reading into that? Because the question wasn't really about commitment and wanting the same thing over and over for the rest of ever, death till you part. It was about tacos. Wasn't it? Like tacos... soft shell, hard shell, answering questions hell—"

He barked out a laugh. "Yes, it was about tacos."

"Oh motherfucker. It totally wasn't about tacos. But even if it was, having tacos forever is fine. There might be all different kinds of tacos, but the bottom line is, a taco is a freaking taco. And I would be committed to tacos because I have no issue with that kind of commitment. I'm a one taco at a time kind of guy. And I certainly don't go looking at other tacos when I have one, if you know what I mean. And let's be real, because of the whole asexual thing, it's usually the taco I'm interested in that goes looking for other tacos."

He chuckled and gave me a nudge with his shoulder. "Those kinds of tacos are all jerks."

The bus went around the corner at the intersection and I totally didn't use that as an excuse to lean in a little. "They are jerks."

He met my eyes and bit his lip. "So, um... do you have a question for me?"

"I do. And if this one sucks, I'm not to blame. It's totally Angus' fault." I took a breath as the bus pulled in to his stop. "Okay, if you were arrested without any explanation, what would your friends think you'd done?"

He chuckled and looked to the open bus door and the people getting off. "That's a good question. Um. I'd like to think it was something amazing like breaking into an animal kill shelter and letting all the animals out." He stood up and I turned my legs to the side so he could get past me. He turned and smiled at me. "But it'd probably be for breaching some cyber security law by releasing all financial sponsorship information of politicians, or maybe just the racist, bigoted politicians. Or maybe I'd transfer a whole lotta money from corrupted corporations' accounts and drop it into Greenpeace's account."

I looked up at him. "So, maybe saving defenceless animals, but more than likely toppling governments, saving the world, that kind of thing."

He nodded. "Yeah."

"Good. Because that's not perfect or anything."

He grinned and hopped off the bus, and I sat there for the rest of my bus ride smiling like I was already falling in love.

Which was utterly ridiculous.

So ridiculous.

Unreservedly absurd.

Goddammit.

Motherfucker.

THE THIRD DAY wasn't much better. There was more pressure now. We'd started some kind of milestone, where the next question had to be better than the last, and the answers even more so. There were more people on the bus on Wednesday and some funky wet wool smell that I ignored when I saw Hennessy waiting for me with an empty seat beside him.

"Good afternoon," he said, grinning as I walked up to take my seat.

"Top of the day to you, kind sir," I replied, for no other reason than I'm an idiot.

"How was work today?"

"Great. We had the early learning kids in today. That's always fun, if not rather loud, but I like reading to them. I make it exciting and interactive so they all think books and reading time is amazing, so I'm like a superhero to them. And being a superhero to a bunch of three-year-olds is a civic responsibility I take very seriously." God, what was up with the nonsensical babbling when I was near him? "Sorry. Nervous blathering. It's a chronic illness."

He was still grinning. "I like that blue on you," he said quietly. "It matches your eyes. Some days they're more blue than grey."

I blushed so hard I almost had a stroke.

"And just so you know," he added, "the fact you read to little kids actually does make you a superhero."

"I tried to tell them I needed a cape," I said. "My boss, that is. The kids already know I need one. My boss isn't convinced."

"If you were a superhero, what would your name be?"

"Is that my question for the day?" I asked.

"It could be."

"Well, my superhero name would be something completely awesome. Like Super Book Man but in Latin."

"Super is Latin," he replied casually. "Etymologically, the Latin word for super is super."

I gasped loud enough the woman in front of us turned around, but I ignored her. "You can't say that kind of stuff to me. Word porn in public could get embarrassing."

"Word porn?"

"The only kind I'm into," I said, then turned a dozen shades of red. "I mean, not physically into it. I'm not really into anything like that. You know why." I cleared my throat. "I think I've embarrassed myself enough for one day, so never mind." God, I almost considered getting up and finding another seat, and I probably would have if I could've got my legs to work.

But then he took my hand and gave it a squeeze, not letting it go. "I'm glad you're not," he said quietly. "Into anything like that. Word porn is fine, I can appreciate that."

I was stuck staring at his perfect face, with his perfect hand still holding mine. I couldn't form words.

"Do you have a question for me?" he asked, almost smiling.

It took a second for his words to compute in my brain, and I realised we were almost at his stop. "Uh, sure. It's another one of Angus' questions. And it is in itself somewhat questionable, but then again, so is he. But he genuinely wants to know the answer to this."

"Who's Angus?"

"My flatmate and one of my best mates."

Hennessy smiled. "And his question..."

"Well, at first he wanted to know why everyone hated Nickelback so much. I told him that wasn't a valid question.

He said it started with why and ended with a question mark and that made it a valid question, but the thing about Angus is, he... well, he's just Angus. And his other question. God. He wants to know why cereal isn't considered to be or called a soup."

Hennessy stared at me for a full few seconds, then he laughed. "I really don't know. Some actual soups are made from just one ingredient and some are served cold, so I don't think there's any reason it couldn't be called a soup. Maybe there's a gastronomical reason. Maybe soups have some qualifying factor that takes them from a drink to a meal."

I shrugged. "What about porridge? It starts out as a liquid, grains are added, and it's heated to a thicker consistency. But we don't call it oatmeal soup. And a few differing ingredients aside, what separates a Bloody Mary from gazpacho? That one is consumed from a glass or straw and the other with a spoon. Angus and I discussed this at great length the other night, and he thought you might be able to shed some light."

Hennessy laughed. "I'm not sure I'm really qualified to answer that question."

I sighed. "I knew I should have just stuck to one of my own."

"And what would that have been?"

"My questions? Easy ones like do you have any tattoos? Or what's the coolest place you've ever travelled to? You know the basic, getting-to-know-you, gaining-some-insight kind of questions."

The bus pulled into his stop and he let go of my hand, stood up, and squeezed past me. "Yes, I have one. And Nepal."

I watched him get off the bus, and my heart banged in my ribs when he looked up and smiled at me as the bus pulled away. Again, my mind was stuck on how my hand felt empty now he'd let it go, and it took a few seconds for his answers to the questions I'd asked to make sense. Yes, he has one tattoo, and he's been to Nepal.

The lady in front of me turned and said, "I couldn't help but overhear your conversation. And yesterday's. I think the questions are cute."

Then a guy across the aisle leaned across and said, "He's been to Nepal? That's smooth."

The lady behind me tapped me on the shoulder. "I think he has a crush on you."

I side-eyed the three of them. "Is this *The Truman Show*? Am I on television right now? Because what even is my life?"

An older man one seat back across the aisle answered. "I heard your soup question, son. I think there's a pretty good chance your life is a mess."

And so, for the remainder of my bus ride home, random strangers on the 353 bus discussed my life, *The Truman Show*, and soup.

Fuck my life.

CHAPTER EIGHT

HENNESSY

I READ our text exchange for what must have been the tenth time.

Just so you know, we may need to find a new bus to catch. People on this one are discussing our questions, gazpacho (which one lady keeps calling gestapo), and Nepal. They've heard our questions every day, and I think they're more invested in us than Merry and Angus. Which is a lot.

That's a shame. I like that bus. There's a cute guy that gets on at the library.

Tell me about it. There's a total hottie that gets off on Cleveland. He wears headphones and I like to think he listens to audiobooks and not music.

That reminds me. I need a new audiobook recommendation. Know anyone at the local library who can give me suggestions?

Maybe... There might be a guy.

Is he cute?

Kinda. A bit awkward tho. Says motherfucker a lot.

LOL I have a joke. Wanna hear it?

Sure!

What do Oedipus and Hamlet have in common?

IDK. What?

They're both motherfuckers.

HAHAHA best joke ever! I'm cry-laughing. Actual, physical tears. People on the bus have stopped talking about soup and are now staring at me.

You're welcome.

I'm going to have that printed on a shirt. And a literary joke? You win all the points.

Glad you liked it.

I'll have the best question ready for you tomorrow, so be prepared.

Can't wait

I SLID my phone onto my desk and Michael caught me smiling at it.

"Is that what's-his-name? Jordan?" He fluttered his eyelashes.

"Shut up."

"So that's a yes. I think I might need to meet this guy."

"What? I've been out with him once."

"And you talk on the bus every day, and you get hearts in your eyes every time you think of him, you have conversations via text, and you never smiled at your phone like that with Rob."

I wanted to roll my eyes but refused to give him the satisfaction. "Can I ask you a serious question?"

His smile faded. "Yeah, of course."

"Why isn't cereal considered to be or called a soup?"

He stared. "Cereal?"

"Yeah, like rice bubbles or corn flakes. It's a grain product immersed in liquid and eaten hot or cold."

His eyes narrowed. "Are you feeling okay?"

I laughed. "I feel great."

He stared out the window at the grey Sydney day. "Well, I guess soups are vegetable or meat based, like the broth part. Whereas cereal is dairy based, like the broth, er... liquid part."

"So what does that make cream of mushroom soup?"

"Gross, that's what that is."

"Or cream of chicken soup? It's dairy."

"It's savoury," Michael said. "With meat. Cereal isn't and doesn't have meat in it."

"Not all soup is savoury. And not all cereal is sweet."

"That's true."

"Jordan asked me this yesterday, and it's ridiculous but I can't stop thinking about it."

Michael stared at me for a long second, then opened my office door and called out to his personal assistant. "Hey, Rach. Why isn't cereal called or considered to be a soup?"

There was a pause, then her voice sounded down the hall. "Seriously?"

"Yeah, seriously," Michael replied.

"Like milk soup and Weet-Bix croutons?"

"See?" I said. "It's an unanswerable question."

"Not sure about unanswerable," Rachel offered, appearing at my door. "More like, random and not altogether too important."

That made me laugh. "True. But interesting."

Michael sighed. "He's playing a game of Q&A with his new love interest on the bus every afternoon and it seems to be a contest of who can ask the weirdest question."

"Oooh, that's so cute!" Rachel said, her face lighting up. "Ask him why we send something by car and call it shipment but send stuff by ship and call it cargo? Or why do our feet smell and our noses run? Or why the number eleven isn't pronounced onety-one? Is Disneyland a people trap operated by a mouse?" She nodded. "I can keep going."

Michael squinted at her. "Did you take a class on random questions?"

"Kind of. I took philosophy at university and we used to have these drinking games where—" She composed herself. "You know what, never mind."

I laughed. "I'll keep those questions in mind."

BUT AS THE afternoon wore on, rain settled in and the bus was crowded. I couldn't save him a seat, and that was not part of my plan at all.

He climbed on the bus and I watched as he scanned through the crowd and he spotted me and smiled, but I could see he was disappointed when he saw there was an older gent sitting next to me. He held onto the vertical handrail near the step and gave me a pouty frown.

"Sorry," I mouthed.

He shook it off with a bit of a smile, but he was soon jostled by another passenger and kind of got half turned around. And I hated that he was right there, so close, but I couldn't talk to him, and he was wearing a grey scarf, and although I couldn't see his shoes, I had no doubt they'd match, and it bothered me that grey was a muted, sad colour, and he was anything but.

I stood up, excusing myself to get past my seatmate. I tapped a lady on the shoulder and offered her my seat, which she gratefully took, and I squeezed my way through the aisle, apologising to everyone. But then I was near him.

"Do you mind if I stand here?" I asked.

"No, that's fine," he said as he turned around. He broke out in a grin but we were impossibly close, and as the bus jolted, he bumped into me. I put my hand on his arm to keep us both steady. He looked up into my eyes, a little dreamily. "Hi."

"I couldn't not speak to you," I said, not exactly hating how close we were. "And our question game..."

Jordan nodded to the crew up the back. "They'll be disappointed they didn't hear."

I looked over my shoulder to the back of the bus to see a few smiling faces watching us. "I think me coming to stand with you made up for it."

Just then, the bus lurched to a stop and Jordan all but fell into me, my arm going around his back. "Sorry," he said quickly.

"Don't be," I whispered. "I can't say I am."

He shot me a look and he blushed. He swallowed hard. "I'm trying not to say anything inappropriate or embarrassing, but you're really close and incredibly good looking, and you smell amazing." Then he blanched, obviously not meaning to say any of that out loud. "Like that. All of what I just said. Not embarrassing at all."

That made me laugh. "Thank you."

He groaned. "I'm a nervous rambler, remember? And before I forget, I'd like to commend you on the Oedipus and Hamlet joke. It's like some comedic geniuses got together and formulated a joke designed just for me. And wow, you look even better this close up."

I laughed again. We were close, close enough that I could see some faint freckles on his nose, but the crowded bus was to blame. Or in my case, to thank. "Oh, and just so you know," I said, "I was curious and googled soups. Did you know there are about forty kinds of cold soup? Even a cold banana soup." I grimaced at the thought. "I have serious concerns."

"Did they have cereal listed as a cold soup?"

I shook my head. "Nope."

His gaze went from my left eye to my right. "It's the conundrum of our times," he whispered, like he was no longer talking about soup. "Your eyes are really pretty."

Now it was I who blushed, and it made me look away, which made me see how close my stop was. "Would you like your question now?" I asked.

"Yes, please."

"If animals could talk, which would be the rudest?"

"Cats," he answered quickly. "Or those monkeys in tourist spots who steal your things. Or sharks. I can't imagine them being overly pleasant company."

"The smartest?"

"Uh, elephants because they never forget a thing. Or octopi. Personally I think octopus are from outer space and landed here a few thousand years ago by mistake. If they came here looking for intelligent life forms, they missed the mark. Humans might have opposable thumbs and mastered how to make fire, but as a species, we're pretty fucking stupid."

I snorted. "Funniest animal if it could talk?"

"Lemurs. Or Tapirs. Maybe giraffes. Or zebras. Oh wait, maybe that's just because of *Madagascar*. I don't know."

"Most political animal if they could talk?"

"Pigs. But again, maybe that's just an Orwellian response."

"I love how your mind works."

He blinked. "You do? Because it's a scary place sometimes."

We turned right at the intersection, which meant our time was almost up. "Okay, your turn with my question."

"Oh, okay. And again, this one is from Angus, so I apologise in advance. Which sport would be the funniest to add mandatory amounts of alcohol to?"

I chuckled. "Um, I'm not a huge fan of any sport really, but I think drunk synchronised swimming would be hilarious. If they didn't drown, of course. Floor gymnastics would be pretty funny. Except for the injuries."

"Yeah, I could imagine if I tried to do that ribbon twirling after a few wines, it wouldn't end well. And the balance beam..." He shook his head. "That was a lame question, sorry."

"No it wasn't." The bus pulled into my stop. "But, if that was Angus' question, what was yours?"

"Well, it's kind of stupid too."

"I highly doubt that."

"Merry will probably kill me for asking this but this is something I've often wondered but never asked anyone, so okay," he said. "Do you think maths is something we invented or something we discovered?"

His question took me by surprise. "Um. Okay, first, wow. Wasn't expecting that." People were getting off at my stop and there were only a few people to get on. I had to go. Shit, shit. "Secondly, I think it's a human construct, like time. We are bound to it, it gives us order and clarity, and its importance is probably what confines us as a species. And thirdly, I think that's a great question and I think you should ask the questions you want to ask because you're really some kind of wonderful."

I had to grab the door to stop it from closing on me as I raced to get off the bus. And by the time I could look back up through the window, all I managed to see was Jordan staring back at me with his mouth open like I'd rendered him speechless.

And he could look at me all starry eyed and get all flustered and ramble on about how good looking he thought I was, but it was he that did that to me. It was he who left my heart hammering and soaring at the same time.

He wasn't like anyone I'd ever met. And normally I'd be reserved and hesitant, but it felt different with him.

Yes, I was in trouble. I was, without doubt, taken by his charm, his intelligence, his smile. But unlike the many times before, there was no dread lurking, lying in wait for disappointment to take its place. There was only anticipation and excitement of what was to come. Which was perhaps a little premature, given we hadn't really discussed some critical issues, but I had the feeling this was the beginning of something amazing.

He might have said he wanted to start as friends, but there was a spark between us. He had to feel it. I wasn't stupid. I could see how he looked at me, how his breath caught, how his pupils dilated. And even if it was only to be fleeting, I would still grab it with both hands. We definitely needed to have a conversation about expectations and limits, and I needed to know where his head was with the whole asexual thing. He'd mentioned it again in passing, so maybe he was getting more comfortable with it. But I wouldn't force him, and I wouldn't lead him down a path he was not meant to travel.

But holy hell, my heart skipped a beat when I thought of him, when I pictured his smile, his laugh. When I was near him, when he looked at me.

I threw on my running gear as soon as I got home, and I was just about to select a playlist on my phone to run to when my phone rang in my hand. My pulse spiked when I saw his name and I grinned as I answered. "Hey."

"I almost died, just so you know. On the bus. You look at me and you stand too close and you say something sweet like I'm some kind of wonderful, and not only do I forget to tell you about the audiobook recommendations, I also forget how to breathe. It's supposed to be an automatic and involuntary anatomical response, Hennessy, but oh no! You told me I'm some kinda wonderful and my brain stopped telling my respiratory system how to function. The soup crowd made me take a seat and practice Lamaze breathing just so I could tell them all about the questions game we play."

I chuckled. "The Soup Crew?"

"Yes, the Soup Crew. That's what I call the five people who spent twenty minutes yesterday discussing soups and Nepal after your stop. They're very invested in our... well, how our relationship is progressing. I hope it was okay for me to call you, by the way. I was going to text but it was going to take too long, and thanks for the concern about my respiratory failure."

I laughed. "I am very sorry about that."

"You don't sound it."

"I'm making a mental note right now to give due notice if I intend to ever say anything sweet, which I probably will, just so you know."

"Well, I'll try to be prepared."

"How did you go with the Lamaze breathing?"

"Really well, actually. Mrs Petrovski taught prenatal classes for thirty years."

"Who?"

"Mrs Petrovski. She's one of the Soup Crew. Nice lady. She was very impressed that you stood up and came down the bus to talk to me. She said it was, and I quote, 'very *Love*

Actually.' She hasn't been this excited since Scott and Charlene's wedding in *Neighbours*."

"Wow. That's some pressure."

"Well, not for you. Apparently your questions are great. Mine was okay today, by their standards, but they don't rate Angus' much. I don't have the heart to tell him."

I snorted. "I liked it. You can tell him I thought it was great."

"He'll like that, thanks."

"I was just about to go for a run," I said.

"A run? Like walking, but faster?"

I laughed. "Yep."

"Oh, the audiobook recommendations," he said. "Do you run to music or books?"

"Usually music, only something for background noise. I like to savour books."

"Like *Flowers for Algernon*?"

"Yes." I sighed. "Will you ever let me live that down? I should have known better than to listen to that chapter in public."

"Live it down?" he scoffed. "Absolutely not. It will live forever in infamy as number one on the list."

"On the list of what?"

"On the list of things that make you some kind of wonderful."

My heart did that banging thing in my chest again.

"So, did you want audiobook recommendations or music? To be quite frank, I don't think I'm qualified to give recommendations on music. Especially music to run to. If it were me, the theme song to *Jaws* would get me going. Or the intro music to *The Walking Dead*. I'd run like Forrest freaking Gump then."

"Not a fan?"

"Of *Jaws* or *The Walking Dead*? Or of running?"

"Pick one."

"All three, really."

I laughed again. "Okay, I'll pick my own music. What are your expert recommendations for audiobooks?"

"Well, given the titles you've already chosen, I have a few. If you want classic, you could do *The Screwtape Letters* by CS Lewis. Or if you want something more contemporary, a little dark but riveting, *Eleanor Oliphant is Completely Fine*."

"Completely fine? That's hardly a glowing review."

He snorted. "That's the name of the book. It's quite compelling, but it isn't for everyone. I'd suggest skimming some reviews for some trigger issues." Then he paused. "Do you? Have trigger issues? Because I could recommend a whole catalogue of lighter-themed books; there are thousands. I probably should have asked that before—"

"No, it's fine. I don't have any triggers. I'm not into erotica. I don't knock it at all, it's just not my thing." I scrubbed my hand over my face. "You know why."

"For asexual reasons."

That made me smile. "Yeah." Then I sighed. "Okay, so if you were to download an audiobook right now, which one would you choose?"

"Oh, probably *The Odyssey* or *Atlas Shrugged*. Maybe even some Dickens or Hemingway."

"You really love it, don't you?"

"I do. Though for a rainy weekend, I'd probably prefer to savour one of my favourites in book form on the couch. So for a commute or the like, I'd probably choose something from the bestsellers list or the editor's choice. Something sci-fi or historical."

I smiled at how passionate he was about his industry,

and just imagining him curled up on a couch with a book made my chest all tight. "Sounds perfect."

"I better let you go," he said. "For your run."

"Yeah, I probably should, before it gets too dark and cold. But I'm really looking forward to tomorrow's question. Yours this time, not Angus'. Not that I don't think they're good questions, I'd just rather hear your mind in action."

He was quiet a moment, then spoke softly. "I'm looking forward to it too."

"And I'm glad you called."

There was a brief pause, like neither of us wanted to say goodbye or for this conversation to end. "Tomorrow, then."

"Tomorrow."

FRIDAY WAS CRAZY-BUSY AT WORK. One of my biggest clients was gearing up for an interface change on their website, which meant hours of examining computer coding and scanning target networks and systems with both commercial and custom vulnerability scanners, amongst hours of simplifying reports for board directors and ensuring their IT department was up to speed. The fact that the client was my ex didn't help any.

It had been months of intricate planning and hard work, and thankfully, we were pretty much down to the final touches. But I had been so busy, I barely realised what time it was until Rachel knocked on my door and tapped her watch.

Shit. I was going to miss the bus!

I shut down my system, grabbed up my laptop, shoving it in my bag as I ran for the elevator. "Good luck!" Michael called out after me. I ran for the bus, smiling as I stepped aboard with only seconds to spare. I made my way up to the back of the bus where seats were spare, and I slid into one and put my bag beside me, keeping it for Jordan. It was then I noticed a few people watching me, smiling. I smiled right back, politely nodding in their direction, wondering if they were the soup crowd, but pretty sure they were.

More people got on the bus and I had a feeling I'd have to give up Jordan's seat. A guy came up confidently, expecting me to move my bag, and with a reluctant sigh, I did. But the small lady in the backseat intervened. "No, this seat is taken," she said, putting her handbag on the seat. "You can sit here." She moved over, giving him a seat beside her. He looked confused, but she grinned at me. "I look out for you," she said, just about beaming, then she nodded to the front of the bus. "Here he is."

And yes, there he was. His coat was blue, his scarf and boots were tan, matching his aesthetic perfectly. His smile lit his whole face when he saw me, and he made his way up the bus. He nodded to the woman who had saved his seat. "Mrs Petrovski." Then he nodded to the faces who had smiled at me. "Charles, Becky, Sandra, Ian." And then he sat down. "Hey."

"Hi."

"I think we have an audience," he said quietly.

"I think so too." God, my heart was hammering. "You look really good today."

I was rewarded with a rich blush. "Oh. Um, thanks." He let out a rush of breath. "You do too. How was work?"

"Busy." I patted my messenger bag. "I'll be working late tonight."

He wrinkled his nose. "Ew."

I chuckled. "It's not so bad. You?"

"It's my turn to cook dinner, or buy it, I haven't decided

yet. I kind of feel like carbs, and I make a mean rigatoni so I might make that."

"Sounds good. Do you share cooking?"

"Yeah. We have done for years." He made a face. "Angus and I are very different. Actually, you couldn't probably get two people who are more opposite, but as flatmates we get on really well."

"So, did you and he... ever..."

He stared at me, then snorted out a laugh. "Oh my God. If you ever met him, you'd realise how funny that is."

"Sorry. I didn't mean to... imply anything."

He put his hand on mine, just briefly. Far too briefly. "It's fine. So, questions? Should I go first, given it's the last day."

"The last day?"

"Of the week."

"Oh."

Mrs Petrovski swooned behind us, and Ian looked a little like a proud dad.

"Guys," Jordan hissed at them.

"You can go first," I told him, fighting a smile.

"Oh, okay. Well, it's kind of silly, but people always say it's the best thing since sliced bread. Like today, I might have said to Merry I think Hennessy could possibly be the best thing since sliced bread, and it got me thinking, what was the best thing *before* sliced bread?"

Sandra grimaced, but Charles nodded. "Fair question."

"Fair, but not overly romantic," Becky added.

Mrs Petrovski gasped. "He just said Hennessy was better than sliced bread." She shrugged. "In a roundabout kind of way."

Jordan sagged. "That's not embarrassing at all, and I

didn't think it was possible but my life is even weirder now than it was before."

I laughed and took his hand, threading our fingers. "It's a great question, and given that bread was first sliced in the 1920s, I think, I'd guess the best thing before that would be the discovery of penicillin or perhaps the invention of internal combustion engines. Those things are pretty amazing."

He gave me a doubtful look. "Penicillin I get, but engines? The best thing ever?"

"Yeah, sure. The first computer chip wasn't patented until the 50s, so it predates that, but engines, definitely. They didn't just revolutionise the transport industry but every industry; manufacturing, agriculture, not to mention—"

"Okay, okay, I get it. I didn't think of that." He nudged me with his shoulder. "Your question. Quick, your stop is coming up."

He was right. We we're almost at the intersection. "Okay, so it's more than one question. It's ten really fast questions, and I want you to say the first thing that pops in your head."

"That could be really dangerous and probably not safe for kids under the age of sixteen."

I laughed. "Try and keep it PG."

"I'll try, but the first thing that pops in my head is usually motherfucker."

I snorted. "Well, I'll try and ask questions that won't warrant motherfucker as an answer. You ready?"

He nodded, and the bus turned onto Cleveland Street. This had to be quick.

"Dogs or cats?"

"Dogs. No, cats. Both. That's not fair, and we're only up to question one, oh my God!"

"Tomato sauce on eggs. Yes or no?"

He made a face. "What is wrong with you? Of course not."

I snorted. "Comfy clothes or fancy suits?"

"Jeans and a sweater, all day, every day."

"Paperback or ebook?"

He stared. "Don't you dare make me choose."

I laughed. "Sweet or savoury?"

"Both. Together. At the same time. You've had my mango fries." He then shot our audience a frantic look. "That is not a euphemism."

I laughed again. "Favourite season?"

"Autumn."

"Dream job?"

"I have it. Just wish it paid more. Or maybe own a bookstore, but I suck at taxes and all things numerical so I'd probably go broke, which is why I'm probably better off sticking to my job."

"Celebrity you'd love to meet?"

"Percy Shelley but I'll need a priest, a Ouija board, and the blood of a chicken."

I burst out laughing. "Harry Potter house?"

"Ravenclaw," he answered without hesitation. Then his smile became a panicked frown. "That's only nine questions."

"Was it?"

He nodded seriously. "Yes." The bus pulled in at my stop and I had to get up. I squeezed past him. He looked up at me with wide eyes. "Hennessy, you said ten questions. You can't say ten and only ask nine, it'll drive me crazy."

"Will you have lunch with me tomorrow?

His smile was immediate and breathtaking. "Yes."

"I'll text you later," I said, making my way to the door, and the people around us clapped and cheered.

I got off the bus laughing and Jordan was grinning from ear to ear. I'm pretty sure Mrs Petrovski hugged him from behind as the bus pulled away, and Charles gave me two thumbs up.

CHAPTER NINE

JORDAN

THE TEXT from Hennessy came in kind of late. Not that I was checking my phone every two minutes or anything. I was watching TV with Angus—well, he was sprawled on the floor watching TV and checking his phone, and I was lying down on the couch, alternating between staring at the ceiling and checking my phone. I was starting to think Hennessy wouldn't text at all, and then when my phone did buzz in my hand, I dropped it onto my face. Angus cracked up laughing at me and I couldn't even be mad.

"Is it him? Your bus boy?" Angus asked.

"Yep."

"Date tomorrow?"

My grin would have given it away if he had been able to look away from his phone long enough to see. "Yep. And you?"

He pointed his screen at me. "Yep. Tomorrow night, six o'clock. Their place." His grin was wide and smug. He'd been seeing a married couple for some extramarital fun. "You?"

"Eleven o'clock."

"Oooh, an all-day date."

"I hope so."

Angus grinned. "I hope so too, man. I know you like him."

"You be careful tomorrow, and if you need anything, you text me."

"I'm cool, they're cool. You know that."

"Yeah, but you know. I just worry."

He snorted and waggled his eyebrows. "I'll be in very, *very* capable hands." I threw a cushion at him and he snatched it and shoved it under his head. "Same goes to you. If he tries anything or treats you bad, you text me."

I knew he would come to my rescue if I needed him, even if he was in the middle, the very literal middle, of one of his *dates*. Just as I would drop everything to help him, it's what friends do.

"I don't think I need to worry about my bus guy," I said.

Angus craned his neck to give me a long look. "You really like this one, don't you?"

I nodded. "He's different to anyone I've ever met. But he's kind of like me, and he... I don't know. He's just a nice guy and he knows books and—"

"I know, I know," Angus said. "He doesn't expect anything. Just promise me one thing."

"Okay."

"Tomorrow, find out if he's on the same page as you."

I sighed. "Yeah. I want to know because it'll be a step forward, but I also don't want to know because what if he's not on the same page?"

"If he's not, Jay, then you and me can watch that Colin Firth movie on repeat tomorrow and order in pizza and beer."

I smiled at him. "Thanks."

He gave me his serious face. "But if he is on the same page and he expects to be calling himself your boyfriend anytime soon, then I need to meet him, 'kay?"

"Yes, Dad."

Angus laughed. "I usually only let a certain couple call me that."

I snorted. "Jesus, please don't elaborate. There are things I do not need to know."

But ten to eleven the next day, I stepped off the bus at my work stop, and when the bus drove off, I scanned the park across the road to see if Hennessy was here already. But I was early, so I wasn't surprised not to find him.

I crossed the street and said hello to some dog walkers and there was a group of parents and prams with toddlers running amok. Which was fine. I'd take squealing and laughing kids over the screaming and crying kind any day. The sun was out, even though the air was a fresh reminder it was still winter. I shoved my hands in my pockets and waited, wondering what Hennessy had planned for us. His text message last night was short and sweet.

Meet me in the park across from the library at 11am. I have a surprise planned. Can't wait!

Truth be told, neither could I. I was super excited about seeing him and what surprise he had planned, but the conversation we needed to have left me feeling a little anxious. But that all fell away when I saw him walking toward me with a takeout coffee cup in each hand and a stunning smile on his face.

"Hey," he said as he got closer.

I had to do the breathe-in, breathe-out thing because of the effect he had on my not-automatic respiratory system. "Hey."

He handed me a cup. "Soy."

"Thank you."

He was still grinning. "You look great today. Love the white. Haven't seen you wear white before."

I looked down at my white scarf, dark jeans, and white sneakers. "I wasn't sure where we were heading, so I figured my cerise pink might not be appropriate."

He grinned. "I like pink, and I don't care. If you want to wear hot pink, wear it."

"I'll keep that in mind," I replied, happy he had no qualms about clothes and colours. After all, wearing bright colours against my drab uniform was my thing. "So, any clues about where we're going or what we're doing today?"

He bit his bottom lip, looking a little nervous. "I thought we could go to the New South Wales art gallery. There's a new exhibit I'd love to see, but if it's not your thing, I thought we could check out the—"

"Are you kidding? It is so my thing. It's actually like a perfect thing, and the fact you thought of it without even asking me..." I stopped and studied him. "Did you ask Merry what my most perfect date would be? Or did your Truman-Show-perfect hologram program do some weird algorithm to find out what would be the best second date ever?"

He threw his head back and laughed. "No! I promise! There's a Brett Whitely exhibit I wanted to see, and I just needed an excuse."

"Oh my God, I love Brett Whitely!"

He smiled and let out a breath like he was immensely relieved. "Shall we?" He nodded toward the bus stop.

"We shall." I was so excited, I was struggling to rein it in. He looked at me and I laughed. "Coffee and an art gallery. You've won me over already."

We sat on the bus, both smiling like fools, our sides

touching from thigh to shoulder, neither of us in a hurry to put even an inch between us.

"How'd your pasta go last night?" he asked.

"It was so good, and the carb coma was great too."

He laughed. "Maybe you could make it for me one day."

My heart squeezed and I felt a little faint. "Sure. I'd love that. Um, how did your work thing go? Weren't you taking some work home?"

"Got it all done," he replied. "Well, what I could get done. But it'll give me a head start on next week. It's one of my biggest contracts and it's almost done, so it'll be good to wrap it up."

"Are you just being modest, or is it a really big accomplishment that other internet ninjas would be envious of?"

"Internet ninja?"

"Yes, all that dark-net stuff you do."

He laughed, but he also blushed. "I like internet ninja. But okay, yes, I'm being a little modest. It's kind of a big deal."

I bumped his shoulder with mine. "You can be honest with me. If you're the best at something, you can just own it. I won't judge. I'm totally the best librarian in all of Sydney, possibly Australia, just so you know."

He chuckled. "You are?"

I nodded. "Yep. I have trophies and everything."

His grin widened. "They have trophies?"

"No. But they should."

"Like the librarian Olympics?"

"Yes! Oh my God, that is the best idea ever. I can see it now. Merry and I would make a kickarse synchronised cataloguing duo. We would totally smash Mrs Mullhearn."

"Who's Mrs Mullhearn again?"

"She's our boss. She's just recently celebrated her 258th

birthday, and she's an expert on Hans Christian Andersen's fairy tales and Merry and I are almost certain it's because she bound the first editions herself."

Hennessy snorted. "Pray tell, which events would you smash Mrs Mullhearn in?"

"Well, all of them. But I'm taking gold in the Decathlon of Motherfuckers. That's where the contestants have to find ten ways to incorporate it into varying library scenarios. You get extra points for creativity and cadence. Samuel L Jackson is the presiding judge."

He laughed. "Lucky for you he's not competing, because he'd be tough to beat."

"I know, right? He's the master."

"Shit, here's our stop!" he said, grabbing my hand and pulling me off the bus. It all kind of happened so fast I didn't have time to object, not that I would have, but then we were on the footpath and there was no reason for him to be holding my hand. He'd actually held my hand a few times, so I was sure he had no issue with it. "Oh, sorry," he said awkwardly. "I should have asked before now. I don't know if you have issues with holding hands. Some people don't like it, and if I made you uncomfortable—"

"Ask me."

"Ask you what?"

"If you can hold my hand. You said you should have asked before now, which might be true, I don't know, but you've held my hand like three times already."

"Three times?"

"I've been counting."

"Oh, sorry."

"I'm not. But you still haven't asked me."

He smiled, more relieved than happy, I thought. "Would you mind if I held your hand? Do you like holding hands? I don't know what you're comfortable with because we haven't got that far yet—"

I held out my hand. "I like hand holding. I actually like it a lot. And the nervous rambling you have going on right now is kinda cute, but I have the nervous rambling market cornered. There are trademarks and patents pending. In case you were wondering."

He took my hand, feeling the weight of it as though it was quite a monumental thing, before threading our fingers. Then he looked at me with the dopiest grin on his face. "I like holding hands too."

Then we stood there on the footpath for a while holding hands and smiling at each other like a pair of idiots. "Should we?" I asked, nodding toward the stairs to the art gallery.

"We should."

So we did, holding hands. We took in the creations and masterpieces that adorned the walls. We didn't speak much in the few hours it took. Hennessy would stop and stare at a particular piece and I'd wait patiently until he'd taken in every line, every stroke of paint or charcoal, every shade. Don't get me wrong; I admired the artwork too. It really was amazing. But watching him process each piece was kind of amazing too.

"You love it, don't you?" I asked him quietly.

He nodded, then turned from the charcoal artwork to me. "I do. I know the saying is *a picture paints a thousand words*, but it's more than that. It's like a book on canvas. Every stroke of the artists hand is a word, a sentence, a chapter. The whole picture is a story in itself. Don't you think?"

I swallowed hard and nodded. And I knew, I just knew that we had to have that dreaded talk about expectations and limits and what we wanted from each other. There was no going back now. Because there, while the world spun around us, surrounded by white walls and priceless art, holding hands and hearing him talk about the correlation between art and books, well... that was it for me.

Like I took a miscalculated step or like I missed the last stair, I fell headfirst right into love with Hennessy Lang.

Motherfucker.

WHEN WE LEFT the art gallery, we grabbed some lunch at the Pavilion, then set off for a stroll through the Botanical Gardens. It wasn't long before Hennessy slipped his hand around mine. "So how was it? Did you really like the exhibit, or were you bored out of your mind? You can tell me honestly."

"On a scale of one to best second date in the history of ever, it was a nine."

"Just a nine?"

"Well, it's not over yet."

He smiled. "True."

"I liked how much you liked it," I admitted. "The fact you find beauty in art tells me a lot about you."

"Is that so?" he mused. "Do I want to know?"

I saw a bench seat in the sun overlooking the park and pulled on his hand to lead him toward it. We sat, almost touching. "It's a good thing, don't worry. It tells me that you have great visual awareness; you notice smaller details others might overlook. It's probably why you're so good at your job. But also that you can appreciate things you find beautiful, simply for what they are."

He was quiet a moment. "You got all that from one visit to an art gallery?"

I laughed. "I'm a librarian, remember? I can tell a lot

about a person by what books they choose. Like you said, artwork is like a novel, yes?"

He nodded. "I guess."

"It's subjective, though. Art and books," I added. "I'm no expert in art, but I know books, and there is such a misconception about what genre people prefer. I don't give a fuck what people read, as long as they read. From manga to gardening books, it doesn't matter, and why people scoff at romance, I'll never know. Because isn't it a beautiful thing? Romance, that is. People wanting a happy ending. How is that ever wrong? But that being said, I'd like to think I know a lot about a person by what they read. Knowing what people choose to read or study or what books they enjoy in private is akin to seeing someone's browser history, their true selves. Autobiographies, murder mystery, self-help, romance... And then you have sub-genres within those genres, which adds another layer of awareness. Some people like any and all crime and thriller, yet some will only read true crime or fictional crime where the protagonist is a forty-year-old woman with mummy issues." I took a sip of my coffee. "It can say a lot about a person."

"And what do you think my choice of audiobooks says about me?"

"That you have eclectic tastes. That you like a broad range of subjects, so you have a well-versed scope on how humans think, and in world affairs, that you're open minded, always learning. You like some escapism but enjoy being challenged. I'd say you're rather clever, smarter than you like to let on. And I think you thrive in your own company, and you need to be mentally stimulated by some-thing, or someone, before you delve a little deeper."

He blinked. "Holy shit. I'd say... you're not wrong."

"I know I'm not."

"And what does your love for eighteenth-century French poets say about you?"

"I can't answer that for me. You tell me what it says about me."

He let out a slow breath. "I'm not going to lie. I feel a little exposed after what you just said about me."

I baulked at that. "How so? I didn't mean to offend you—"

"Oh, I'm not offended. I just feel—" He let out another breath. "—like you see me. I feel kind of stripped bare, given you dissected me in five seconds with your analogy. But you... see me."

I blushed. "I like what I see, just so you know."

He laughed. "Okay, my turn. What does your love of eighteenth-century poets say about you? I think it tells me that you're a romantic at heart. Perhaps, like the revolution itself and like those who survived it, that despite all the adversity and horrors, there is still hope that love will win in the end."

Oh God.

I chewed on my bottom lip, my eyebrows narrowed, and I wanted to object, but I shrugged with a resigned sigh. "Well, I'd say you're... you're not wrong."

"I know I'm not." He gave me a nudge with his shoulder and he smiled.

"Isn't that what everyone wants?" I asked, looking up at the sky before looking at him. "Not romance or love, exactly. I'm aware of my aromantic brothers and sisters." I raised a fist before letting it fall heavily back to my lap. "But we all strive for something. It might not be hearts and roses for everyone, but doesn't everyone want something to fulfil them or someone to connect with on some level?" I shrugged, feeling less confident now and more vulnerable.

Here it was, the leap into the discussion we needed to have. "Is it not human nature to find our own tribe? We all want that one thing, whether it's someone to meet your every sexual need, or maybe it's someone who loves to cuddle on the couch, or maybe it's someone who knows the last three answers in the cryptic puzzle you can never get every damn time, or maybe it's someone who loves Dungeons and Dragons just as much as you do, or maybe they love olives on pizza and will pick them off yours for you. Finding someone to share your life with doesn't have to be based on sexual compatibility. I mean, if you want someone to pound you into next week while you're chained to a cross, then by all means, I hope you find them and live happily ever after in your red room of pain. Or if you want someone who doesn't want to ever have sex but still enjoys hugs and kissing, hand holding, and snuggling on the couch to watch movies, then hell the fuck yes, you should find that person. Or two people, if poly's your thing. Whatever floats your boat, have at it. Find your one person, your tribe. Be happy, be content."

"You're sex-positive," he said, with the hint of a smile. "Meaning you have no issue with sex itself."

"Totally. If sex gets your motor running, then go have all the sex you want. As long as it's consensual and healthy or whatever, then yes. Go do that." I made a face. "But it's not for me."

He nodded, then sighed and smiled with what had to be relief. "Me too. I just want people to be happy, and I totally respect their desire to want sex, but I also want them to respect my desire to not have sex."

"Exactly." I groaned up at the sky. "I can't tell you how many times I've had people tell me maybe I haven't met the right person, or I wasn't doing it right, or maybe I wasn't even gay. Have I considered fucking a woman instead?" I rolled my eyes. "My great-uncle Brian thought it was hilarious to ask me that in front of my entire extended family until I asked him how he knew he was truly straight if he'd never fucked a man before. I mean, maybe he just wasn't doing it right. Maybe he needed to try bottoming, just to be sure."

Hennessy barked out a laugh. "Oh wow. I bet that was a conversation stopper."

I sighed. "Made him realise how stupid he sounded. And I was uninvited to his Christmas dinner after that, which was a win-win for me. My mum was kinda pissed though."

He frowned. "I've heard all that before too. Mostly from men. Dates, boyfriends..."

I nodded and gave him a smile that I just couldn't quite get right. "Yeah. It sucks. Is it not enough to be gay? But oh no, let's sprinkle on some asexuality just for good measure. I wish I liked sex. I wish I wanted it. But I just don't. And I have stopped trying to pretend."

"It's not easy. I told you at the meeting the night we met that I first told my boyfriend slash best friend in high school that the idea of sex didn't appeal to me."

"And his response was really shitty. Sorry he did that to you."

"Me too. I lost my best friend and the only other gay friend I had in school, so that sucked. And for a few years after that, I tried to like it. You know, sex and whatnot. And I tried to fit in, and I tried to pretend it didn't bother me. But it did. And it's not easy for a guy to fake, you know what I mean?" He waved his hand at his crotch. Then he whispered, "They could see I wasn't sexually aroused."

I made a sympathetic face. "Yeah, been there, done that."

He let out a long sigh. "But it wasn't working for me. I was miserable, and I told my doctor and she suggested I read up on asexuality. So I did, and it was like something clicked inside me. I was nineteen, and I finally felt right. I found an online community group and finally met people who were like me. It was incredible, and I began to embrace that part of my life. It was part of who I am, and so when I met guys, I'd tell them I was asexual. Some had never heard of it, some thought I was joking, some thought I was weird. But I've had a few boyfriends over the years, so it's not all bad."

"Was it an issue for them?" I asked. "In the end?"

"Yes. And I've even tried to oblige, to make my boyfriend happy. It's quite common for asexual people to engage in sexual activity to make a partner happy or to help fulfil their partner's needs."

I swallowed hard. "Boyfriend? You said boyfriend, as in current..."

"Ex, sorry. I should have said ex. It's well and truly over."

"I'm sorry to hear that," I said quietly but so very relieved.

"It was my choice. But he wasn't exactly upset by the news. He went out the very night after I'd left and slept with three guys, so..."

"Ouch."

He sighed again, adding a shrug. "He knew from the beginning about my being asexual. I was upfront, as I'd always been for years. And he said he was okay with it, but..."

"But in the end, they think you'll change or give in or have sex whether you really want to or not. Like you said, to fulfil their partner's needs." I frowned as I looked out over the park.

"Is that what you did?" he asked gently.

I nodded.

"It's okay," he replied. "I've done it too. I thought it would help, and I thought it would make them happy."

I looked at him then, and his eyes searched mine. "But it made you feel like you'd whored yourself out? Like a transaction where sex was the currency but all you got from the deal was a sick feeling in your gut because you'd just sold yourself for sex."

He quickly reached and took my hand. "Their happiness shouldn't come at the expense of your own."

"I left him," I said. "After that night. I couldn't even look at myself in the mirror. That was like, ten months ago. We'd only really been together a month or two, and I'd told him I didn't really want sex and he thought it was weird but he said he was okay with it. And every time I'd hold his hand or hug him, he thought it was foreplay. He couldn't understand it wasn't anything more than just hand holding or hugging. It wasn't a precursor to wanting more. And it messed with my head because I liked him. Well, I thought I did. He was smart and funny, but then I was scared to initiate any kind of contact. I wouldn't hold his hand or touch him, even if I wanted to, because then he'd think it was foreplay. I lived with that kind of anxiety in my gut for weeks, just being around him, because he'd always ask if I'd changed my mind and I tried to tell him it wasn't like that."

He squeezed my hand. "It's not like that."

"But then he asked if I wanted to make him feel good. He said if I really liked him I'd want him to be happy, and I fucking believed that shit." I shook my head. "I know better. I really do. But I was so caught up in him and he did things with me that he didn't actually enjoy, like watching *The Great British Bake Off*, or going to local author readings, so surely I could do something for him, right?"

"Oh, Jordan..."

I nodded sadly. "I felt so dirty," I whispered. "But it was consensual. I did agree to it, but the whole thing was awful. I left him after that."

"I'm glad you did."

I gave him a weary smile. "I know, right? I mean, I should have known he wasn't the one for me. Because seriously, who doesn't like *The Great British Bake Off*?"

Hennessy chuckled. "Only monsters and heathens."

"Exactly. Monsters and heathens." I studied the coffee cup in my hand for a bit. "Anyway, I told Merry, of course, and I'd talked to her before about not being too interested in physical stuff, but always in a kind of joking way. Like, 'Ugh men, they can never get enough,' and we'd laugh it off, and I'd always just said they'd wanted more than I did, which wasn't an untruth. But it all came out after I left Anthony— that was his name. And I admitted to her I'd never been too interested in anything sexual, ever, and I was expecting her to say something smart or funny. But she didn't. She said asexuality wasn't anything to be ashamed about, and I was like *what*? And we talked about it off and on, for a while, she was always asking me if I'd read up on it, but I hadn't. I didn't want another label to wear, ya know? Then a few months later she saw a flyer in the community centre next door about a meeting for asexuals, and she thought I should go." I laughed quietly. "Would you believe I'd never heard of it? Well, I'd *heard* about asexuals and aromantics, but I'd never read the fine print, ya know?"

He nodded, because, yes. He ran the meetings. Of course he'd know.

I took a deep breath. "So I don't know where you're at or what you want, or even if you want anything, I don't even know. God, this is embarrassing, but I think you're kinda great, so I was wondering if you wanted to maybe talk about what you might want with me, or from me. Because you're asexual too and I'm really hoping you're on the same page."

"I think you're kinda great too," he said, his gaze intense. "Truly, you walked into my support meeting and I thought to myself, *He's really cute*, but it was inappropriate of me to be thinking that of a guy who was there for emotional support, but then you got on the bus and you asked me about the audiobook I was listening to, and you knew who the author was without even trying, and it's one of my favourite books. I'm not gonna lie, I was kind of blown away and fascinated, and felt like it was fate or something."

"I couldn't believe it was you," I said with a laugh. "Standing there all cute and shit with your clipboards in that meeting."

"You looked scared as hell," he whispered.

"I still am." I let out a puff of air. "To be honest, right now I'm about five seconds away from freaking the fuck out, just so you know."

He shot me a look and put his coffee down so he could take my hand in both of his. "You don't have to worry or be scared when it comes to anything with me. I will never pressure you for sex. You mentioned cuddling on the couch and watching movies or hugging and kissing?"

I swallowed hard and somehow managed to nod. "I like those things. I want all the romantic things. I like holding hands and I love kissing. I love it. It makes my heart do some pretty weird shit and I get butterflies. And hugs are... well, a good hug can fix a wounded soul."

Hennessy grinned at that.

"So I want all that," I admitted. "But I don't want anything else. I see all the naked pics on Twitter and Grindr, and for the life of me, I can't figure out why they don't put clothes on. Like I have zero interest in that. And the random gifs of porn are like, *Jesus, is that really necessary?* Not one part of it appeals to me. I think I can honestly say I've masturbated like twice in the last twelve months, which is probably far too much information than you ever needed to hear, but one of those times was just to see if I could even get aroused and the other time was, well, more of an attempt at stress relief, which evidently had the opposite effect. But I just want a boyfriend who I can sleep in with on Sundays, whom I can cuddle with or touch just because he's close, and I want all that without him wanting more. And that's probably selfish, I realise that. But I can't be in another relationship where I'm walking on eggshells and praying he doesn't want sex." I shuddered at the thought. "I just can't."

Hennessy smiled and let out the mother of all breaths. He looked up at the sky and shook his head, and I thought for sure I'd blown it.

I'd crossed a line and said I wanted something he won't do... I pulled my hand away and stood up, wanting to leave but not sure my feet would take me. "I'm sorry. Was it the kissing? Do you not like that? Or the idea of sleeping in on Sundays? I mean, not the actual sleeping in part, but the sleeping in the same bed part."

He stood up too and grabbed my arm. "God no. Jordan, everything you said, all those things, it was like you read my list of what I want. Everything, exactly as you said it."

"You like kissing?"

"Very much."

"And hugging?"

"Can fix a wounded soul."

For some stupid reason, my eyes got all watery and my heart was trying to trample its way out of my ribcage. "Really?"

He nodded. "Can I kiss you right now? Because I sure would like to kiss you."

I could barely nod, and he put his hand to my cheek and slowly cupped my jaw. His thumb scraped along my scruff and he smiled before he leaned in real slow. It was that moment before the kiss, where you're sure your heart will pop or your lungs will squeeze too hard, and the butterflies are in a flurry. That perfect pre-kiss moment, where he's close enough that I can see just how beautiful his irises are, and the warmth of his palm on my cheek is keeping me from floating away. His lips, so close they almost touched mine, the barest hint of touch made me gasp, and my heart rate kicked it up a gear, and then he did it. He pressed his lips to mine, soft and warm and slightly open, and his other hand cupped my jaw, and he kissed me so perfectly, all I could do was melt into him.

The most perfect kiss.

He pulled away all too soon and I almost fell forward. He caught me and chuckled. "You okay?"

"I'm um... that was... wow," I put my hand to my forehead, then took Hennessy's hand, and sliding it inside my coat, I held it over my heart. "Can you feel that?"

My heart was hammering so goddamn fast he *had* to be able to feel it.

He sucked back a breath, his eyes grew dark and intense, his pink lips parted, and he nodded. "I can."

"That's what you do to me."

He smiled then and leaned in again, pressing his lips to mine one more time. Chaste and sweet and so utterly perfect. "I'm so glad we're on the same page," he said, his hand still to my chest, he slid it up to my neck, his thumb tracing my cheekbone. "It's a relief I can't even describe."

"Me too. Merry will be over the moon, and Angus will be pleased too. Though I will admit, he said if I found out today you weren't into the same things as me, that we would spend all day tomorrow watching *Pride and Prejudice*, eating pizza, and drinking beer. And I'm not gonna lie, that sounded pretty damn good."

Hennessy took my hand and we started to walk again. "There's no reason we can't do that."

"Really? You would do that? *Pride and Prejudice*? I mean, I'm almost certain it bores Angus to tears, but he said he'd do it if it made me feel better."

Now he laughed. "Well, Angus sounds like a helluva good friend, and yes I would totally watch it. I do prefer Colin Firth as Mr Darcy, though Matthew Macfadyen gets an honourable mention for his voice alone."

I stopped dead in my tracks. "Okay, you win. All the awards. All the points. This date is now a full ten stars on a scale of one to the best second date ever in the existence of dates."

Hennessy barked out a laugh. "And it's not even over yet."

"We may need to modify the rating system. I have a feeling ten isn't going to be high enough. Though it might depend if the date includes dinner. There is a slight chance it could go horribly wrong, though I'm highly doubtful it will."

"There's a small Hungarian restaurant just a block or two from my place. The owner is a little old guy who talks really loud and he has the best laugh, and the food is amazing."

I sighed dramatically and threw my hands up and spoke to a more or less empty park. "Okay, folks, thanks for trying, but the contest is over. All the points have been awarded, the votes have been counted, and we have a winner."

He grinned at me. "Did I win?"

"Hell yes, you did, motherfucker."

He laughed, long and loud, then slung his arm around my shoulders, and we began to walk back to the main road. "So there is a downside to us being on the same page," I said. "And I probably should tell you this now so you have enough time to bail. But Angus said if things went well with us today that he wants to meet you."

"That's okay, because Michael said the same thing."

Oh. "So um, are we doing the meet the friends thing? Because I will need some warning time to get my head around that and possibly enough time to get some Xanax, because my nervous rambling would possibly go nuclear, and under Spanish Inquisition circumstances, that won't end well. Just so you know. Too many questions and the 'you hurt him and I'll kill you' intimidation speech and I will freak the fuck out and you'll probably need to call an ambulance for me while your friends call the *Intervention* TV show people for you, and it will be a total disaster."

Hennessy gave my shoulder a gentle squeeze. "I promise I won't let him. He knows, anyway."

"He knows what?"

He stopped walking, let his arm fall from around my shoulder, and faced me. "That things are different with you. Even from early on, he said he could tell I was already invested. That I'd found an asexual book lover for a boyfriend and that it was different this time."

The butterflies in my chest flooded my throat. "Boyfriend?"

Hennessy let out a laugh and ran his hand through his hair. "Well, I... I um... I'm not terribly opposed to the idea."

"Me either," I whispered.

He beamed. "Then yeah, I think we should do the friend-meeting thing."

"Okay," I said, trying not to overthink actually meeting his friends. "Um, what about family?" Then I realise how that sounded. "I mean, do you have any? Not that we have to do the meeting the family thing. I think friends is more than enough for me not to freak the fuck out over, but I've never even asked you about your family. Or your tattoo. Or why the hell you went to Nepal. God." I put my hand to my forehead. "Way to ruin everything, Jordan."

"You didn't ruin anything." He squeezed my hand. "Yes, I have family. My folks live up on the Gold Coast, and I have two sisters, Siobhan and Saffron. Both older; both live in Melbourne. We're all kind of busy, but we talk on the phone all the time and we see each other for a week at Christmas."

"Siobhan and Saffron," I repeated. "And Hennessy. Did your parents write the book on How To Give Your Kids Cool Names?"

He chuckled. "We got a lot of shit at school, actually."

I made a face. "Oh, sorry."

"That's okay. What about your family?"

"I don't speak to them. I haven't since they wouldn't have a gay kid, and I couldn't be not gay, so that was that."

Hennessy stopped, his face drained, and he put his hand on my arm. "Oh my God, Jordan. I didn't know. Sorry."

"I was eighteen and living on my own at uni anyway, so it wasn't like I had to add the label of homeless to freshly orphaned. But I'd rather cut all ties with those arseholes than spend years begging for them to love me, ya know?"

He nodded. "Yeah. But Jesus. I'm so sorry they did that."

I shrugged. "I'm sorry too, but I'm okay. I knew they'd never accept me, so it wasn't some huge shock. I kind of expected it, to be honest. I'm stronger because of them, and in a roundabout way, they taught me to stand up for myself. Plus, I have a brother in Angus, and a sister in Merry. I made my own family, and they're so much better."

He blew out a breath and studied me for a long second. "You're amazing."

I scoffed and rolled my eyes. "And if you're thinking I'm headed for some kind of breakdown because I use humour and sarcasm as a defence mechanism, you'd be wrong. I've always been a nonsensical rambler, ever since I could talk, and I was funny long before my parents were bigoted arseholes."

Hennessy gave me a small smile. "You're still amazing.

"Not really, but you wanna know what I really am?"

He nodded.

"Hungry. And you mentioned food."

He smiled, more genuinely this time. Then he put his arm around my shoulder again and we began walking to the bus stop.

CHAPTER TEN

HENNESSY

WE WERE GREETED WARMLY by Feri as soon as we stepped inside. "Good to see you again, Mr Hennessy," he said, his grin wide, his arms outstretched. "You bring special someone?"

"I did, yes," I replied, sparing Jordan a small glance, feeling a little proud, a little embarrassed. "This is Jordan."

They smiled politely at each other and said quiet hellos.

"I give you best table, come this way." Feri was a short man, as tall as he was wide, but he had a smile that could light up a room. His restaurant was a small, dank-looking place, and I probably would have thought it questionable if it weren't for the non-stop crowd of people lining up for whatever Hungarian creations he could dish up.

After we were seated, Jordan took his time going over the menu. It was probably the quietest I'd ever seen him. "You okay?"

"Oh sure," he said quickly. "I just don't know what to get. It all looks good, but I've never had Hungarian before. I mean, I've had goulash before, but I don't know what any of these other things are, and what if I order the wrong thing and don't like it. I don't want things to be awkward."

"Want me to order for you?"

He looked up from the menu to me, a little puzzled, but there was a hint of a smile. "Do you think you're good enough? Because if you order it and I don't like it, then it's bound to be awkward."

I chuckled. "The name of this place, Itthon, is Hungarian for *at home*. Like home cooking, soul food. There isn't a bad thing on the menu. And you ordered those mango fries for me, and there was no awkwardness."

"Because they're deep fried heaven sticks." Then he shrugged. "But I'm game if you are."

I folded my menu closed, already knowing what I'd order.

When Feri brought out the lángos and stuffed cabbage and the chicken paprikash on nokedli for us to share, I waited for Jordan to taste it first. He took a tentative forkful of the chicken, then his gaze shot to mine. "Get. Out."

I grinned. "Told you."

Feri let out one of his contagious laughs. "You bring him here to win his heart," he said with a clap of his hand on my shoulder. "My food works every time."

I'm certain I blushed every shade of red known to man, but Feri went on to his other customers, leaving Jordan and me to eat in slightly mortified silence.

"Well, this definitely cranks your rating up to a full ten points," Jordan said. He put his fork down and leaned back. "This is amazing."

"I thought it was a full ten before we got here."

"A full ten on the new scale," he said. "Which would be like a fifty for anybody else, but we have to keep it at ten so they don't feel bad. Not everyone can live up to your standards."

I grinned. "Well, that would be fair. Oh, and your questions earlier. My tattoo is the Marvel Avengers' A, you know, but in black, grey, white, and purple, like the ace flag. Kind of like my superhero shield. It looks better than it sounds. It's on my chest." I pointed to my heart. "And I went to Nepal before my final year of uni. I had two months off, and I knew once I graduated, it'd be competitive, and once work started, my next vacation would be in ten years. So I spent five weeks travelling from Vietnam to Cambodia, Thailand, Myanmar, Northern India, then Nepal. It was crazy but incredible. Best five weeks of my life."

"That sounds amazing. You went with friends?"

I shook my head. "Nope. My travel agent lined up a guide from Vietnam, paid him a year's wages, which wasn't much by comparison. He had an old Jeep I'm pretty sure was left behind from the war. The suspension was shot, but it was all part of the experience."

"You went on your own? Oh my God, I would definitely end up in a bathtub of ice missing a kidney or something. Or I'd end up in the Bangkok Hilton because the customs guys would probably think my non-stop talking was a sign of drug use. It'd be a disaster."

I chuckled and broke off a piece of the lángos. "Here, try this. It's amazing."

He took it, tasted it, and groaned. "Why have I never been here before? I think we'll need to come back and try every single thing on the menu."

"Deal."

He ate a bit more, set his fork down, and sipped his water. "So what have you got on at work this week?" he asked. "You mentioned closing off one of your biggest contracts. I mean, I don't even know what internet ninjas do."

"Yeah, there are things I can't tell you. You know, being an internet ninja—" I winked. "—means there are things I can't tell you."

"So you *are* an undercover cop or a secret agent?" He narrowed his eyes at me. "I knew it!"

I laughed at that. "Definitely not a cop or a secret agent. But I deal with classified information. Big companies, corporations, and the CEOs trust me with passwords and encryption codes. If I wanted to, which I don't, but if I was so inclined, I could take down some pretty big companies."

"So you have access to all of their information?"

I nodded. "Names, addresses, tax-file numbers, bank accounts, offshore accounts, wire transfers. You name it, I can see it."

"Wow. That's kinda scary."

"It is a bit."

"Have you ever been tempted to go to the dark side?"

I smiled. "No. Being a good guy pays well, I get to do what I enjoy, and there are other perks—like not going to prison."

Jordan snorted. "Pretty big perk."

"So there will always be things I can't tell you. Don't think it's anything against you, because it's not. It's just my job. There are all kinds of NDAs and contracts where I guarantee silence and anonymity."

"No, that's completely fine. I get that."

"But yes, I will be wrapping up that contract this week, which will be a hell of a relief for a whole range of reasons," I said. "The biggest reason being, the boss of the company I'm working with right now is my ex. But despite our differences, he wanted the best, and me being ever the professional..." I waved my hand.

He made a face and shifted in his seat. It clearly made him uncomfortable. "That can't be easy."

"No. Especially after I moved out, and having to see him again, it wasn't easy at all."

"You lived with him?"

"Yep. For six months. It was kind of crazy, and I think moving in with him was a last-ditch effort to save the relationship. Which in hindsight was stupid. I thought it might make us closer, and apparently he thought it might make me want to sleep with him. We broke up, he moved on, and I moved out."

"He's the guy that slept with other people right after you broke up?"

"Three people. That day." I threw my serviette onto my empty plate. "I know that because he brought them home. I don't know if he wasn't expecting me to still be there..."

"That motherfucker."

I nodded. "Yep. I didn't stick around to watch. I was gone before his bedroom door was even closed."

"Good."

"I went straight to Michael's place, and he and Vee fed me Chinese food and vodka till I felt better."

"They sound like my kind of people."

"You'd like them. I know you and Michael would hit it off, and Vee would adore you."

"Is she the one who is trying to set you up with dinner dates?"

I nodded. "Yeah. She just wants me to be happy."

"Are you?" he asked.

I met his gaze and held it for a long moment. "I am now."

He blushed and rolled his eyes. "Well, I am a total catch."

I sighed happily. Happier than I had been in a long time. "Can I be totally honest with you?"

He looked stricken. "Oh God. This never ends well."

I moved my foot to the outside of his under the table and kept it there. "It's not bad. It's just... this is probably going to sound corny, and it's probably too soon to dump this on you, but I'm so glad I met you. To finally find someone who not only understands me, but is like me... it feels like I won the lottery." He looked about to say something, and maybe this was crazy-fast, but I felt something in my very core for Jordan. I put my hand up. "Maybe I'm not saying this right and I don't want to scare you off. But for me to meet someone who not only gets me but who is the same as me, well that's pretty amazing."

He frowned at his plate. "No, I get it. I really do. I thought there was something wrong with me. I thought I was just different and that was who I was. And like I told you at the support meeting, I have so many labels already, I didn't really need another one. But I'm thinking now maybe it wasn't the label I had the issue with. Maybe it was finally admitting there was something different about me, because if I admitted it, it made it true and then I had to face it. Know what I mean?"

I nodded. "I do, yeah."

He smiled. "And that right there is why I'm glad I met you too. Because you're like me. There *are* other people who are like me. There's nothing wrong with me, there's nothing abnormal about me."

"No, there's not. The word normal should be thrown in the garbage."

"I'm thinking of writing Merriam-Webster a sternly

worded letter," he joked. "It needs to be removed. Along with the word baccalaureate. Not for any other reason that I just don't like it, and I can never spell it right on the first go."

"Do you have to use it often?"

"Too often. You'd be surprised."

"Then it should be abolished immediately."

He smiled at me, a half-smile. A comfortable, lazy kind of smile that made him look as cute as hell. "But getting back to my point," he said. "You've shown me that it's okay to have hard limits and likes and preferences, and that I don't have to endure unwanted sex just to feel like society tells me I should feel. Because that's not who I am; I know that now, and I know it's not a defect. So for that reason, I'm really glad I met you too."

I grinned at him.

"I mean there are other reasons I'm glad I met you, the most perfect second date in history, notwithstanding."

"Such as?"

"Loves books, has great taste in books too, I might add. You're kind and thoughtful, and you notice things about people that most people wouldn't."

"I do?"

"Sure. Like Feri," he said, nodding toward where Feri was talking to another couple at the counter. "Most people would have described him as short, kinda round, Hungarian, or loud. All they see are obvious physical descriptors. But not you. You said he has the best laugh. You see a trait that embodies him as a human being."

I was a little stunned by his assessment. He had an uncanny way of stripping away the bullshit and seeing the real me.

"Oh," he added, then leaned across the table. "And you're a great kisser."

I snorted out a laugh and let my smile linger as I studied him for a moment. "It was kinda great."

His cheeks drew a nice pink, and he rolled his eyes. "Actually, it was terrible. It was so bad, I think we might need to practise a whole lot more until we improve. And the hand holding needs work; there should be much more of it until we have it mastered. And we haven't got to hugging yet, but I'm confident enough to know there will probably be a need for much training. I hear repetition is key."

I laughed. "Most definitely is key."

Just then Feri came over to ask if there was anything he could get us, but we were done. We halved the bill, bid Feri good night, and walked out into the street. The night had gotten dark and cold, and we both shoved our hands in our jacket pockets for warmth as we began walking back toward Cleveland Street.

"So we should try and organise a meeting of friends," I suggested. "For me to meet Angus, and for you to meet Michael. Or do we leave it a while and just enjoy being us for a bit."

"I don't mind," he replied. "I'd say you could meet Angus right now, only he's getting his itch scratched and won't be home until morning."

"An itch?" I asked. "Does he need antibiotics?"

Jordan snorted. "He probably will after." Then he explained. "He has a couple he meets up with every other weekend when they have an itch or when he does. If you get my drift."

"Oh."

"Yeah. When I said we're very different, I meant it," he said with a smile. "He doesn't really want a relationship, I don't think. He just likes to hook up when it's convenient. And the fact that there's two of them isn't such a great surprise, knowing Angus. A husband and wife who enjoy his company every so often, maybe every second or third weekend, with no strings attached. But apparently they're super nice and they treat him well, so that's all I care about. Plus, it's how Angus likes it; he doesn't want complications or anything but mind-blowing sex every so often. So when I say he's getting an itch scratched, it's getting scratched very thoroughly."

I chuckled. "Sounds like it."

"So if the universe has a quota of the amount of sex allowed, then Angus evens out my loss," he said with a laugh. "I don't want any, and he does two at once. Like I said, we're very different, but maybe that's why we get on so well."

"How did you meet?" I asked. "If you don't mind me asking."

"Well, it's a bit weird, but the real estate agent who manages rentals hooked us up."

"Hooked you up?"

He made a face. "Not like that, God no. I meant hooked us up. She knew I was looking for a new place and the unit was perfect, but I needed a flatmate to help cover rent and she knew of someone else who was looking and she asked me if I'd seen *Notting Hill*..." He grinned. "The rest, as they say, is history. That was three years ago."

"*Notting Hill?*"

He nodded. "Yep. You know Hugh Grant's flatmate? The tall, weird Welshman?"

"Yes."

"Well, that's Angus. Except he's not tall, and he's Australian, not Welsh."

"Sounds... fun."

"Never a dull moment, that's for sure."

I had wondered about his dynamics with his flatmate, or best friend, or brother as he'd called him. Jordan had said they were close but very different, and I'd wondered if they had some kind of history. I couldn't deny the selfish stab of relief when he confirmed there'd never been anything physical between them. I knew everyone had a past and exes. I had my own. But I wasn't sure how I'd feel about them still living together.

We'd somehow managed to walk ourselves to my place. "Oh," I said, rather stupidly. I pointed to the townhouse I called home. "Um, this is me."

"Oh!" Jordan looked kinda horrified, and if I could read him properly, he looked anxious. "I um, I should, uh..." He glanced up the street.

"Jordan," I said gently. "I can call you a cab or an Uber right now, and I'll even pay for it so I know you get home safely. Or you could come inside? I can promise you there will be no pressure for sex or anything, really. Although I wouldn't be opposed to maybe some more kissing or hand holding. And I'm pretty sure *Deep Space Nine* is on Netflix, and I haven't seen it in years." I was nervous and it was very obvious. "I've just had a really great day and I don't want it to end yet, but if you want to go, it's totally fine and I understand, I really do. It is kinda late, but if you do want to leave, please let me pay your Uber fare because as much as I love this place, it can be kind of sketchy at night and—"

Jordan put his hand on the gate to my front door and pushed it open. "After you."

I let out a relieved laugh but went through the gate. My stomach tightened with nerves. "Um. Thank you."

"The nervous rambling is cute," he said. "But like I said, that's my trademark. You'll need to get your own."

Smiling, I took out my key and unlocked my front door,

and this time, I held the door for him. "I'm not normally the nervous type," I admitted as I stepped inside. I flipped on the light and closed the door behind him, then leaned my back against it. "But I am around you. I mean, I'm comfortable like I've known you forever, but I'm nervous because I don't want to fuck this up."

He turned and eyed me for a moment. "Why would you fuck it up? Because believe me, if there's anyone who is a walking train wreck, I'm pretty sure it's me."

I put my hand to my forehead, trying to get myself in order, and pushed off the door to close the distance between us. "You're not a walking train wreck," I whispered, putting my hand to his jaw. "You're kind of awesome and really cute. And I probably should find my manners and ask you if you'd like a drink or something, but I'm pretty sure if I don't kiss you right now, my heart will explode."

He sucked back a breath and licked his lips. "Well, we can't have exploding hearts. I mean I know CPR and I can keep a heart beating until the ambulance gets here but I don't think there's much I can do for an exploding heart and I'd much rather you didn't die right now because the cops might think I did it and I'm far too cute to go to jail."

I chuckled as I leaned in. His eyes fluttered shut and his lips parted slightly just before I kissed him. He responded, leaning into me and kissing me back with a restraint and tenderness that made my knees weak. I had one hand cupping his jaw and the other at his waist, and he felt so right against me.

There was no arousal; my body didn't usually react like that. But my heart was beating triple time, my blood singing, and my chest bloomed with a warmth I'd only felt a few times before. He took my breath away.

I slowed the kiss, and keeping my forehead pressed to his, I swiped my thumb along his jaw. "Wow."

He laughed and his blue-grey eyes swam as if he were drunk. "Yeah. Wow."

I hummed and licked my lips, enjoying the thrum of sensations kissing him had given me. Like he'd done to me before, I took his hand and placed it over my heart. "Feel that? That's from you."

He blushed and laughed it off, sliding his hand from my heart down my arm. It took him a moment, but he eventually met my eyes and there was uncertainty in his.

"You okay?" I asked.

He nodded and looked around the room, taking in the TV, the couches, and the small dining table. "I um..." He let out a breath.

I might have thought he was nervous but it wasn't that. He was anxious. "Want that drink?" I asked, figuring he could use the distraction. I walked into the kitchen and hit the lights before opening the fridge. "I have bottled water or lemon-flavoured mineral water, which I sometimes add vodka to? Or Corona if you want beer, and tea or coffee."

He was still standing in the living room where I'd left him, his hand in his back jeans pocket. "Um... water'd be great, thanks."

I took two bottles and handed him one, then picked up the TV remote. "So, *Star Trek: Deep Space Nine*. Should I start at the first episode, first season? Or do I just skip straight to season three?"

It seemed to take a second for his brain to kick into gear. "Oh, episode one, season one, of course." He walked around to where I was and sat slowly on the sofa. "Um, you can't be a true fan if you skip anything."

"True." I waited for Netflix to load and found the

thumbnail I was after and hit Play. I sat beside him, on the same couch, but not too close. I leaned back, put my feet on the coffee table, and plonked a cushion on my lap. "So, Sisko is the best captain or commander, whatever his rank ended up? What about Picard, or Kirk and Spock, or Janeway? There has to be a reason you picked Sisko."

He smiled at me and seemed to relax before launching into a spiel on consistency and compassion and how Sisko's being a father in the show made him more relatable. He was animated; the light in his eyes was back, along with his smile. We watched two episodes before I couldn't fight another yawn. "I think it's time for bed," I said, trying to shake off my tiredness.

"Oh," Jordan said, quickly getting to his feet. He swallowed hard and took a small step back. "Yes, I should be going. I didn't realise how late it was."

His anxiousness was back, and I think I knew what it was. While we'd been standing close and touching, he'd become anxious, but as soon as I put some distance between us and made no move to get cuddly on the couch, he'd relax.

I sat up and put my feet on the floor. "Jordan, can I ask you something?"

He opened his mouth but shut it again and he glanced to the front door. "Uh, sure."

"Are you worried that I want more?" I looked up at him. "Because I don't. I mean, that kiss earlier was amazing and I'd like to do more of that, but not tonight. And maybe we'll work our way up to cuddling on the couch." I gave a pointed nod to the TV. "Maybe by season two? But not tonight."

He let out a loud breath and almost swayed. He sagged back onto the couch next to me. "Am I that obvious?"

"You're like a rabbit in front of a fox."

He barked out a laugh. "That's an apt description, because it's how I feel."

I gave him a sad smile. "I'm sorry. I want you to feel safe around me. But I get it. I do."

He frowned and spoke to his hands. "It's just that things always start like this, and there'd be hand holding and kissing, and I'd say that's all I want and they'd agree, but then they'd think kissing was just a tool for foreplay. Like no one can just kiss because they like it. It has to be a prelude to wanting more, and they'd always think I was playing hard to get, and then I'd have to say no, again, because how could anyone not want to have sex, right? And then they'd say, 'But you like kissing, it's not that different,' but it really fucking is. Kissing and having sex aren't mutually inclusive. Just because I want one doesn't mean I want the other or have to partake in sex just because I want to enjoy kissing." He took a breath. "And you kissed me and it was incredible. Like, seriously, it may have been the best kiss of all time and I was floating. Seriously. You have skills. But then habit snuck in and I thought for sure you'd ask for more and I didn't want to have to say no to you because well, this has been the best date ever and I didn't want to ruin it."

I shook my head. There was quite a lot to unpack in that. I took his hand and waited until he looked into my eyes. "Okay, first things first, you saying no wouldn't ruin anything. Don't ever think you're doing something wrong by saying no. Blame should fall on the person with the expectation that they are owed sex. Secondly, kissing is not the same thing as sex. Not even close, and if someone tries to guilt you into something you're not comfortable with, then they're a piece of shit and witches should put a hex on them so that every time they get a hard-on, they cry for their mummies."

Jordan snorted. "If they don't already."

I laughed and the tension was now, thankfully, gone. I squeezed his hand. "Jordan, I don't want to have sex with you."

"Oh." He jolted back, shocked, frowning and upset. His voice was quiet. "Is there something wrong with me?"

I would have laughed at that, except it really wasn't funny. It was a very stark reminder that he was still coming to terms with his asexuality and that he had a lot of years of rejection and stereotypical demons to conquer yet.

I lifted his hand and rubbed my thumb over his knuckles. "Jordan, there's absolutely nothing wrong with you. You're perfect just as you are. My not wanting to have sex with you isn't personal. I don't want to have sex with anyone. That's where I am on the spectrum of sexuality, and there's nothing wrong with me either. It's just who I am." Now for the tricky part. "Your knee-jerk reaction to thinking there's something wrong with you because I'm not attracted to you sexually tells me you've spent a lot of time dealing with arseholes who told you you weren't normal for not wanting sex."

He chewed on his bottom lip and conceded with a small nod. "You're very good at this support-group-mentor speech."

I chuckled. "Thank you."

"But yes. I've been told too many times to count that there's something wrong with me."

I scooted a bit closer so our knees touched, and still holding his hand with one of mine, I put my other to his cheek. "There's nothing wrong with you, Jordan. Actually, you're pretty damn close to perfect."

He blushed. "Well, then that's such a coincidence because I think you're pretty damn close to perfect too."

I grinned at him and we both took a second to just take it in. "You feel better?" I asked.

He nodded. "Much. Thank you for not letting me freak out and ruin everything."

"You were about ready to bolt for the door."

"I was working out the mathematical equation of hurdling your couch and escaping."

"It takes maths to jump a couch?"

He nodded. "Yep. Distance of the jump required times the height of the couch, divided by the energy and exertion necessary. I'm sure there's a cos, tan, sin equation in there somewhere but I failed year-eight maths so I really wouldn't know. And you'd need to subtract the amount of food I ate at dinner and my absolute lack of athletic ability to do anything, really, so I'd also need to allow for an inevitable crash over the back of the couch, hitting your floor, possibly denting the wall, and in all likelihood, any bones that break when gravity reminds me that I'm no longer a teenager, fit, or agile."

I laughed, because right there was the real Jordan I knew; all hint of anxiousness was gone. "Then how about I walk you around the couch and see you out." We stood and I took my phone out. "Let me book you an Uber. It's late." I handed him my phone. "Your address?"

He quickly thumbed it in and handed it back to me. "Thanks." Then he was quick to take my hand again. "We still need to practise."

"Oh, true. Practice is key."

He swung our still-joined hands and smiled. "You can stop trying now. I stopped scoring this date. It passed a solid ten at lunchtime. You've lapped ten several times."

I turned to face him, leaning my back against the front door. "I'm not trying. I just want you to get home safe, that's all." I held my phone up. "Your driver is three minutes away."

"Well, if you're not opposed to it, I think I'd like to kiss you again," he said.

"I'm not opposed to that at all."

He leaned his front against me, pressing me against the door, and kissed me. I let him lead this time, and he was slow and languid, deep and thorough. There was the right amount of pressure, the right amount of tongue, soft lips and rough stubble, gentle hands and a gentle nudge of his nose when he pulled away.

"Damn," he breathed. He lifted my hand to his chest this time so I could feel the thump of his heart.

"Damn," I echoed. My entire body was buzzing and warm, alight with the memory of his kiss. We stared at each other for a long moment, our smiles growing wider. I turned the door handle and stepped in closer to Jordan so I could open it. He didn't move, just kissed me again, chastely this time. Then he took a step to the side so I could open the door fully. "I have had the best day," I said.

"Me too."

"What are you doing tomorrow?"

"Laundry, groceries. All that super fun adulting stuff."

I groaned. "Same."

"You can text me though," he said. "Or call me. I won't mind at all."

A car honked its horn out the front. "That's your ride."

He nodded and cupped my face before pressing his lips to mine once more. "'Parting is such sweet sorrow,'" he whispered, quoting Shakespeare as he walked to the gate.

I couldn't let him beat me. "'The pain of parting is nothing to the joy of meeting again.'"

Jordan stopped and turned, put his hand to his heart,

and groaned. "And he quotes Dickens? My heart, my heart!"

I laughed and he shot me a grin before he got in the Uber. I waved goodbye and closed the door, my smile lingering. I put my fingers to my lips, still feeling the ghost of his kiss, and I laughed.

My heart, my heart, indeed.

CHAPTER ELEVEN

JORDAN

"HE QUOTED DICKENS!"

Merry gasped and narrowed her eyes at me. "That motherfucker."

"I know!" I swooned—again—pretty sure I was still grinning and damn sure my feet hadn't touched the ground yet.

Merry and I were at work, cataloguing new arrivals, and we had the science of talking-whilst-working down to such an art that Mrs Mullhearn couldn't get mad at our constant yabbering because truthfully, we got more work done the more we talked. We were making short work of the books while I gave Merry all the details about my weekend.

"And how did Angus' date night go?"

"Well, he has that sated-swagger thing going on and a smile that reminds me of that time we all ate hash brownies and did the Ru Paul's *Drag Race* marathon."

Merry snorted so loud it scared me. "Sorry," she said with a laugh.

I had my hand to my heart. "Jesus, warn a guy next time."

"Do you remember that time you, me, and Angus got

really drunk on champagne with Midori on Saint Patrick's Day and Angus bought those space cakes," she said, still chuckling.

"Oh my God. Last time he ever trusts an Irish guy dressed as a Leprechaun selling four-leaf-clover-shaped edibles," I said, laughing.

"He was so funny."

"He's seeing them again this weekend," I said. "His couple. They have such a great time with him apparently, they've cleared their schedules to do it again."

"How long has he been seeing them?"

"For six months or so, just whenever the need arises."

"As long as he's happy," Merry said. "And that they treat him right."

"Mmm," I agreed. "What about you, Merry? Are you happy?"

"I am." She put the book she was holding on top of the final pile. "I can live vicariously through you and your new romance, all from the comfort of my couch in my PJs and messy hair. It's all I need."

"If you wanted—"

"If you finish that sentence, Jordan O'Neill, I will forever associate you with my mother and her velociraptor colony of people who think I need someone to make myself complete. I am very happily single and free to do whatever the hell I want, whenever I damn well want to."

I put my hand up in surrender. "Uh, yeah, I was just going to say if you want to come over anytime, I'll have Angus get some more brownies and we can do a *Great British Bake Off* marathon and order take out and eat ice cream. From the comfort of our couch in our PJs and messy hair."

She glared at me and slid the pile of books onto her trolley. "You were not going to say that at all, you lying liar who lies."

I laughed. "Well, no. I wasn't. But your mum's colony of velociraptor people scares the bejeezus out of me."

"You and me both," she said, wheeling her trolley to the door. "But that invite might be good for Hennessy to do the meeting-of-friends thing you talked about."

I loaded up my trolley, smiling at the thought of seeing Hennessy again this afternoon on the bus. We'd talked on the phone twice yesterday, once when he called when I was in aisle three of the supermarket having a conversation with Mr Collins, a guy who frequents the library, about the importance of psyllium husk in a man's diet—which, believe me, was promptly added to my list of things I never needed to know—and Hennessy had laughed for a solid minute, and then I called him last night. I totally did not call him when I was lying in bed just to hear the sound of his voice. It just so happened I was artfully reclined in my room and his voice in my ear is what happens when you speak to someone on the phone.

But it was nice and it made me feel all gooey inside, so shut up.

And my heart just about galloped out of my chest when I got on the bus and saw him, grinning at me with a vacant seat next to him. I made my way up to the back of the bus, thankful I didn't trip over my own feet and ignoring the ridiculously giddy grins the Soup Crew were giving me. I mean really, Mrs Petrovski was about bouncing in her seat, and when I sat beside Hennessy and he leaned in real close, giving me a slow, gentle nudge, she just about expired.

"Hey," he said, all casual-like while my insides were a full-on carnival parade.

"Hey."

"How was work?"

"Great. And yours?"

"Busy. The contract should wrap up this week. Next week at the latest."

"That'll be good, right? You won't have to see whatshis-name again?"

"It'll be so good. I spent three hours with him today, going over parameters and firewalls."

"Sounds painful," I said.

He grimaced. "I'd rather be rolled in honey and tied over a nest of fire ants, but going home to have an acid bath will have to suffice."

"Whatever works." I chuckled, not even remotely guilty for being pleased he hated having to spend time with his ex. "Though I hope they know how professional you are for enduring that every day. It can't be easy."

He shrugged. "They do know. But I don't mind," he said wistfully. "Because Michael told him all about how I've been seeing a new guy and how I was never this happy when I was with him. So if that's any kind of bonus, I'll take it wrapped with a big-arse bow and a side of gleefully spiteful."

I gasped, giving him a nudge, ignoring how my innards were now re-enacting a circus acrobatic routine. "I hear gleefully spiteful is the new black."

Hennessy grinned at me. "Maybe after my acid bath, I could call you while I'm artfully reclined in my bed."

"Will you ever let me live that down?"

"Probably not."

I sighed. "Well, I can't even be mad after the 'I've been seeing a new guy and was never this happy' comment."

"Michael said that, not me," he said. Then blanched. "I mean, I would have said that if we'd talked about it, but apparently Michael beat me to it and whatshisname never asked me after that."

I snorted. "Good save."

"I thought so."

"So I was thinking maybe you could come over on Thursday night for dinner to meet Angus, if you wanted to, because we have the ace support meeting on Friday and he'll be busy all weekend with his 'couple with benefits,' if you follow my meaning. But if you're hammered with work, we could leave it until Sunday or even next week if you want."

He chuckled. "I thought you said Angus only met his couple every other weekend?"

"You're not the only one getting hammered, apparently. If the glazed-over look Angus wore yesterday was any indication."

He put his hand to his mouth and bit back a laugh. "Apparently not."

"But anyway, dinner on Thursday at my place is still on offer, if you want. Merry wants to be there as well, just so you know. We can order in and eat ice cream from the comfort of our couch in our PJs and messy hair, and there will be no velociraptor-colony people or Leprechauns with hash edibles." I put my hand to my heart. "I promise."

Hennessy cracked up laughing. "Sounds good." Then he grabbed his messenger bag. I wasn't even aware we were at his stop already, but he leaned in and gave me a quick kiss. "I'll call you tonight," he said, then dashed off the bus.

I blushed so hard I feared the capillary damage would be permanent, but I also grinned so hard my cheeks hurt.

Mrs Petrovski clapped and wiggled in her seat before she leapt up and shooed me over so she could sit next to me. "Tell us everything! You two are so cute!"

I looked around at the other passengers. The Soup Crew were smiling and nodding at me, and even a few random people were smiling along with the others. This was getting ridiculous, but the inner carnival in my insides was now a full-on Mardi Gras and my excitement bubbled out in the form of a butt-wiggle with my fists to my face, eyes peering over my knuckles like an anime character. "He's the most amazing guy in the history of the world and we had the best date ever—I mean, evvvvvver—he took me to an art gallery exhibit and the botanical gardens, and then he took me to a Hungarian restaurant—"

"Itthon's?" Ian asked. "On Marlborough Street?"

I nodded. "Yep."

He groaned. "Oh, that is smooth."

"I know, right? Smooth doesn't even begin to describe it."

Mrs Petrovski put her hand on my arm and looked up at me with stern, hopeful eyes. "He kiss you?"

I put my hand to my heart. "Oh, boy. Did he ever."

She cheered and others clapped and laughed, and I laughed too because this was how bizarre my life was now.

"So what will you do when it's your turn to plan the next date?" Becky asked.

My smile died a slow death and I clutched my heart for completely different reasons. "I... I um... I can't live with that kind of pressure. Oh God, what am I supposed to do to live up to his date. Because we had to reinvent new scales of ratings for his date. I'm not even kidding."

"Like the Richter scale?" Sandra asked seriously.

I nodded, equally serious. "Exactly like that. But to the power of ten. It really was that good."

"Don't you worry," Charles said. "We got you." And for the rest of the trip home, they all chipped in with the best-worst ideas ever. So God help me. The Soup Crew really were a bunch of weird and wonderful motherfuckers.

"NEED ME TO BRING ANYTHING?" Merry asked. I'd just told her about our dinner plans on Thursday and told her she had to be there for moral support.

"Nope. I was going to have it at home and cook something, but the Soup Crew thought it would be better if we went out."

"The Soup Crew?"

"Yeah, Mrs Petrovski, Charles, Becky, Sandra, and Ian. They catch the bus with us and they're very invested. They're like the Avengers..." I made a face as I reconsidered. "Okay, more like the cast from *Cocoon*, but whatever. They're very invested, and they clap and cheer whenever Hennessy does anything sweet before he gets off the bus. Like yesterday, when he kissed me."

"Wait." She put her hand up. "Hennessy kissed you on the bus yesterday?"

I swooned at the memory. "He did. Just a sweet peck before he ran off the bus."

Merry gave me her puppy dog eyes. "Awww."

"I know!"

"And people on the bus clap and cheer for you?"

I nodded.

"What even is your life?"

"Fucked if I know."

"Jordan!" Mrs Mullhearn said, frowning at me. "Is there any emergency reason for the language?"

"Well, emergency is subjective. I'm sure what *I* would

deem as an emergency and what you might deem as an emergency—"

"Is anyone in a life-threatening situation?" she said over the top of me.

I looked around the room. "Um, no. Unless we count Merry's lunch in the fridge. She cooked it last night and believe me, I've eaten her cooking before and although life-threatening is a strong word—"

Merry whacked my arm. "Hey!"

"Ow!"

"Is there work to be done?" Mrs Mullhearn asked.

"Always," I replied with a smile, knowing my tactic of talking until she made me leave would make her forget about my swearing.

Merry and I shoved out into the hall and she pushed my back. "What's wrong with my cooking?"

I laughed. "Absolutely nothing. So, Thursday? You in? I was thinking of that café with all the vintage stuff, on King Street."

"Oooh, I love that place. And after your comment about my cooking, you're paying."

I laughed. "Deal."

THE BUS WAS CROWDED and Hennessy gave me an apologetic shrug when I locked eyes with him, because there was a guy in the seat next to him. "It's okay," I mouthed.

But then the guy nodded at me and rolled his eyes and smirked before standing up. "I can find another seat," he said. "I've been telling my wife about you guys, and if she ever found out I was the reason you couldn't sit together, she'd kill me."

I tried not to turn too red, but well, it was awkward and I was the king of that shit. "Thanks," I said. "And tell your, uh, wife I said hi?"

I sat next to Hennessy and he was looking a little bewildered. He whispered, "He told his wife about us? What does that even mean?"

"I don't even know. Apparently our lives are now like *The Truman Show* meets *Cocoon*." I cleared my throat. "I've stopped questioning the weirdness."

He laughed. "You look great today. Love the purple. Very ace."

"Ace? Oh." Ace, as in asexual. I freaking blushed again and looked down at the offending purple scarf. "Thanks."

"So Thursday night dinner? Are we still on?"

"Yes, for sure."

"I'm looking forward to it. Tell me again, Angus is okay with it?" He made an adorable face like he was freaking out.

I grinned at him. "I told you last night on the phone. He's more than okay with it."

He let out a relieved breath. "I know. I'm just nervous."

"I know, and it's utterly ridiculous to me that you would be nervous about anything."

"Why?"

"Because you're the cool one, and I'm the one who is definitely punching above his weight."

"Cool one?"

"Ah, yes, with the cool name, like Hennessy who is paid to be an internet ninja." Jeez, did I have to spell it out for him?

He snorted. "Says the guy who has the best dress sense

and can name and quote any literary reference off the top of his head."

"I'm not sure that's a qualifier."

"Well, I disagree. And you're not punching above your weight, I assure you."

"We'll let Angus be the one to decide that."

His mouth fell open; a look of horror crossed his face. "Oh God. No pressure then."

"That's why these guys—" I waved to the Soup Crew who were listening intently to every word. "—thought meeting at a restaurant or café would be less pressure on you than being at my place."

Mrs Petrovski patted Hennessy on the shoulder. "We got you. Mutual ground is best for these things."

Hennessy's eyes went wide and he laughed. "Ah, thanks?"

I chuckled and nudged his shoulder with mine. "Embrace the weirdness."

His whole face was smiling. "I'm trying."

I nodded pointedly to his messenger bag. "Working from home again tonight?"

"Yep. Mostly coding stuff." He glanced up the front of the bus, seeing we were nearly at his stop. "But I'll call you?"

"Yes, please."

"And I'll tell Michael he'll be meeting you next week, probably. When we're not so busy with work and we can have a relaxing dinner that doesn't involve talk of network security fundamentals, digital forensics, and intrusion detection."

Now it was my turn to make the adorable face like I was freaking out. He laughed and stood up. "I'll call you later."

"Okay," I said.

He took a few steps toward the door when Mrs Petrovski called out. "Wait, stop!" He stopped, a little scared. Every person on the back half of the bus watched and waited. "You not kiss him today?"

"Oh," he mumbled, blushing every shade of red known to man. He took a few quick steps toward me, leaned in to kiss my cheek. Everyone cheered, and my whole face burned so hot I'm surprised I didn't catch fire, and he grinned and ran off the bus.

Mrs Petrovski patted my shoulder. "I got you too."

Oh God.

I really had to find me a better bloody word than motherfucker.

IT RAINED ON WEDNESDAY, which usually meant the bus would be full, and even though I had held out hope there'd be a spare seat, I wasn't exactly surprised to see it was standing room only. Not surprised, but disappointed.

I found a handrail to hold on to and gave Hennessy a frowny-smile and he gave me one right back, but like he did before, he stood up and made his way through the standing passengers to me. He just kind of slotted himself in right next to me, up close, our bodies bumping and swaying with the beat of the bus.

"Hey," he said.

"Oh, hey," I said. His face was right there, so close. "I'm kinda not sorry there were no seats."

He grinned that spectacular Hennessy Lang grin. "Me either, to be honest." The bus braked for traffic and he pushed right up close and our noses were barely an inch apart. "I really do like your face."

That made me laugh. "Um, thanks? I'm kinda glad, I guess, because it's the only one I have."

He chuckled. "What part of the face is your favourite?"

Random, but okay. "Mine or yours?"

"Oh, um, I don't know. Both I guess."

"I like my eyes. They're a crazy grey colour, and they're just like my grandad's. And my favourite part of your face, well, gee. Just this—" I waved my hand at his ridiculous face. "—whole general area. I mean, you have great eyes, and your nose is straight, and there's a dimple, and who doesn't love a good dimple, and even your beard scruff is great. And your ears are slightly elfish, which speaks to my inner geek, just so you know, and your lips..." Of course, then I got stuck staring at his lips. "Um..."

He bit his bottom lip, which made his smile crooked. I'm pretty sure he did that on purpose. Fair, he did not play. And then he was staring at my lips and for one horrifyingly exhilarating moment, I thought he was going to kiss me. Right there on the bus. Like a proper, proper kiss. I wouldn't have said no, but I wasn't sure if the other passengers would appreciate it. Well, the Soup Crew would. I was pretty sure they'd clap and cheer...

But then the bus came to an abrupt stop and he had to hold on to me to stop from falling. Or maybe it was me who was at risk of falling... which was far too late because I'd already fallen for him.

Wait, what?

"What?" I asked. "That's not at all correct."

Hennessy looked around us. "What's not at all correct?"

Shit.

"Oh, nothing, I was just thinking about something totally not related to you at all."

"Okay, though that doesn't sound very convincing," he said with a bit of a laugh.

"Well, it's just that falling... on the bus..." I put my hand to my forehead, trying to will my stupid mouth to shut up. "What I meant was that falling on the bus could be hazardous to one's health."

He stared at me for too long. He knew I was bullshitting. "Okay, yeah sure. I mean, we should think of the children and the elderly."

"Exactly."

He was so close. Did he need to be that close? Did he have to smell that good? God, he was so inconsiderate. "Do you really have to be that handsome?" I asked. "Because it's so unfair on the unsuspecting public. I mean, I'm kinda used to it, but these poor other people..."

He chuckled. "Well, it's the only face I have, so..."

"Me too."

He jostled into me again, not looking the least bit sorry. "I'm looking forward to tomorrow night. Despite the nerves and the fear that your friends won't think I'm good enough, I'm looking forward to spending time with you."

My heart did that squeezing thing that made my brain unable to brain and my lungs unable to lung. "My friends will think you're great because I do."

"You do?"

I could barely even whisper. "Jesus, motherfucker, you are too close, I can't think straight."

"Well, I would move, but...," he said, looking down between us, and there was my traitorous hand, fisting his shirt and pulling him closer.

"Oh."

"It's my stop," he said. "I have to go."

"That's generally what happens when it's your stop, yeah."

"So, um..." he chuckled. "Did you wanna let go of my shirt, or no?"

"Oh!" I said, having to consciously unpeel my fingers from the fabric. I patted it down. "Sorry about that."

He glanced up the back, nodding to Mrs Petrovski before kissing my cheek, then he hopped off the bus, grinning with a bounce to his step.

Which was great. He had bouncy legs and I had jelly legs. I had to hang onto the railing, and a pregnant woman offered me her seat. I didn't take it, of course. But I seriously considered it, not gonna lie.

I HELD my nerves together pretty well, considering. But as five o'clock drew near on Thursday, I was starting to get that giddy, filterless brain-mouth thing and having trouble standing still.

Then my phone beeped with a message.

I fumbled with my phone when I saw Hennessy's name. Jesus. He was going to cancel.

I won't be on the bus.

"Oh God, he's going to cancel," I mumbled.

I'm not cancelling.

"Oh."

Work is crazy and I'll meet you at the restaurant. Is that okay?

"Yeah, of course," I said stupidly before I realised I actually needed to text my reply not say it.

Sure. I'm sure I'll survive the bus ride home, alone. All by myself. By my lonesome. Without you.

LOL The Soup Crew will assist, I'm sure. No taking seats from pregnant ladies.

I won't need to if you're not there, I replied. Then mumbled, "Cheeky motherfucker," only to realise there was a lady at the counter, watching me, hearing me swear. And not just any woman, but the one with the feline buttholitis. "Oh, sweet mother of God," I said, horrified at the way her lips pursed together like that... and that damn coral-coloured lipstick. What was she thinking? I was fairly certain that hadn't been on the open market since Avon sold it in 1985.

Merry appeared from nowhere, springing up like the Hobbit she was. She shoved me out of the way. "Hello, Mrs Peterson," Merry said brightly.

God, Mrs Cat Bum Face had an actual name that wasn't directly related to feline buttholitis?

"Jordan's been called out the back and I'll be helping you today," Merry said. "Did you find what you were after?"

I didn't hear any more than that. I took my cue and got the hell out of there. I grabbed my coat and my scarf, and I grabbed Merry's too. I even washed up her lunch container as thanks for dealing with Mrs Peterson and her dreadful choice of lipstick and lack of lip filler. I mean seriously, would a little Botox have hurt?

Merry met me at the front door, shoving me out it. "Oh my God, Jordan, you owe me big time."

"I'm sorry you had to look at her face. I'm buying you dinner and drinks tonight. Double shots if you want. God, her mouth looks like she's been sucking lemons for twenty years. Do you think if she wore a hat with a tall feather in it, it'd look like a cat's tail to complete her cat's-arse look?"

"Jordan O'Neill," Merry said, "you are a terrible human being." It didn't help that she laughed as she tried to push me in front of the bus. I took her arm and dragged her on the bus, which was surprisingly empty.

Mrs Petrovski had a terrible frown on her face. "He not on the bus today. I asked the driver to wait but he no-show."

I took a seat and Merry sat next to me. "Uh, no. He has to work a little later tonight."

"He still meeting you for dinner?" She really was quite concerned.

"Yes, he is meeting us there. Mrs Petrovski, this is my friend Merry."

"Are you meeting Hennessy for the first time tonight?" she asked.

"No, I've met him before. Only briefly though." Merry gave me a what-the-hell? kind of look.

So I explained. "Mrs Petrovski is the leader of the Soup Crew."

"Oh." Recognition dawned on Merry's face. "Riiiight."

"We help the boys fall in love," Mrs Petrovski said. She looked to Becky, Charles, Ian, and Sandra, who all nodded earnestly. "It's better than *Home and Away* or *Neighbours*."

Merry gave me a wide-eyed, you-weren't-exaggerating stare, but before I could speak, Mrs Petrovski took some slips of paper from her handbag. "Oh, before I forget, I wrote these out for you. We all swap recipes now," she said, and literally fifteen people at the back of the bus nodded.

I read the first. Mayal's green chicken curry. The next was Richard's homemade lentil dal. Then Ian's pork mince dumplings, and there were several more.

Oh my God. They were all swapping recipes. And they were no longer weird, no longer invasive, no longer over-invested in mine and Hennessy's relationship. Because this was really cool, and sure it was still crazy and a little bit weird, but these people started out as strangers.

Now they were friends.

I was a little surprised at how emotional it made me. I swallowed down the lump in my throat. "Wow. This is awesome. Like really freaking cool, guys."

Mrs Petrovski let out an, "Awww. I just wish Hennessy was here to see your face right now."

"Me too. I'll show him these recipes tonight, and maybe we can write a recipe out to you guys."

"We would love that," she said. Everyone else nodded.

When we got off the bus at my stop, Merry asked if I was okay. "Sure," I replied.

"You weren't kidding about the bus fan club."

I snorted at that. "No. They're pretty cool though, yeah?"

"Are you kidding me? Jordan, that was the coolest thing ever! And I think it's an omen."

"An omen for what?"

"For tonight, silly. It's gonna be perfect."

Except it wasn't. It was going to be a disaster. Because Angus was late getting home, and apparently he'd spent the entire day in a closed, confined space with industrial glue.

He was as high as a motherfucking kite.

He walked in with the glazed smirk, slits for eyes, and greeted us with a "Heyyyyyyy" that would put Fonzie to shame. "Are we still meeting your bus boy for dinner? Because I have some serious munchies."

After it took Angus ten excruciating minutes to get his boots off, he moseyed on into the shower, and I practised my Lamaze breathing techniques. "Oh God, Christ on a cracker, this is going to be a disaster. I'm going to call Hennessy and cancel. He'll understand, I'm sure."

Merry laughed at me. "Are you kidding? Oh my God, Jordan, it couldn't be more perfect."

I gawped at her like she'd lost her mind. Which she had. Obviously.

She sighed. "A stoned Angus is a happy, placid, agreeable, hungry Angus. If at any point before now he was thinking he could interrogate Hennessy, you certainly don't have to worry about that any more. Just keep a plate of fries or corn chips in front of him, and you won't hear a word out of him."

I let out a long exhale. "Well, we could hope so. If he calls him Bus Boy, I will die, just so you know. And in the unfortunate event of my untimely demise, please delete my browser history."

She snorted. "What for? It's not like you have some kinky, nasty pig porn to delete. I don't think anyone is going to consider seventeenth-century French poetry as some kind of debauchery."

I gasped, my hand to my heart. "Don't underestimate the comedic brilliance of Voltaire."

"Please, for the sake of my sanity, do not quote him."

"'It is difficult to free fools of the chains they revere.'"

Merry sighed, long and loud. "You are relentless."

"Thanks."

Angus appeared from his room wearing underpants and a brightly coloured Hawaiian shirt that looked like it had gone twelve rounds with a packet of Skittles. "Okay, I am ready for food."

Merry squinted at him. "Aren't you forgetting something, dear?"

Angus shot me a look. "Oh, yeah, sorry. And I'm totally ready to meet the bus boy guy."

"You're missing something else," Merry deadpanned. "Like maybe some pants?"

Angus looked down at himself and laughed while being

genuinely surprised, like we'd somehow made his pants disappear. He toddled back into his room, and I had to steady myself against the wall while I did Lamaze breathing again.

"Disaster," I wheezed.

Merry gave me a sympathetic nod and patted my shoulder. "Breathe, Jordan. It'll be fine."

CHAPTER TWELVE

HENNESSY

I LOOKED across the table at the man sitting opposite me, wondering what on earth I'd ever seen in him. Rob was conceited, self-absorbed, and arrogant. He took himself far too seriously and assumed he was better than everyone else in the room. Maybe it was his confidence that originally attracted me; there was always something about a guy who carried himself well. But I'd soon learnt that he expected perfection not only from himself, but also from everyone around him. And that had included me, in and out of the bedroom.

Yes, he was wealthy and successful, but he was also an absolute jerk.

He viewed people as a means to an end. If he couldn't benefit from them, he simply walked away. Much like he'd done with me. At the time I'd been devastated, but with the view of hindsight—and now that I'd met Jordan—breaking up with Rob was the best thing to have ever happened to me.

I'd finally found someone who accepted me. The real

me. And speaking of which, if this meeting didn't wrap up soon, I was going to be late for dinner.

As Michael and Rob discussed business, I checked my watch for the tenth time.

"Am I keeping you from something?" Rob asked.

I'd stopped listening to his droning on, and his question caught me by surprise. "Oh, um. Actually, yes."

Michael looked at me in a way that was almost as effective as a kick under the table, so I amended with, "If you'll both excuse me for just a moment, I'll just make alternative arrangements and I'll be right back." I didn't wait for a reply. I wasn't asking permission. So I slipped out of the room and out of sight and pulled out my phone. I was already going to miss the bus, that was obvious, and I knew Jordan would assume the worst.

I won't be on the bus. I hit Send without really thinking it through. He would assume I was bailing on him, so I quickly thumbed out another. *I'm not cancelling. Work is crazy and I'll meet you at the restaurant. Is that okay?*

I could see his reply text bubble and let out a relieved sigh.

Sure. I'm sure I'll survive the bus ride home, alone. All by myself. By my lonesome. Without you.

I laughed at my phone. *LOL The Soup Crew will assist, I'm sure. No taking seats from pregnant ladies.*

I won't need to if you're not there.

"Hennessy?" Rachel asked from the hallway. "Everything okay?"

"Oh, yeah, sure. I was just..."

"Laughing at your phone? Skipping out on a meeting with Mr Sleazebag to text your new guy?"

I chuckled, totally busted. "Guilty as charged. I'm meeting him for dinner and didn't want him to think I was gonna be a no-show if I'm not on the bus." I sighed. "I better get back in there."

"Good luck," she said with a wink.

I went back into the room, and the report I'd given Rob still sat on the desk, untouched. "Did you sort out your personal life on my time?" he asked, smug and smiling.

"Your time?" I questioned. "No, what I did was waste my time when I wrote you a full, extensive report that you didn't even read."

He didn't even flinch, but his tone took a cruel turn. "How've you been, Hennessy? You settling into your new life okay?"

I smiled at him. "Perfectly, thank you. It's almost like minimal living, getting rid of the useless shit that cluttered your life. Does wonders for the soul."

His gaze hardened and he shifted in his seat. "I'm not paying you a fortune to be insulted."

"No," I replied flatly. "You're paying me to evaluate the security of your website, your brand, your livelihood, and identify vulnerabilities in your system, networks, and system infrastructure. You wanted me to run extensive penetration measures to find security exposures within your system configurations, hardware and software vulnerabilities, as well as operation witnesses in process for technical countermeasures." I shrugged. "If you had read the report, you would know this."

"The report was eighty-two pages of scripting, coding, and hardware engineering jargon."

"There was a detailed summary on page seventy-nine."

He smiled like he was enjoying this. "I hired you to give me a report from the fundamental understanding of our network vulnerabilities."

If he thought challenging me to be some kind of game, I

wasn't here to play. "Then let me dumb it down for you," I said, not breaking eye contact. "I skimmed ports to find vulnerabilities, scrutinised patch installation processes, performed detailed traffic analysis, and fixed your intrusion detection and prevention systems. What I found were eight bugs spread across four main access ports on your site. One was a clickjacking vulnerability, which could easily become a sitejacking if not stopped. Several others were cross-site scripting liabilities, an especially flexible and malicious type of attack in which hackers inject their own code into the domain web application, gaining access to not only your staff's personal information but that of your clients as well. The staff login portal was susceptible to infiltration, making it relatively easy for hackers with malicious intent to steal data from other visitors' browsers and possibly even impersonate them. And all the usual phishing scams."

Rob stared at me and it took him a second for what I'd just said to register. "Did you fix it? Oh my God. Tell me you fixed it!"

"Of course I did."

"And we're still right to transfer and go live next week? We have so much depending on this—"

"Of course, everything is fine. You wanted the best and you got it."

Michael smirked before he schooled his features. "Thanks Hennessy. Did you, uh..." He smiled. "Didn't you have somewhere to be tonight? We're almost done here."

I shot to my feet, unable to keep the grin from my face. "I do, thanks." I walked out without even pausing, grabbed my laptop, my messenger bag, only pausing at the elevator to say goodbye to Rachel. "Bye!"

"You could cab it," she called. "Or Uber it! It's the twenty-first century, you know?"

But I was already in the elevator, and as soon as the doors opened, I ran for the next bus.

———

I RACED HOME, dumped my gear, changed my shirt, freshened up, and not knowing much about Newtown, I booked an Uber. I got to the restaurant barely two minutes late, feeling a rush of relief when I saw Jordan sitting at a table with Merry.

Merry nodded pointedly at me and Jordan turned around, and his whole face lit up when he saw me. He stood just as I got to his table, and I couldn't resist putting my hand to his back and kissing him hello. "Sorry I'm late."

"Oh," he said with a little laugh, blushing beautifully. "Hi."

I nodded to Merry and said, "Nice to see you again."

She smiled cheerfully. "Same."

Jordan pulled out a seat at the table for me. "And not to worry, you had a crazy day at work, huh?"

I nodded as we sat down. I sat next to Jordan, Merry sat across from him, and I had an empty chair across from me. "Yes, busy with demanding, obnoxious clients." Then I noted the vacancy at the table. "I thought I was meeting Angus? Did he not come with you?"

"He's in the bathroom," Jordan said, "and before he comes back, I would like to apologise in advance for anything he may say or do."

"Um, why?"

"Well, I told you he's a painter," he said. I nodded, and Jordan sighed. "He's high as a kite on industrial adhesive."

I snorted a laugh. "Really?"

Merry nodded. "Really. And anything he says or does

on a good day is questionable, but he's adorable and we love him."

"I'm sure he's not that bad," I said before pouring myself a glass of table water and taking a sip.

Jordan grimaced. "Just please promise you won't hold me accountable."

"I promise," I said, smiling at him.

"Good, because here he comes."

The only guy walking our way from the bathrooms was short and stocky, well-muscled, well-built, tanned, and handsome in a rugged, outdoorsy way. He had sandy-blond hair that was short and mussed up, brown eyes—well, I think they were, they were barely slits—and he had a wide smile. He was also wearing a Hawaiian shirt that was so bright it could possibly be used to land aircraft, and faded jeans with a hole at the knee that didn't look artfully created. More like he'd tackled someone and ripped them. He also wore work boots. Again, not the stylish Timberland variety, but more of the 'just came from the building site' kind.

When Jordan had said he and Angus were complete opposites, he wasn't joking. They were poles apart.

"Man, those lights in the bathroom are freaky," Angus said as he sat down across from me, a slow drawl to his husky voice. "Heyyyy, you must be Hennessy."

"I am. Nice to meet you," I said, offering my hand for him to shake.

His hand was rough and calloused. Definitely had tradesman's hands. "Like the cognac," he said, nodding.

"Yep, like the cognac," I replied. I wasn't sure if him being high was the reason he spoke slow and spaced out or if that was just him, but it was hard not to like him.

"You're the guy who's got Jay all tied up in knots."

Jordan groaned. "Thanks, Angus. That's not embarrassing at all." I slid my hand onto Jordan's thigh and he gave me a smile.

"So many knots," Angus said, then he snorted and laughed. "And all the smiles and there's been gliding."

Jordan's eyes closed slowly, but Merry tilted her head and squinted at Angus. "Gliding?"

Angus nodded enthusiastically. "Much gliding. He gliii-iiiiiiides." He panned his hand across the horizon. "He never used to glide. The gliding is new. As is the smiling. But then—"

"Thanks, Angus," Jordan said, then cleared his throat. He shoved a menu in front of him. "Have you looked at the menu yet?"

Angus nodded slowly. "Indeed I have. I'm feeling the eggplant, the lamb, and the chicken."

Jordan looked at his menu, then to Angus. "That's three mains."

Angus stared at Jordan. "I'm a tad peckish. You really shouldn't judge or food-shame me, Jay. It's not like you, and frankly, I'm a little surprised."

Jordan and Merry both stared at Angus, and I tried not to laugh but it won out in the end. "He's right," I said with a grin. "Food-shaming isn't cool."

Then Jordan and Merry turned their wide eyes to me, and Angus laughed. "See? My man Hennessy is a'ight."

I nudged Jordan's shoulder and leaned in really close to whisper, my lips brushed his ear. "I like him, and he thinks I'm a'ight."

Jordan blushed and he opened his mouth to say something, but Angus beat him to it. "Hennessy, are you familiar with limericks?" he asked.

That was one hell of a subject change. "I am."

Jordan whisper-hissed across the table. "Angus, there will be no limericks."

Angus laughed and nodded. "There once was a man called Hennessy," he said, grinning. "Who caught the bus numbered three-five-three."

"Oh, God," Merry said, looking around the restaurant. "We need a waiter."

Jordan cringed and I laughed.

"Now Jay here was smitten."

Jordan rubbed his temple and Merry looked on with horrified resignation.

Angus leaned in and put his hands in the shape of a ball. "Like a cute little kitten."

Jordan squeaked. "Such a disaster."

But Angus raised his hands, waving them to me with a flourish. "But Hennessy was too, as anyone can see."

I burst out laughing and Angus offered me a fist bump. Jordan slumped in his seat but nudged my thigh with his. "Don't encourage him."

"That was pretty good," I said to Angus. "Are limericks a specialty?"

"I have lots more," he said. "There was a man called Jay. Who liked men because, you know, he's gay."

"This is going to end terribly," Jordan mumbled.

Merry was now trying not to smile and I put my arm around Jordan's shoulder.

Angus grinned. "But they were all out of luck, because Jay don't like to—"

"Angus Walter Spears," Jordan whisper-shouted across the table. "You will not finish that line."

Merry put her hands to her mouth to hide her laugh, but I laughed right out loud, giving Jordan's shoulder a squeeze, and I kissed the side of his head. "They weren't *all* out of luck. I certainly am not."

Merry snorted. "The night's not over yet."

Jordan let out the mother of all sighs and closed his eyes. "Siri, what is the definition of disaster?"

I cracked up laughing and Angus was still nodding, still smiling.

A waiter appeared at our table, pen and pad in hand. "Oh, thank God," Merry said. "Please bring us food. It doesn't matter what kind. Any kind. The fastest thing on your menu, times four."

"Oooh, food," Angus said, sitting forward and looking over the menu again. "There once was a man who was famished..."

I laughed again and Jordan put his head on the table. We did manage to order something, and we spent the next few hours eating and laughing... well, mostly laughing. Angus' high eventually waned, leaving a headache in its wake. Merry had some Panadol in her bag, which he took, and our conversation was quieter after that. The restaurant was almost empty when Jordan excused himself to go to the bathroom.

"So," Angus said. "Tell us, what's the story?"

"Story of what?"

"Of you. What's your life story?" He turned his empty water glass on the table. "I'm guessing you could be around for a while, so what do we need to know."

"Oh." My lip drew down. "I'm kind of boring, really. I grew up on the Gold Coast with my parents and two sisters, Saffron and Siobhan. And yes, Saffron, Siobhan, and Hennessy—we got a lot of shit at school for our names," I said with a laugh. "I was always interested in computers and coding, even in high school. I have a masters in computing science and security, and now, I work with my best friend. Actually, I work *for* my best friend. It's an internet security company and it's like a partnership; I run the technical side but he owns the company and deals with the finances and taxes. It suits me. I moved to Surry Hills when my ex live-in boyfriend decided being with an asexual person wasn't enough for him. I take the bus because it minimises my carbon footprint. I run four kilometres every day, and I have two Siamese fighting fish and a cactus."

"What are their names?" Angus asked.

"The fish are Ali and Bruce," I said, a little embarrassed. "After the only two fighters I could name."

"Mohammed Ali and Bruce Lee," Angus said, like he got points for knowing that.

"Yep. And the cactus is called Spike."

Merry smiled but there was an edge to her brow. "Tell us, what have you learned about Jordan tonight?"

I let out a breath through puffed-out cheeks. "Well. A lot, actually. That he has not only a love of classic literature and seventeenth-century French poets, but he also loves Yaoi graphic novels. I didn't know that before tonight." I met Merry's gaze, then Angus'. "To be honest, I'd been worried that he might turn out to be different when he was with you guys than he was with me. My ex would be like two different people. You know, the guy who he was in public and the guy who he was with me, and it used to bug me. But Jordan's not like that. The Jordan I've spent time with alone is the same Jordan he is with you guys. I've learned he has a spectacular sense of humour, that there's minimal rambling when he's completely comfortable. He's *really* smart, and I learned that he has some pretty amazing friends."

Merry and Angus both smiled, but said nothing, just as

Jordan came back from the bathrooms and slid into his seat. "Am I interrupting anything?" he asked, looking moderately scared.

"Your friends were just giving me the interrogation test," I said, unable to stop the smile.

He shot them a look of horrified surprise. "They better not have. I gave strict instructions. Strict instructions in point form. It wasn't difficult. There was only one instruction. No interrogation. We. Are. Not. ASIO."

I snorted and Merry rolled her eyes at him. "Oh relax. He passed."

"He did?" Jordan asked.

"I did?" I asked.

Merry nodded and Angus gave us a sly smile. "Yep. Flying colours and all that."

Jordan visibly relaxed and turned to face me, his hand on my thigh. "I hope it wasn't too bad. I'm sorry, I shouldn't have left you alone."

I laced our fingers on my leg. "It was fine, really. Glad I passed though."

"Are you ready to go?" he asked.

"Yeah."

He smiled all shy-like. "Did you want to... come back to my place?"

"Oh yes, please." Angus leaned back and patted his belly. "I need to take off my pants."

Jordan's mouth drew into a thin line and he turned back to me. "Or we could go to your place, perhaps?"

I laughed. "Sounds great. Why don't we cab it? We can drop everyone off at their places on the way."

And that's what we did. We dropped Angus off first, then Jordan and I went to my place, and we left some cash with Merry for the final drop-off. We waved her off and

Jordan sighed up at the night sky, his breath billowing in the cold night air. "So, it wasn't a complete disaster."

"Are you kidding?" I asked, opening the gate to my townhouse. "Your friends are great."

We got inside and I flipped the lights on, shut the door behind us, and pulled him into my arms. "I had a great night. Your friends are funny as hell. I can see why you like Angus."

"He's one of a kind, that's for sure."

"Can I get you a drink or take your coat?"

He shook his head. "No. You could kiss me though."

I laughed and cupped his face before bringing our lips together. It was soft and warm and tender, and it made my knees weak. Eventually I pulled away, smiling at the dazed look on his face. "We could move to the couch? I have a lot of *Deep Space Nine* episodes to catch up on. Maybe we could make out some more? Hold hands? Cuddle?"

He nodded, so I took his hand and led him to the couch. One episode later, we were lying down—me on my side, Jordan at my front—but he seemed distracted. "You okay?" I asked.

He nodded but scooted up so our faces were close, and this time he kissed me. I let him lead and set the pace, but we pressed together and it was suddenly very intimate. He deepened the kiss, and as soon as our lips met, there was a hint of tongue, and he pulled me closer against him, tangling his tongue with mine and moaning into my mouth.

His reaction surprised me. It wasn't entirely unwelcome. We both liked to kiss, that much had been established, but I think his reaction surprised him even more. He pulled back and there was fear in his eyes. He put his hand to his lips. "Oh God, I'm sorry." He swallowed hard and scrambled off the couch to get to his feet. He looked around the room, scared as hell, before taking a step back. "Um, I don't know where that came from."

He looked about two seconds from bolting out the door. "Jordan," I said softly, sitting up. "Don't apologise for kissing me like that. You can kiss me like that any time you like."

He squinted his eyes shut before scrubbing his hand over his face. "Maybe I should go," he said. "I... I need to go."

I stood up, confused by his reaction, but before I could reply, my phone buzzed in my pocket with an incoming call. I ignored it. "Why? Did I do something wrong?" I asked him. I wanted to reach out and touch his arm but didn't want to startle him even more.

"No, no," he answered quickly. "It's just, I um..."

"You weren't prepared for your own reaction to kissing me like that?" I prompted.

He barked out a laugh and shifted his weight on his feet, a little panicky. "Something like that."

My phone rang again and I groaned as I took it out of my pocket. It was Michael. Knowing it was more than likely work-related—if it was conversational, he'd text me first—I really should have answered his call, but Jordan was right there in front of me and kind of freaking out, so I let it go to voicemail.

"Please don't go," I said. "Can we talk about what's wrong? You didn't do anything wrong."

He licked his lips and he was about to say something when my phone rang again. I considered throwing it across the room, but three calls back-to-back from Michael meant it was something important.

"I'm sorry, I have to take this," I said, hitting Answer.

Jordan nodded. But the way he bit his lip and shoved

his hands in the back pocket of his jeans told me he was on edge. He stopped closer to the door.

"Hennessy," Michael said in my ear.

"Michael, what's up?" I said, not taking my eyes from Jordan. "Please don't go," I whispered to him.

"Everything okay?"

"Um, now's not a good time."

"Oh, man, I'm sorry to interrupt," Michael continued. "But it's Rob. He just got home to find his place ransacked. They took his laptops."

My heart sank and I sighed. "Fuck. You at the office?"

"On my way as we speak."

"I'll be there in fifteen," I said and disconnected the call. Jordan had got the gist of the phone call, but I needed to explain. "That account I was hoping to wrap up this week? Well, there's just been a massive security breach. I have to go."

He nodded quickly. "Yeah, that's fine. It's probably for the best. I really should be going anyway. I can see myself out."

He had to step around me to get to the door, so I grabbed his arm. "Jordan." He looked at me and there was a look of resignation on his face. "What just happened? What did I do wrong?"

He shook his head. "Nothing. You didn't do anything wrong."

"Then talk to me."

"I had a great night. The best, really. But I think I need some time... And I don't think I can be what you need, or something. I don't even know."

"What does that mean?"

He shook his head, pulled his arm away, and took a step to the door. "I should let you go. You have to go anyway."

"I'll have the taxi drop you off. On my way to the city," I tried, thinking it would give us time to talk in the car.

"My place isn't on the way. It's the opposite direction," he said. "It's fine, I can get home. No big deal."

"Jordan…" I shook my head, not knowing how to fix this.

"I'll call you tomorrow," he said. He opened the door and stopped. He gave me a parting glance before studying the door, and it looked as though his eyes were glassy. "I'm really sorry."

And he left. The door clicked closed behind him, leaving me heartsore and completely at a loss about what the fuck just happened. I stood there for a few seconds, blinking at where he'd just stood moments before, trying to get my head around it. But my phone rang in my hand again. This time it was Rob. I growled at his name on my screen before I answered his call.

"Did Michael get hold of you?" he asked, no hello, no apology.

"Yes. I'm on my way to the office right now."

"I'll see you there then."

Fucking great. I ended the call without another word, sneering at my phone before pocketing it again. My night just went from shitastic to fucking worse. I grabbed my coat, checked my pockets for wallet and keys and, finding both, picked up my messenger bag and walked out.

CHAPTER THIRTEEN

JORDAN

MOTHERFUCKER, motherfucker, mother-fucking-fucker.

I'm so stupid.

I felt awful. My stomach was in knots, my heart was aching, my mind was a motherfucking mess.

I was glad Angus wasn't up when I got home. As much I probably should have talked to someone, all I wanted to do was crawl into bed and pretend I wasn't such a goddamned disaster.

But I was.

And it wasn't bad enough that I could be a hot mess on my own, but I had to bring Hennessy into it. Dear God, the look on his face when I left was something I wouldn't ever forget. I hurt him. I led him to believe I was someone I'm clearly not.

I wasn't who or what he needed.

I hurt him, and I hated myself for it.

When I walked in my room, I left all the lights off, kicked off my shoes, but crawled into bed fully dressed, jeans and all.

I reached down to give my dick a squeeze. I wasn't hard, not even close to it. I slipped my hand under the waistband and cupped my balls and palmed my dick, and... nothing.

Mother fucking nothing.

My head swam, my mind turned in circles. I was so confused. I thought I'd found who I was. I thought I'd found out what I was and found my people like me. And for the first time in years, I'd felt like I'd belonged. Like all the little pieces of me slotted together to complete my bigger picture.

But I was wrong.

I didn't belong with them, and the picture of my identity was, once more, in a thousand disassembled pieces.

I had a lump in my gut, an ache in my chest, and my eyes burned, so I rolled onto my side and cried myself to sleep.

"I KISSED HIM."

Merry stared at me. We were in the staffroom. She'd come bounding in, all excited for gossip of how my night ended up with Hennessy. She took one look at me and dragged me into the corner; her smile was gone, replaced by pure concern.

"I thought you were both okay with kissing," Merry asked gently.

"I am," I said. "He is." God, I felt nauseous.

"So what went wrong?" Merry pressed. "Did he want more?"

I tried to swallow, but my mouth was too dry. I shook my head instead. "No. I did."

Merry blinked and I could see it on her face as she tried to get the pieces to fit. "What?"

"I did," I repeated. "I ravaged his face like an alien face sucker and I pulled him close and I'm pretty sure I moaned and that's not even the worst of it because I think I wanted more." God, I was actually going to vomit. "So of course I freaked the fuck out and he got an emergency work phone call, but he was trying to ask me what was wrong, but how can I tell him that?"

"Tell him what?" Merry asked.

I gaped at her. "Have you even been listening?"

She did that patiently not-sighing thing she does. "Jordan, what can't you tell him?"

"That I'm not what he wants. He said, pretty much from day one, very clearly, he only wants to date asexual guys."

"And?"

My eyes burned again with tears. "And I'm not." I tried really hard not to cry, but my chin did that wobbling thing and I waved my hand at her, trying to stave off my emotions. Which was futile. "I thought I'd found where I belong, ya know? I thought I'd found who I was, who I really was. But then my body betrayed my brain and I basically ran out the door. Fucking hell, Merry. You should have seen the look on his face." I pushed my hand against my stomach, my eyes burned with tears. "I feel ill."

Merry put her hand on my arm and looked me dead in the eye. "You need to speak to him."

"What am I supposed to tell him?"

"The truth."

"I don't want him to end this."

"So you want him to think you're ending it?"

"What?"

"What do you think he's feeling right now?" She did her real-talk eyebrow thing. "He's probably at work wondering what the hell he did wrong. He'll be so confused. At least you know what the issue is. He has no clue. How can you expect him to fix something if he doesn't know what's wrong?"

"He can't fix me, Merry. It's not something that went wrong. It's me. I'm not what he thinks I am."

Merry took a deep breath. "How many texts or phone calls has he sent you since last night?"

I took out my phone and handed it over to her. There were four missed calls and five texts the last time I looked. Right then, Mrs Mullhearn came in with a clipboard. She took one look at me. "Jordan? Something wrong?"

I scrubbed at my face. "No. I'm fine, I just..."

She straightened. "Aren't up for dealing with the public?"

I didn't even have to nod. She just handed me the clipboard, which I now realised had about twenty spreadsheets on it. "These titles need to be archived. In the basement. Should take you—" She looked at her watch. "—oh, about eight hours."

So of course my eyes chose that particular moment to leak saltwater. "Thank you."

"Off you go," she shooed me out.

I was so thankful, I didn't even stop to think. Being in a dark basement surrounded by stacks and boxes, with a list as long as my arm to keep me busy for an entire day, was exactly what I needed. I wanted to be busy, distracted. I wanted to lose track of time. I wanted to hide away where I didn't have to pretend to be all-smiles.

I didn't even realise Merry still had my phone.

CHAPTER FOURTEEN

"WHAT THE HELL HAPPENED?" Michael asked.

I'd just arrived at the office at a quarter to eleven at night. Jordan had just done a runner on me, leaving me stunned and confused, and I had to come into work because of a possible security breach on the job I'd busted my arse on. Who just happened to be my ex, who was the very fucking last person I wanted to see right now. I'd sent Jordan two texts on the cab ride into the city, but he hadn't replied.

"I don't know," I answered with a shrug. "We had the best night. His friends are great, we laughed for ages, and I even got the feeling that they could one day be my friends too, ya know?" I swallowed hard. "Then we go back to my place and everything's fine. And then he kissed me and it was... amazing. But then he freaked out. And I mean *freaked* out. And then you rang and he bolted."

"Without telling you why?"

I shook my head. "He said he didn't think he could be what I needed. He said he needed time and that he was sorry. Said he'd call me."

"The fuck?"

I shrugged. "I don't know. I thought we had something. I thought..." God, I couldn't believe I was going to admit this. "I was thinking long-term, ya know? I thought he could be all that for me."

The elevator pinged at the other end of the floor and I sighed. Michael clapped my shoulder. "Put your game-face on. Rob's here."

Michael was right. The very last thing I needed right now was Rob gloating in my face that I'd had another failed relationship.

Failed relationship. Fuck. Is that what Jordan and I were? I couldn't believe it. I wouldn't. Not until he looked me right in the eye and told me it was over.

I couldn't even take any joy from Rob's misery. He looked terrible and stressed. I'd imagine coming home to find your place ransacked would suck for anyone. Even arsehole ex-boyfriends.

We met in the waiting room. The entire building was empty, save security downstairs who had been instructed to grant Rob access. "What happened?" Michael started.

"I'd been at The Greenroom," he said. I rolled my eyes, not giving a single fuck if he saw. The Greenroom was a notoriously sleazy gay club for executives, rife with drugs and hookers. "I left at nine with..." His gaze darted to me before he looked back at Michael. "With company. We arrived back at my place to find the door ajar. They took anything they could carry. TVs, computers, jewellery, watches. They even took my juicer. Trashed everything, upended everything. Cops took fingerprints, but they have security camera footage."

"They got caught on camera?" I asked.

He shrugged. "The police said the men, there were two

of them, didn't even seem to care about the cameras. And that they should be able to get an ID."

Michael looked at me and I smiled. "If they were stupid enough to get their faces on camera, then it's very likely they won't know how to get past the password access."

"That's good, right?" Rob asked.

"For now," I replied. "But who they sell the laptops to might have a different set of skills."

"You have the police report number?" Michael asked.

Rob nodded. Then he looked at me. "They um, the cops wanted to know the names of everyone who had access to my apartment in the last six months." He frowned. "I gave them your name but told them you weren't involved."

"My name?" I asked.

"Yeah, sorry if that affects your security clearance or your reputation," he said, and he did look legitimately sorry.

And it was true. In my line of work, reputation and integrity were my entire business. Yet I couldn't help but laugh. "Believe me, after you told the police you take guys from The Greenroom back to your place a few times a week, they won't even look at me. And why would they? If I wanted access to your laptops or any of your financial accounts, I could do it without getting off my couch."

Rob looked as though he was about to snarl at me, but he bit it back. Maybe he could tell I wasn't in the fucking mood. "Sorry my home being robbed, my privacy being violated, is such an inconvenience to you," he said. His tone was neutral, but his smirk gave his intent away. "Did I interrupt a date or something?"

"Okay," Michael said flatly. "One, what Hennessy does in his private time is none of your business. Two, this incident, while unforeseen and out of all our control, undermines weeks of work that Hennessy has done." Michael looked at me and asked a question he already knew the answer to. "Can you fix this before the relaunch next week?"

I gave him a grateful smile. "Of course I can. I'll let you two sort out the legal details. I'll be in my office where I will, no doubt, be for every hour of the next six days."

I left them to it, went into my office, and pulled up the dozen files that would need new passwords throughout, new firewalls, new encryption patches, and coding rewrites. I didn't have to redo anything from scratch. I just needed to run scans and patches, check ports, and I'd probably spend more time amending the final reports and data for his IT team. It wasn't a total loss. It was just a huge pain in my arse.

It was also a great distraction from my sore heart. Yes, I had to speak to Jordan. I just needed to deal with this mess first.

Three hours later, I'd confirmed there'd been no immediate breach and had started on the long and tedious path to fixing this whole mess. Michael had gone home an hour ago —there was no point in us both being zombies tomorrow—so I shut everything down and went home, not even feeling the bite of cold as I left the building and slipped into a cab.

My alarm went off a few hours later, and the first thing I did was check to see if Jordan had replied.

He hadn't.

He hadn't replied when I trudged my sorry arse back to the office, and he hadn't replied when Michael passed a fresh coffee to me just before nine. "Still no reply?"

I shook my head. "No."

"Did you try calling him?"

I nodded. "Five times. It just went to voicemail. Any more and I'll look like a crazy man. It's now up to him."

"I'm sorry," he offered. "I know how much you liked him."

Liked him? I think it had well exceeded that. I didn't admit that though. Not out loud. I just nodded and went back to work, hoping to get lost in codes and data files. Until my phone rang and Jordan's name flashed on the screen.

I fumbled with my phone, almost dropped it, then almost hit the ignore button by mistake.

"Jordan?"

"No, it's Merry."

My heart sank like a stone, then panic set in. "Oh my God, is he okay?"

"Yeah, he's fine. Well, not really. He's a freaking mess."

The ache in my chest burned. "Oh."

"God, Hennessy, what happened last night?"

"He freaked out. He shot off the couch and bolted. I don't know what happened."

"Oh dear."

"Oh dear, what? What does that mean?"

She sighed. "You care for him, don't you." It wasn't a question.

"Yes. I do. He's... everything I could ever want. And I have no idea how to fix this. He won't even speak to me."

She was silent a moment. "And he'll kill me if he finds out I'm talking to you. You have the ace support group meeting tonight, yes?"

Oh fuck. I'd forgotten about that. And it was supposed to be at the library. Where Jordan worked. Fuck! I rubbed my temples trying to stave off the headache that threatened to split my skull. "Yes."

"Good. So here's what's going to happen."

CHAPTER FIFTEEN

JORDAN

AS I WAS GETTING my coat and scarf, Merry handed me back my phone and gave me a hug. "Call me if you want to talk," she said, her hands on my shoulders.

I nodded sadly, dreading catching this bus. I even considered waiting for the next one, or even walking home, but I knew I had to be an adult about this. I'd told Hennessy I'd talk to him today, and even though it was a conversation I didn't want to have, it wasn't fair on him to put it off.

But he wasn't on the bus.

And that was so, so much worse.

I fell into a seat and clutched at my messenger bag on my lap, mentally telling my heart not to squeeze so damn tight.

A hand patted my shoulder. "No Mr Hennessy today," Mrs Petrovski said. I couldn't bear to meet her gaze.

"Uh, no. I um... I don't..."

Don't cry, Jordan. Don't cry.

Just make up some random bullshit story about how he was really an art insurance broker who was caught up in some multi-million dollar heist with international thieves and how it read like Oceans Eleven *meets* Thomas Crown *and, and... and... motherfucking fuck.*

"He's probably avoiding me and I wouldn't say I blamed him because I fucked it up, and let's be honest here, we all knew I was going to be the one to fuck it up. I mean, he's completely perfect and sweet and lovely, and I'm not what he thought I was. And I'm not what I thought *I* was, so I can't be what he needs and it totally sucks because I'm pretty sure he's the guy who was designed and made just for me, like he's so ridiculously perfect, and it's worse than *Me Before You*. I mean, being left behind because of assisted suicide must be awful because, you know, death and all, but that's fiction and this is real life and it hurts so much worse in real life than it ever does in books. I wish I could turn to the last page and see how it ends, and even though I normally call people who do that, absolute monsters, I would totally do that if this were a book. But he was reading *Flowers for Algernon* and that..." My voice fell quiet. "Well we all know how that ends."

Mrs Petrovski frowned. "I don't know how that ends."

I sighed. "Probably just as well."

She leaned in. "Did he tell you he not want to see you?"

"No, I... I walked out on him," I mumbled. "I... it was..."

"You not talk to him?"

I shook my head.

"You must talk to him. Sometimes talk is not easy, but you must. Communicate is most important!" she declared to the entire bus, her pointer finger held high.

Charles, Sandra, Becky, and Ian all nodded. "It is," Ian said.

Jesus Christ. Was everyone on the bus invested in our relationship? Had I let all of them down too?

"Sorry if I've disappointed you all," I mumbled.

"You didn't let us down," Charles said. "You let yourself down."

"And Hennessy," Mrs Petrovski added.

Oh great. Because that's so much better.

"I'll see what I can do to fix it," I lied. Then I willed myself not to cry, and I ignored how everyone now frowned, so I stared out the window until it was my stop.

I got home, stripped the doona off my bed, and cocooned myself on the couch, and stared at that nowhere space between me and the TV. The room grew darker, and when I heard Angus come home, I didn't even sit up.

His face appeared in front of me, concerned and sad. "Hey, is my Jordan Burrito alive in there?"

"Yeah." My voice cracked.

His frown grew deeper, but he sat on the coffee table so I could see him. "This is the saddest burrito I've ever seen."

"I was going for cocoon. A chrysalis, even. Just waiting to turn into something prettier before I come out."

"Bad day?"

"The worst." Which was totally dramatic, considering the horrors some people were living through in the world that very moment, but I was wallowing, so shut up.

"Well, I was hoping..." He twisted his hands in his lap. "Never mind. Another time."

"You were hoping what?"

"Well, considering we did the 'meet the friends' thing for you, I was thinking maybe you'd like to maybe do the 'meet the friends' for me?"

"Your sex-couple?" I wasn't sure what else to call them. "Is it getting serious...? I didn't know that, sorry." Then I felt a whole lot worse because he'd always been a good friend to me and I'd been so caught up in my own fucking world, I hadn't thought to ask him how things were in his world.

He shrugged. "Maybe."

"I've been a shitty friend, sorry."

His face softened. "No you haven't."

To be completely honest, leaving my cocoon, leaving the couch, and leaving our apartment was the last thing on the planet I felt like doing. But this was Angus, and at the end of the day, I'd do anything for him. "You were meeting them tonight?"

"Yeah, well, we talked about it..." He seemed so unsure. He bit his bottom lip and couldn't look at me, so it was pretty clear he was nervous about it.

"I'll go," I said, still not moving my burrito cocoon on the couch. "You make the arrangements, and I'll wallow a little bit more, then we can leave."

He smiled, relieved. "Okay, I'll just go shower."

"Maybe you should let them see you all covered in paint and your hair filled with plaster dust. You know, the real you."

He laughed. "Nah. If there's body-licking involved, I don't wanna taste like a building site."

I buried my face into my cocoon and mumbled through my doona. "Too much information."

His laughter disappeared, and a moment later, I heard the shower start. I took some deep breaths and tried to fortify the resolve to at least sit up.

Small steps.

But who knew... maybe being forced out of the house and being made to socialise might do me the world of good. I'd literally spent the entire day in the basement at work, hiding away from the world, and that had been a blessing. Maybe tonight would be too.

Twenty minutes later, we hit the pavement, our breaths

puffs of steam in the cold winter air. I shoved my hands in my jacket pockets. "So, where are we meeting them?"

"Oh," he replied. "Um, at the Clock Hotel."

Right across from my work. "Well, on the bright side, Sunan's will be open and we can get some of his mango fries, spicy beef salad, and green curry to help soak up the fuckton of alcohol I plan on drinking tonight."

Angus laughed and it was an uneventful bus trip in. There was no Soup Crew, which I was thankful for, because I wasn't sure I could face another lecture about my failings. The closer we got to the stop in Surry Hills, the more eager I was to get shitfaced.

As we were stepping off the bus, Angus' phone rang. He answered it, all cheeky smiles, and grabbed my arm. "This way first," he said. Instead of crossing the road to the pub, he was taking me toward the library. "Okay, we'll see you soon."

"Angus, where are we going?"

"Just a quick stop first. And believe me, if it all turns to shit, you can drink all the Midori Leprechauns you can drink, and I'll pay for it."

Weird, but whatever. Sounded like a fucking plan to me.

CHAPTER SIXTEEN

HENNESSY

IT WAS possible I was going to puke. I eyed the wastepaper bin in the corner of the room, just in case. Everyone was there already—Bonny, Leah, Sabina, Nataya, Glenn, and Anwar. And Merry.

She stood at the door, peering out every so often, her phone in her hand. "He's on his way up," she whispered.

Fuck. The nausea was real.

I fiddled nervously with the clipboard to some curious glances. "You okay, Hennessy?" Nataya asked.

"Oh yeah, just a lot on my mind," I replied, then took my place at the front of the room. "I like the new meeting room," I said, trying for calm and casual. "No chance of being interrupted by drunk people dry humping."

Everyone laughed, and I took a deep breath just before the door opened and Jordan fell into the room. Well, more like he was pushed. "What the hell...?" he said, then straightened up and saw me. He froze, fear and horror all over his face. He stared at everyone in the room, landing on Merry. "You!"

She grabbed his arm, pulling him into the room, and

Angus appeared behind him, pushing him forward. Merry plonked him in a seat. She sat on one side, Angus on the other. "Is this a...," Jordan said, wide-eyed. "Holy mother-fucking fuck, is this an intervention?"

"Yes, it is," Merry said, holding his arm like a vice. "Hennessy has something to say and you will sit here and listen, so help me God, Jordan."

Everyone else—Bonny, Nataya, Leah, Sabina, Glenn, and Anwar—sat there gobsmacked. Possibly horrified. "Dude, are you okay?" Anwar asked.

Jordan leaned forward to look at Anwar. "No, they're holding me against my will. It's like kidnapping, so if anyone knows Liam Neeson, that'd be great, because he *will* find me. I left the safety of my burrito chrysalis on my perfectly good couch, on the promise of as many Leprechauns as I could drink." Then he shot Angus a glare. "You lied to me."

"Yes, I did," he replied, giving me a not-too-discreet wink.

Then Jordan stared at me. "You're in on this?"

"It was my idea," Merry said before I could reply. "Don't blame him."

Jordan turned slowly to face Merry. "The evil master-mind. I should have known."

Merry rolled her eyes. "Just shush and listen. These good people would like to get home sometime this year." Then Merry leaned forward and waved to Bonny and Leah and the others. "Hi, by the way."

Bonny laughed and waved back. "Hi."

But then there was a moment of silence, and that was my cue. I was so nervous. My mouth was so dry, I could barely speak. Jordan looked like he hadn't slept a wink. He looked miserable and wired and hopelessly resigned.

Thank God I'd found some valid posts on line and printed them off. If I had to speak from the heart, it'd be a train wreck for sure.

"What I wanted to talk about today is really important," I started. "There's a huge misconception about what being asexual means. Asexuality is such a huge and broad spectrum. It isn't black and white. There is no right or wrong.

"To be asexual is simply defined as sexual orientation characterised by a persistent lack of sexual attraction toward any gender. To simplify a complex subject, an asexual person doesn't experience sexual attraction. But the important difference is that sexual attraction and sexual desire are not the same thing, okay? That's the tricky part. Let me say that again. Sexual attraction and sexual desire are *not* the same thing.

"To experience sexual desire doesn't make someone *not* asexual. Sexual desire does not make your asexuality invalid."

I paused and Jordan looked up at me then, and I knew, I just knew I'd hit the nail on the head. So I kept reading straight from my notes. It helped that I could just read and didn't have to look at him. "In the ace community, we are neither entirely with or without sexual desire, with or without engagement in sexual activity, with or without sexual drive. The stereotype of asexuals being wholly non-sexual or without any hint of attraction towards others is not who we are. Being asexual is varied and diverse, as is the complex relationship between sexuality and attraction."

I swallowed hard. "To some extent, we all come with a sexual expectation attached to our bodies. It becomes internalised, reinforced, and replicated through the major veins of society: in the workplace, the doctor's office, at home, on TV, movies, in books. I haven't met one other asexual person who has not, at some point, internalised their sexuality with social narratives and expectations. Sometimes we don't even know we do it. Sometimes we're our own worst gatekeepers."

I sighed and parked my arse on the table. "I didn't mean to sound like I was lecturing, sorry."

"You look really tired," Bonny said kindly.

"I didn't sleep much," I admitted, then scrubbed my hand over my face, trying to focus. "Sorry. I just want to say one more thing before we open up discussion." I looked down at my clipboard but didn't see the words.

"Like I said before, desire and attraction are not the same thing. To experience sexual desire does not make someone less asexual than someone else. Asexual people can engage in sexual pleasure. It doesn't make them any less asexual. Sometimes our bodies betray our minds, and it's okay. There's nothing wrong with you. Your asexuality is still valid."

I looked at Jordan then, and he was staring at me, his face drained, his eyes were glassy. I took a deep breath and shook off my tears. "Does anyone have anything they'd like to contribute?"

Glenn spoke first. "I think we've all had sex because we thought we were supposed to. Well, I know I have," he said. Others nodded. "We're pressured into it, told we're abnormal if we don't."

"Yeah," Leah agreed. "And sometimes I want to engage in sexual release. But not with another person. It took me a long time to realise that was okay."

"And that it doesn't revoke your A-card," Sabina added. "I still don't feel sexual attraction to people, but taking the edge off once in a while is okay."

Bonny nodded. "I spent two years in a relationship

where I willingly participated in sex. I never initiated it; it never actually occurred to me to initiate it. They were very sexual, and I wanted them to be happy. I *still* want them to be happy," she said with a smirk. "Just happy with someone who is not me."

There was quiet laughter, then Jordan cleared his throat. "I um... I'm still trying to figure this whole asexual thing out. I'm like, almost certain, I am. Asexual, that is." He let out a breath and his eyes filled with tears. "Well, I did. I was sure I was. And I was with someone who means the world to me, and he's said before—he's been very clear about it—that he can only be emotionally invested with someone who is asexual, because it just got too complicated otherwise, and hearts always get broken. And I thought, great, because that's what I am, right? I'm asexual. I don't want to have sex with anyone. I don't want to even think about having sex with someone. It kinda freaks me out and makes me uncomfortable. And everything with this guy was going great. Like really great. But then last night we were on his couch and I kissed him and we both like kissing. We've established that kissing is great and he can kiss like a motherfucker, you have no idea." He put his hand to his forehead, his lip trembled and a tear rolled down his cheek. "But then my body... it wanted more, like you said; our bodies betray our minds. And I freaked out, and I left him. Because he only wants someone who's asexual, and..."

I hadn't even realised a tear had slipped down my cheek too. I scrubbed it away. "Did you want to have sex with him?"

Jordan looked at me like I was crazy. "What? No! God, no. I don't want that. My mind doesn't want that at all. But if my body did... Doesn't that mean I'm not asexual?"

I shook my head. "Oh, Jordan. You're as asexual as you need to be."

He sobbed and put his hands in his face. "Oh mother-fucking fuck. You must hate me."

"How can I hate you?" I said, half laughing, half crying. "When I'm in love with you."

Sabina gasped. Well, I think it was her, and all heads turned like they were watching a tennis match.

Jordan looked up at me, stunned. I shrugged and held my arms out and Jordan shot out of his chair and walked straight into my embrace. He sobbed against my neck and I held him as tight as he was holding onto me. Merry did some crying-clapping thing in her seat, and Angus raised both hands like he'd scored a goal in soccer. "Hell yes, that's how it's done!" he crowed.

CHAPTER SEVENTEEN

JORDAN

"I TOLD you he'd forgive you for lying to him," Merry said, swatting Angus' arm before she came over and joined our hug. Then Angus joined in. Then Bonny did and Anwar, all laughing, but eventually I pulled back and wiped my face. I looked up into Hennessy's eyes. "I'm so sorry. Do you forgive me?"

He nodded. "Next time, talk to me."

"I will. I promise." Then I turned around to the other group attendees, knowing I should explain or apologise or something. "I'm sorry. That's two group meetings and two episodes of tears. Two for two, because that's how I roll. Stay tuned for next month's party trick. No crying though. It's so last season."

They laughed, which was a relief. "So," Glenn hedged, looking between me and Hennessy. "You two are a thing?"

"Yes," Hennessy answered. "We met at the last meeting, but I couldn't figure out where I knew him from. Turns out we catch the same bus, and we started talking."

Bonny tilted her head, then squinted at us. "Oh my God! You're Jordan... You're the boys on the bus!"

"The what?" I asked.

"My mum has talked non-stop about two boys who fell in love on the bus! Every day this month, it's like a soap opera. Every night she tells us all what happened. There's been recipes too! It's like the craziest thing!"

Oh God. Soap operas and recipes... "Is your mum Mrs Petrovski?" I asked.

Bonny nodded. "Yes!"

"She lectured me this afternoon. She wanted to know why Hennessy wasn't on the bus and I word-vomited all over her. She told me I had to communicate better."

Bonny grimaced. "Yep, that's my mum."

"Well, she's not wrong," Hennessy said, pulling me against him in a side-on kind of hug. "He does need to tell me what's bothering him."

I fisted his shirt at his back and inhaled deeply before looking at Bonny. "Well, you can tell your mum it all worked out."

"She's going to be so pissed she missed this," she said.

"I also owe her a recipe," I added. "I'll have something for her on Monday, I promise."

Bonny grinned and shook her head. "I can*not* believe it's you two. What a small world."

Then Hennessy cleared his throat. "I just want to say that while tonight's topic was personally motivated, it's still relevant. No matter where we are in our realisation of our sexuality, sometimes a reminder can do us all a favour."

"I think it proves how relevant it is," Sabina said. "I first realised I was asexual years ago, but having social expectations and internalised sexualities reaffirmed every now and then is important. My circumstances have changed since I first came out. I'm not the same person. But I'm still valid."

Nataya put her hand on Sabina's arm. "You are."

It was then I noticed that Merry was standing back and that she was crying. I left Hennessy's hug and collected Merry in my arms. "I still hate you," I said. "Even if you're amazing and fabulous and know what I need better than I know myself."

She snorted into my shirt. "Thanks."

"You okay?" I whispered.

Merry nodded against my chest. "I'm just happy it all worked out."

"I think we need Thai food and unlimited Leprechauns," I suggested.

She sighed. "Sounds perfect."

When the meeting wrapped up, everyone wished us well and promised to see us next month. It was agreed that the library was a great location, and they all agreed that Hennessy and I made the cutest couple.

Of course we fucking did.

I knew Hennessy and I had a long conversation ahead of us, and I was willing and happy to lay it all on the line. But I also owed Merry and Angus a whole bunch and a night of Thai food, a few drinks, and great conversation with my three most favourite people on the planet sounded like heaven.

We went to Sunan's, just a few doors down, and took a table. I sat with Hennessy, Merry and Angus sat opposite us, and we ordered a bunch of plates to share. When the waiter left us, Merry winked at me. "So, interesting day, huh?"

"The worst," I answered. I looked to Hennessy and smiled. "And the best."

"It started pretty shit," he said. "But it's ending better."

I nodded, and taking Hennessy's hand on the table, I looked directly at my two best friends. "Thank you. Both of you. Merry, for concocting this whole plan, being the evil mastermind that you are. And Angus, for lying through your teeth and promising me copious amounts of alcohol and not delivering."

"I did," he said with a grin. He waved his hand at Hennessy. "Six feet of cognac, did I not?"

Hennessy laughed and conceded a nod. "That's true. He did."

"Anyway," I said. "Thank you both. If it weren't for you, I'd still be cocooned on my couch being the saddest wallowing burrito ever."

"You were pitiful at work too," Merry said.

I shrugged. "That's true. I was. I wallowed in the basement for eight hours."

"Because Mrs Mullhearn didn't want you near the public, given your mood and your tendency to swear," Merry frowned. "It wouldn't have ended well."

"Remind me to thank her on Monday."

Our food arrived and we ate in silence for a while. "So, Angus," I said. "Any chance of me meeting your couple? When you told me that's who we were meeting, I kind of got my hopes up."

Angus chewed thoughtfully, then set down his fork. "They've been asking for a while."

"They have? Why haven't you mentioned it?"

"Dunno if it's what I want," he said.

"Are you not happy with them?" I asked. "Do you not love spending time with them?"

"Well yeah. But they're fancy and smart. Smarter than even you, Jay," he said. "And they've got this big flash house, and..." He shrugged.

"And what?"

He met my gaze. "What if I do the meet-the-friends

thing, and what if I tell them I will move in with them, and what if I love them, and then what if they don't want me anymore."

"Oh, Angus." I reached over and squeezed his hand. Then I— Wait, what? "Have they asked you to move in with them?"

"It's been mentioned, but I don't wanna. They have a big place and said they wanted me to, but I said I have a Jay, and I like living with him. He's like my big brother, and I'm not too smart, but he looks out for me and won't break my heart like they could, ya know?"

I was speechless. "Angus."

"So if you want to meet 'em, you can."

"Only if you want me to." I gave him a smile. "And you're like a brother to me too. And Angus, I can't really offer any advice for navigating a relationship between three people. I mean, I can barely get one right with two people, as we've all borne witness to in the last twenty-four hours." I gestured broadly to Hennessy. "But what I do know is this: if you're happy and if it works for you, then take the chance. Because it could just turn out to be the best thing that's ever happened to you."

Hennessy squeezed my thigh, and Merry fanned her eyes. "Jesus, what is it with the tears today? You're all arseholes."

I laughed, and Angus gave me a shy smile. "I'll speak to them and let you know."

"You also have to meet Michael and Vee, and Saffron and Siobhan," Hennessy said, giving me a nudge. "But maybe friends first, then family. I don't want to throw you in the deep end."

Angus tilted his head and studied Hennessy. "How did you know their names? I never said their names."

"Who?" he asked. "Michael and Veronica? Or Saffron and Siobhan?"

"Well, Michael and Vee." Now he looked confused. "The couple I've been seeing..."

My eyes almost popped out of my head. "What?"

Merry gawped. "What?"

Hennessy's eyebrows almost met his hairline. "Michael and Veronica Hawke. They live on King Street."

Angus nodded, a mix of disbelieving and stunned. "Darling Harbour Apartments."

Hennessy sat back in his seat and a slow smile spread across his face. "You're the one."

"The one what?" I asked.

"The one Michael's been talking about. He was being all weird, and a few weeks ago he asked me if it were possible to love two people. At first, I was like what the fuck, dude. You can't be cheating on Vee. That's not cool. And he laughed and said he wasn't cheating. And the whole conversation was weird, but then we got busy, and then I met you," Hennessy said, looking at me. "And I've been kinda absorbed with that. And not to mention work's been crazy and stressful."

"He's been stressed," Angus said, nodding slowly. "That's why I've been seeing them so much. It... helps—" He shrugged. "—relieve stress."

"Wait," I said, putting the pieces back together. "Your best friends Michael and Vee are Angus' couple?"

Hennessy laughed. "I think so." Then he pulled out his phone and hit a number. It answered on the second ring. Still smiling, Hennessy said, "Michael, my dearest friend in all the world. ... Yes, yes, it all worked out really great, actually. I'll be in first thing in the morning to catch up. ... Nah, it's fine. I'm here with Jordan right now and his two best friends. ... Yeah, me too. Hey listen, if I said to you right this minute I was sitting across from a guy called Angus, what would you say?" Hennessy grinned as he listened to whatever Michael was saying. "Well, he's a painter by trade, brown hair, brown eyes, cute as hell."

I snorted at that, and Angus blushed. Hennessy handed his phone over to him, then Hennessy laughed and nodded. "Turns out it's a really, really small fucking world."

"No way," Merry whispered excitedly.

"You're not kidding!" I cried. "Holy shit."

Angus was smiling and blushing and whispering into the phone. "Okay." He ended the call and handed Hennessy back his phone. He was three shades of red but his smile gave him away. "Uh, this um, meeting thing we talked about?" He cleared his throat. "Dinner at their place next weekend..." He bit his lip. "If you want?"

I was stunned. "And I thought today couldn't get any weirder. Hell yes, I want to meet them." Then I blanched. "Oh God. I'll be meeting your best friends and his couple. At the same time." I put my hand to my forehead, already about to panic. "I need to give them the 'don't fucking hurt him' speech for Angus, and they need to give it right back to me for you. Fuck. This could be a disaster."

Hennessy burst out laughing and slid his arm around my shoulder. "They'll love you."

"I need an invitation to this dinner party," Merry said. "There is no way in hell I'm missing this."

I squinted at her. "You really get far too much enjoyment from my anguish. But God, yes, you're coming. I'll need all the moral support I can get."

Merry shook her head sadly. "I'm not going for moral support, honey. I'm going because if it's an utter train wreck, I want first row seats. And if I have to hear about it for the next five years of my life, I'd rather be an actual witness so I will know if I have to be supportive or if I need to tell you to pull your head out of your arse."

I considered arguing, but everything she just said was pretty much true. "Fair enough."

Angus was positively glowing. "Well, I hate to bail on you guys, but I just had a better offer, so I'll um... be heading into the city. I probably won't be home till morning. Just so you know."

"And as much as I'd like to inhale a bottle of vodka right now," I said. "I think we need to go back to your place and talk, yeah?"

Hennessy smiled. "Yeah."

I put my hand up to get the waiter's attention. "Can we have the bill, please?"

AS SOON AS Hennessy opened the door to his townhouse, my nerves were back. But it was different this time. I wasn't nervous or anxious wondering what his expectations were on a physical relationship. I was nervous because I was about to tell him how I felt about him. But I was excited too. It wasn't lost on me what he'd said in the group meeting, in front of everyone. He'd said he couldn't hate me when he was in love with me.

"So?" he said, throwing his keys and wallet on his table. "Angus, huh? What are the chances?"

"I know! How freaking freaky is that?" I replied. "Do you really think... do they...?" I sighed. "I worry about him. He's just a teddy bear who some people might take advantage of. And he's not stupid. I mean, he sees the best in people and he has a heart of gold and I'd hate to see him get hurt. I think he's really falling for them, and I have no idea about the dynamics of throuples, but I—"

Hennessy put his finger to my lips, then replaced them with a soft kiss. "Michael and Vee are two of the best people I know. They're kind and decent, and there's probably not a better couple suited for Angus. Michael told me weeks ago about the loving two people thing, long before we knew it was Angus. And if Michael says he loves someone, it's with all his heart. He and Veronica are devoted to each other, and if they've introduced a third person, then I can only imagine they'll be equally devoted to him."

"I hope so."

Hennessy pulled me in for a hug that I could literally feel balming my soul. "It's been a weird day, huh?"

"So weird," I said. I pulled back and looked up into his eyes. "And I'm sorry. I really need you to know that. I should have stayed and talked to you, but I panicked and basically ran away. I was an idiot."

"You're not an idiot," he murmured. "You're still navigating where you are with your asexuality, and that can take ages. There's no right or wrong."

"Not talking to you was wrong," I replied. "Leaving you without an explanation was wrong."

He made a face that kinda said he agreed with me. "It could have saved us both a lot of heartache."

I nodded. "I'm sorry I hurt you."

He gave me a kiss. "I forgive you."

"When I thought maybe I wasn't asexual, I panicked. You've said before that you don't want to date anyone who wasn't, and I thought I'd blown it. My stupid dick liked the attention, or something, I don't even know."

He snorted. "I don't think your dick is stupid."

"Well, I can tell you, it's no Einstein either," I replied,

and he chuckled. "But I don't want to have sex. I really don't—it makes me uncomfortable even thinking about it, to be honest. I want to be able to cuddle and kiss on the couch while we watch *Deep Space Nine* without my dick getting any ideas."

Hennessy kissed me again, this time with smiling lips. "That sounds perfect to me. And if your Einstein gets any bright ideas, we can cool it a bit. Or go into the bathroom and get rid of it."

I gasped, horrified. "I'll pass on that."

"Would that be a *hard* pass?"

I gave him a playful shove. "Really? Dick jokes?"

"Yes. Dick jokes. I'm asexual, not dead. We're allowed to joke about these things. And we're allowed to talk about sex. And we're allowed to get hard-ons, as inconvenient as they sometimes are. We can't change being human."

I pulled him against me, fitting right into that groove of his body like perfect puzzle pieces, and sighed. We stayed like that for a while, just holding each other, breathing each other in. Now for my moment of truth. "In the meeting tonight, I asked if you hated me for being such an idiot, and you said you couldn't hate me because you loved me. And that was the single most romantic moment of my life, and it's a gift I will never take for granted. I promise you that. And Hennessy?"

He pulled back so he could see my eyes. "Yeah?"

"I love you too. I think I loved you from the beginning. When I found out you were reading *Flowers for Algernon*. That was like bam! Cupid fucking shot me. And you know, at first, I thought coming to terms with being asexual would turn my world upside down. But I was wrong. It kind of set it the right way up."

His eyes were a little glassy, but his smile was brilliant.

"I love you too." He cupped my face and he drew me in for a kiss. "And you knew who Daniel Keyes was. And bam! Cupid shot me too."

"He's such a motherfucker."

Hennessy laughed and pulled me to the couch, where we fell into a heap of legs and arms and cuddles and kisses and two episodes of *Deep Space Nine*, until I fell asleep in his arms.

THE NEXT WEEKEND

HENNESSY

"DO I LOOK OKAY?" Jordan asked. He was breathing hard, a little pale, and this was his fourth outfit change.

"You look fine."

He grimaced and made a weird strangled sound, then disappeared back into his room. We were heading into Michael and Vee's place for dinner. Angus was already there, having left a few hours ago.

When I'd gone into work on Monday, I'd held my phone out to Michael, showing him a selfie we'd taken the day before. "Me, that's Jordan, and this guy..."

Michael sighed, turned, and shut my door, then sat on my desk. He took my phone and stared at the photo on the screen, a smile pulling at his lips. "We used to play around with a third person when we were in college," he said absently, still staring at Angus. "It was a lot of fun, and the sex was always amazing, but it was only ever me and Vee. We were rock solid. We still are. Then we got engaged and we stopped inviting people in, if you know what I mean. We just didn't think it was something married couples did, you know? It was weird. And we didn't for a long time.

Years. But then on New Year's, we were out at a bar down-town and Vee went off to dance, and she met this guy. She said he had a smile that could light up the room and his laugh..." Michael grinned as he spoke, still holding my phone, his eyes trained on Angus. "God, his laugh. And you know, she wasn't wrong. She never is."

"And one thing led to another," I prompted.

"And it led to another, and another." He let out a long sigh and slid my phone back across the table. "It was never supposed to be permanent. But he was so much fun, and he's great in bed, like wow, and he's... he's... addictive. But he's also genuine, and he's kind, and he's considerate—"

"And he's Jordan's best friend."

Michael nodded. "I know. Well, I know now. He's only ever called him Jay, not Jordan. But yeah..." He shook his head and let out a long breath. "Angus is... I love him. And Vee loves him, and we love him together. And I know that's weird, and it's not conventional, but bringing him into our marriage doesn't detract from anything. It makes it better. It's another dimension and another layer. I don't expect you or anyone to understand, but you don't have to. We don't need permission and I won't defend how I feel about him. I—"

I put my hand up to stop him or surrender, or both. "I would never ask you to. If you've brought a third person into your bed, then I'm glad it's him. Angus is a great guy. How can anyone not like him?"

Michael's grin was instantaneous. "I know, right?" He swallowed hard. "So? We're cool?"

"Of course we are."

"And dinner this weekend?"

"Looking forward to it. Jordan is already having a nervous breakdown," I said with a laugh. "But he'll be fine."

"And things with you and him are all sorted?"

I nodded. "Yep. We're good."

"For what it's worth, I've never you seen this happy."

"Thanks."

"And something to make you even happier, we're signing off on Rob this week."

"And I cannot fucking wait."

"You've been the utmost professional." He smirked. "Not that I expected anything else."

I snorted. "Thanks."

"And we've got two smaller contracts for immediate start," he said. "So, if you want, I'll do the handover with Rob so you don't have to see him. I'll be sure to remind him that you've moved on to bigger and better things."

"Deal."

"Oh, and Vee said you don't need to bring anything this weekend. Just this new man of yours. We'll take care of everything else."

"ARE you sure we don't need to bring anything?" Jordan asked when he came out wearing the first outfit he'd had on. It was dark jeans and a blue-grey sweater that matched his eyes perfectly. "Not even wine or flowers, or chocolates, or something?"

"No, nothing." I looked him up and down. "You look great, by the way."

There was a knock at the door. "That will be Merry," Jordan said.

I got up to get the door while Jordan put on his shoes. "Hey," Merry said brightly when she saw it was me. "Oh, don't you look dashing."

"He always looks great," Jordan mumbled from the living room. "And I look like a potato. They're going to think Hennessy is dating a potato. They'll probably stage an intervention—"

"Jordan, shut the fuck up," Merry said, still smiling. "Or you'll be a late potato."

"Oh God, what's the time?" he said, appearing somewhat panicked.

"We have plenty of time," I said to him. "And you look great."

Merry appraised him. "You actually do."

He looked down at himself. "Do I actually look like a potato?"

Merry rolled her eyes and ignored him. "You look great too," I told her. "Love the dress." It was purple, and her yellow cardigan and orange shoes somehow kind of all worked.

"Thanks!" She said, shoving her hands into the pockets. "It has pockets!"

"Okay, let's go," Jordan said, patting down his pockets, double checking for the fifth time that he had his wallet, phone, and keys. "We ready?"

I nodded and held out my hand for him to hold. "Relax. They'll love you."

"How do you know that? You can't know that. You just wait until I open my mouth and word-vomit all over everyone. It'll be a disaster."

"They'll love you." I kissed him. "Because I do. Now come on or they'll wonder where we are."

And the funny thing about Jordan was that he definitely had two varying degrees of nervousness. There was the ordinary kind of nervous where incessant rambling ensued, and then there was the petrified, holy-shit kind of nervous where he went unusually silent.

He'd stopped talking when we got close, barely made a sound when we got out of the cab, and as we rode the elevator up to their floor, his lips were pressed into a thin, very-shut line.

"You okay?" I asked, pulling on his hand.

He nodded, then shook his head, then nodded. Then the elevator pinged and the doors opened and he shook his head. "Nope. Not okay."

We stopped just outside Michael and Veronica's door, and I cupped Jordan's face and kissed him softly. "They will love you because you're an amazing guy. Because I love you, because Angus loves you. You have nothing to worry about, okay?"

He nodded but hardly looked convinced. I pressed the doorbell anyway, and Michael answered. He wore jeans and a white button-down shirt, looking handsome and casual and very, very happy. "Hey, come on in," he said, opening the door wide. He didn't even wait for introductions. He just stuck out his hand and said, "You have to be Jordan. The guy I hear about all the time, from Hennessy, from Angus."

"Oh," Jordan said, shaking his hand. "Yes, the one and the same. It's nice to meet you."

"And this is Merry," I said, making introductions.

Once that was done, Michael waved his hand inside. "Come on in and let's see if we can find my beautiful wife."

Their apartment was very nice. Not only had Michael made his own fortune, but Vee had too, and it showed in their style of tall ceilings, white tiled floors, dark furniture, and floor-to-ceiling glass that showed off one of the best views in

Sydney. Vee was in the kitchen, wearing dark tights and an off-the-shoulder, oversized sweater, looking glamorously casual, her dark hair in waves to her shoulders, her smile wide.

And there was Angus, looking just as at home in his jeans with the knees out of them and an old T-shirt, no shoes. His whole face lit up and he walked over and collected Jordan in a crushing hug, and I gave Vee a kiss on the cheek. "You look... Well, jeez, you look ridiculously happy."

She beamed. "I am."

Michael walked behind her and kissed her bare shoulder. "We are."

"You do too," she said quietly. "Introduce me to the man who puts that spark in your eye."

We all made small talk and had a glass of wine and few canapés, but Jordan was still quiet, and the stiffness of his shoulders told me he was incredibly nervous.

"Oh, Vee," I said. "You have to show Jordan your Miyazaki set."

He perked up at that. "Hayao Miyazaki?"

"Oh, you know his work?"

He put his hand to his mouth. "I love it."

"I have *The Art of Howl's Moving Castle*. Leatherbound, first edition. Signed."

Jordan gaped. "You do not!"

Vee laughed. "And that's not all."

"Noooo," Jordan breathed.

Vee nodded.

Jordan gasped. "Shut. Up."

She laughed and took him by the arm and they disappeared down the hall with Angus in tow. Merry and I helped Michael serve the main meal, and when Jordan reappeared with Vee and Angus, he was so much more relaxed. And chatty. And smiling.

We ate dinner, drank some wine, laughed, and chatted until our plates were empty and our bellies were full. It was actually amazing to watch Michael, Vee, and Angus all interact. There were soft glances, the brushing of hands, lingering looks. It was clear to see they were all happy.

"Thank you," Jordan whispered to me later. "Vee's library is amazing. I want one."

"You're welcome."

"I like your friends," he murmured. "They treat him well."

I spared a glance at Angus and he was laughing at something Merry had said, and he had his arm around Vee's chair and Michael had his hand on Angus' thigh. "Yeah. I knew they would. He's happy."

Jordan let out a sigh and smiled, leaning into me a little. "So am I."

I leaned in and kissed him. "Glad to hear that."

There was silence, which made me and Jordan look around the table. All eyes were on us, and I couldn't even be embarrassed. "Yes, I'm so ridiculously in love," I said. "It's actually gross."

Vee laughed. "I think we need music!" She picked up her phone, and a few screen-taps later, music began to play out of the ceiling speakers. Then she offered her hand to Angus, which he took with a grin, and they danced over to the living room, sliding the coffee table out of the way. Michael shot up and offered his hand to Merry, which she happily took, and I stood up and held out my hand to Jordan. "Mr O'Neill, if I could have the privilege of this dance."

He blushed and made a face but we danced, and it was

fun and crazy and we all laughed as we danced, but a few songs later, Jordan and I were slow dancing, lost in each other's eyes. I hadn't even noticed Merry leave, but Jordan looked around suddenly. "Where's Merry?"

Vee answered. "She thought it was time to go. I ordered and paid for her Uber. She said to say goodbye and you owe her coffee on Sunday. Something about lunch with a velociraptor." She shrugged, and Jordan and I chuckled and went back to slow dancing.

"I like dancing with you," he whispered below my ear.

"We should do it more often."

Half a song later, I tapped Jordan's arm and pointed with my chin. "Look."

And there, near the wall of glass stood Angus, Vee at his front with her hands on his hips, and Michael behind him with his arms around Angus' chest. They were slow dancing, three bodies moving as one. Angus had one hand on Vee's hip, grinding against her while grinding Michael's crotch. His head was lolled back on Michael's shoulder, his eyes closed to the pleasure, and Vee kissed down his neck.

"I think we should leave them," I whispered.

Smiling, Jordan nodded. "Probably a good idea."

We grabbed our coats and waved goodbye to Michael, who now had Angus turned around. His smile was his only farewell, and we laughed out into the hallway.

"I don't think we need to worry about those three for a while," Jordan said with a laugh.

I took his hand as we walked to the elevator. "Do you miss that? That kind of intimacy? That kind of sexual bond?"

Jordan stopped and met my gaze. "Not at all. Do you?"

My smile was slow and full. "Absolutely not. They can

have what they've got, and good luck to them. But what we have? Is perfect for me."

"It's perfect for me too. And you know what would make it even more perfect?"

"Season two of *Deep Space Nine*, hot chocolates, and cuddles on the couch?"

Jordan laughed and hit the elevator button a few times. "Goddammit. You shouldn't speak dirty to me."

I laughed just as the elevator doors opened, and we stepped inside, hand in hand, and ridiculously, grossly, fucking happy.

THREE YEARS LATER

JORDAN

NOT MUCH HAD CHANGED. Angus and I still lived together, only now we rented a bigger apartment in Surry Hills, and Hennessy lived with us too. We still had Bruce and Ali, the Siamese fighting fish, though they were now Bruce the Second, and Ali Prince Junior, because apparently fish only had teeny-tiny mortal coils. And Spike still sat on the windowsill, and Hennessy still talked to him every day.

Angus was still involved with Veronica and Michael, and while he was still resisting making the final move in with them, we all knew it wouldn't be long. He was at their place three or four nights out of every week, and they now considered their marriage—not just relationship—to be between three people. It was kinda weird, but it really worked, and the three of them were utterly, ridiculously happy.

Just like me and Hennessy. My family tolerated him just as much as they tolerated me, but his family had totally adopted me as their own. It was all I'd ever need.

Merry had met and fallen in love with Jodie, and they

were sickeningly happy, living together for almost two years, and Merry and I still drove Mrs Mullhearn crazy five days a week.

Hennessy still worked with Michael, still jogged in the evenings, still listened to audiobooks, and he still kissed like a motherfucker. He still ran the Surry Hills Ace Support meetings, and the Soup Crew had established a recipe and garden community group that now met every month at the library.

And life was, somehow, perfect.

We'd spend lazy Sunday afternoons cozied up on the couch, me reading a book, Hennessy would do a crossword, or choose recipes and write shopping lists, or one of his many lists for every little thing. Sometimes he'd pull my feet into his lap, or sometimes he'd rest his head on my chest, and sometimes he'd fall asleep when I ran my fingers through his hair.

But sometimes he'd have to work late, which was totally fine, and I'd have to run the support group at the library. I'd done it a few times without offending or injuring anyone, so when he called me to say he had to work late and asked me to run the group, I didn't think anything of it.

The usual faces were there, plus a few more we'd collected over the years. There were now eleven regular attendees, and they knew Hennessy and me well. According to the general consensus of the group, we were the poster boys for an ace relationship.

We were just like any other couple. We did everything they did. We held hands, we kissed, we hugged, we argued over cleaning and laundry, and we shared a bed. The only thing we didn't do was have sex.

Hennessy had tried to explain that there couldn't have been one ideal ace relationship because everyone had

different limits and preferences. Not everyone liked to kiss
or hug, and not everyone fought over laundry—because they
wouldn't fold the damn towels wrong like Hennessy does,
and chances are they'd pick up the bathmat, for fuck's sake,
because every person on the planet apparently knows how
to pick up the damn bathmat, Jordan—but the sentiment
was the same.

We were far from perfect. But we were proof it was
possible to be happy. To be perfectly happy.

Utterly, pristinely, perfectly happy.

I wouldn't change one thing.

Not one iota of a thing.

Okay, so maybe I'd change the way Hennessy folds the
damn towels, but he may have possibly been correct about
me leaving the bathmat on the bathroom floor. Not that I'd
ever tell him that. He was incredibly organised and planned
everything meticulously, and my attitude of 'just wing it
because what could possibly go wrong' made his eye twitch.
Which was why he had the support group meeting notes all
printed out in bullet form, even though the SMART Board
PowerPoint presentation was more than adequate.

I stood at the front of the room with Hennessy's clipboard as everyone filed in. They were early, but the Power-
Point presentation was ready to go.

"You holding the fort today?" Bonny asked.

"Yep. Hennessy's stuck at work. Any and all complaints
need to be written on a twenty dollar note and handed in to
me before you leave, thanks."

That got me a few laughs. I knew these people, and they
knew me. They knew I had a tendency to get off track, and
sometimes there was nonsensical rambling. But I liked these
people. They were my people. My tribe. Where I belonged.

"Okay, so," I started, opening the clipboard. "Hennessy

kindly made notes on a clipboard for me. In point form, and he even noted when it's a good time to pause and encourage discussions." I turned the clipboard around and showed them. "See? I'm not overly familiar with the vacuum cleaner at home, but I can operate a SMART Board."

They all smiled, and I continued to read. "And today's meeting topic is Can Asexual People Get Married?" I stopped reading. That was a weird subject choice, but whatever. We had discussed all sorts of things at these meetings. I looked at the audience, hit the button that started the presentation, and read the first bullet point that was written on the screen for everyone to see. "*Sometimes you drive me crazy.*"

I stopped again and frowned. "Wait a minute," I said. "I think I have the wrong file or something."

"Here, let me," Nataya said, getting up and quickly taking control of the laptop. She was some computer engineer wizard at Hogwarts or something, so if anyone could fix it...

The next screen appeared. *Sometimes you make me mad.*

"The fu...?"

Nataya pressed the next screen. *You never pick the wet bathmat up.*

"What the...?"

And I know you used my toothbrush that one time, even though you said you didn't.

"I bought him a new one," I said, defending my honour. "And it was a different colour, and he is a lying liar who lies."

But you make me laugh.

I looked at everyone in the room, and they were all smiling at me.

The next screen appeared. *And you recommend the best audiobooks.*

"I work in a library, genius," I mumbled. "But that is actually true. He loves audiobooks."

And there's a hundred little things...

Nataya pressed the next screens, one after the other.

You give the best foot massages.

You buy the bread I like, even though it's not your favourite.

You make the bed every day.

I nodded. "That's true. I don't think he's ever made it once."

Because you're the last out of it.

I gasped. "I resent that!"

You are the light in my dark, my missing puzzle piece.

Awww. I put my hand to my mouth.

But something's missing, Jordan.

I blinked a few times. "What?" I looked around the room. My heart rate skyrocketed. "What?"

Breathe, Jordan. Yes it said *Breathe, Jordan* on the actual fucking screen.

I put my hand to my heart just as Nataya pressed the next screen. *There's something missing from our relationship...*

I couldn't breathe, and I felt sick, and the room was getting smaller and darker, and someone cleared their throat. I turned around, half a second from blind panic setting in.

And there was Hennessy. He was holding his hand out with something in his palm. He smiled at me. "There is something missing, Jordan."

I shook my head. "No there's not. Everything is perfect.

Unflawed, without fault. No longer upside down, remember? But the right way up."

He took a step closer and I could see he was holding a book —a small book—and I was scared to take it, but he was giving it to me. "The part that's missing is inside," he said quietly.

I looked at the book. It wasn't a real book. It couldn't be. It was too small for that particular edition. It had to be a replica. The book was *The Poetical Works of Percy Bysshe Shelley*. The 1880s New York printed edition. My all-time-favourite cover of my all-time-favourite book.

"Inside this book? It's poetry, Hennessy. You know this. It's my favourite. What does that mean?"

"No, inside the book," Hennessy said.

Merry snorted from near the door. Merry was here? And Jodie. And was that Angus, and Michael and Vee? Merry opened her hands like she was opening a book. "Inside," she mouthed.

I opened the book, and the pages were hollowed out, and inside lay a black ring.

"The only thing missing from our relationship is a wedding and the next sixty-something years of our lives together," Hennessy said, going down on one knee. "Jordan,

Nothing in the world is single;
All things by a law divine
In one spirit meet and mingle.
Why not I with thine?

"MARRY ME. Say you'll spend your life with me."

I put my hand to my mouth and burst into tears as everything clicked into place. The slideshow, everyone arriving early and taking their seats. And then he quoted my all-time-favourite poem. "You planned this? The Power-Point presentation?" I sobbed, snot and all. "And I didn't use your toothbrush, I promise, but I do make good coffee, that's true, and I buy that bread because it's your favourite. But you're the light in my dark, and you're my missing puzzle piece too. When everything was out of place and upside down, you made everything right. Nothing really made sense until you."

He laughed. "Is that a yes?"

I nodded. "Of course it's a yes. Holy motherfucking shit, Hennessy," I sobbed. "You quoted Percy Shelley. Of course it's a yes."

Hennessy crushed me in a hug and everyone cheered and clapped around us. I cried into his neck. This man, this perfect, sweet, sweet man wanted to marry me. He pulled me back, wiped my tears, and planted a kiss on my lips. "You just made me the happiest man on the planet." He took the small book, which looked just like the real thing only a little smaller, turned out to be a ring box. "I had this made, just for you."

"If you had sacrificed a real book, I would have said no."

Hennessy laughed, but we both knew it was true.

He took the ring out. A wide black band with a brushed finish and a narrow polished finished edge. It was...

"It's black to symbolise asexuality and how we met. And it's titanium, because it's one of the strongest things on earth." He slid it onto my finger and the weight of it was new and somehow grounding.

"It's perfect," I mumbled through more tears.

We were then, in turn, separately hugged by everyone,

and by the time my tears had stopped, I'd made my way back to Hennessy. And after a while, the only people left were our dearest friends.

Angus put his hands on my shoulders. "There once was a guy called Jay."

We all chuckled because Angus' limericks were a classic.

> "Who was the best friend a guy could ask for.
> He deserves to be happy,
> and he found that with Hennessy.
> So I don't feel so bad about moving out."

I laughed because it didn't rhyme, but then what he actually said made sense. "You what?"

"I'm moving out," he said quietly, but he glanced to Michael and Vee and smiled. "I've put it off long enough."

"Yeah, you have. But what will I do without you?" I asked, not sobbing at all.

"I'll be around. We'll still do pizza and movie nights, yeah? Like on Fridays or something."

"Yes, please."

Angus shrugged. "And I think Hennessy wants a kitten, and you can use my room to put your bookcases in and get that library you've always dreamed of."

So of course I started to cry again, and I looked at Hennessy. "You want a cat?"

He nodded. "Mr Collins' cat had kittens, remember? He showed us the photos?"

"They were cute!" I said. "And we're going to get one?"

"Well, yeah," Hennessy said, all adorable and shy-like. "I asked Mr Collins and he said yes, and there's a little boy cat that's the cute one and I've already named him Lord Byron."

Again with the tears.

So many tears.

Hennessy pulled me in for a hug and tucked me snug into his side. "How about we all grab a table at Sunan's?" he said, kissing the side of my head. "We can order bowls of mango fries and bottles of wine. It seems we have much to celebrate."

"Yes!" I said, trying to pull myself together. "Like the next sixty-something years."

I took Hennessy's hand, and surrounded by our very best friends, we walked, laughing out into Crown Street. Together, as I imagined we always would be, into the rest of our lives.

THE END

ABOUT THE AUTHOR

N.R. Walker is an Australian author, who loves her genre of gay romance. She loves writing and spends far too much time doing it, but wouldn't have it any other way.

She is many things: a mother, a wife, a sister, a writer. She has pretty, pretty boys who live in her head, who don't let her sleep at night unless she gives them life with words.

She likes it when they do dirty, dirty things... but likes it even more when they fall in love.

She used to think having people in her head talking to her was weird, until one day she happened across other writers who told her it was normal.

She's been writing ever since...

ALSO BY N.R. WALKER

The Spencer Cohen Series, Book One

The Spencer Cohen Series, Book Two

The Spencer Cohen Series, Book Three

The Spencer Cohen Series, Yanni's Story

Blood & Milk

The Weight Of It All

A Very Henry Christmas (The Weight of It All 1.5)

Perfect Catch

Switched

Imago

Imagines

Red Dirt Heart Imago

On Davis Row

Finders Keepers

Evolved

Galaxies and Oceans

Private Charter

Nova Praetorian

A Soldier's Wish

Titles in Audio:

Cronin's Key

Cronin's Key II

Cronin's Key III

Red Dirt Heart

Red Dirt Heart 2

Red Dirt Heart 3

Red Dirt Heart 4

The Weight Of It All

Switched

Point of No Return

Breaking Point

Starting Point

Spencer Cohen Book One

Spencer Cohen Book Two

Spencer Cohen Book Three

Yanni's Story

On Davis Row

Evolved

Free Reads:

Sixty Five Hours

Learning to Feel

His Grandfather's Watch (And The Story of Billy and Hale)

The Twelfth of Never (Blind Faith 3.5)

Twelve Days of Christmas (Sixty Five Hours Christmas)

Best of Both Worlds

Translated Titles:

Fiducia Cieca (Italian translation of Blind Faith)

Attraverso Questi Occhi (Italian translation of Through These Eyes)

Preso alla Sprovvista (Italian translation of Blindside)

Il giorno del Mai (Italian translation of Blind Faith 3.5)

Cuore di Terra Rossa (Italian translation of Red Dirt Heart)

Cuore di Terra Rossa 2 (Italian translation of Red Dirt Heart 2)

Cuore di Terra Rossa 3 (Italian translation of Red Dirt Heart 3)

Cuore di Terra Rossa 4 (Italian translation of Red Dirt Heart 4)

Natale di terra rossa (Red dirt Christmas)

Intervento di Retrofit (Italian translation of Elements of Retrofit)

A Chiare Linee (Italian translation of Clarity of Lines)

Spencer Cohen 1 Serie: Spencer Cohen

Spencer Cohen 2 Serie: Spencer Cohen

Spencer Cohen 3 Serie: Spencer Cohen

Punto di non Ritorno (Italian translation of Point of No Return)

Confiance Aveugle (French translation of Blind Faith)

A travers ces yeux: Confiance Aveugle 2 (French translation of Through These Eyes)

Aveugle: Confiance Aveugle 3 (French translation of Blindside)

À Jamais (French translation of Blind Faith 3.5)

Cronin's Key (French translation)

Cronin's Key II (French translation)

Au Coeur de Sutton Station (French translation of Red Dirt Heart)

Partir ou rester (French translation of Red Dirt Heart 2)

Faire Face (French translation of Red Dirt Heart 3)

Trouver sa Place (French translation of Red Dirt Heart 4)

Rote Erde (German translation of Red Dirt Heart)

Rote Erde 2 (German translation of Red Dirt Heart 2)

CPSIA information can be obtained
at www.ICGtesting.com
Printed in the USA
LVHW011136120519
617538LV00001B/27/P